MURDER
in
NEW YORK

BOOKS BY HELENA DIXON

HELENA DIXON

MURDER
in
NEW YORK

bookouture

Published by Bookouture in 2024

An imprint of Storyfire Ltd.
Carmelite House
50 Victoria Embankment
London EC4Y 0DZ

www.bookouture.com

The authorised representative in the EEA is Hachette Ireland
8 Castlecourt Centre
Dublin 15 D15 XTP3
Ireland
(email: info@hbgi.ie)

ISBN: 978-1-83525-693-0
eBook ISBN: 978-1-83525-692-3

For Maisie, with love.

PROLOGUE

Telegram to Mrs Kitty Bryant

December 12th, 1936

Your father seriously ill. Advise you come at once New York. N. Dangerfield.

Torbay Herald December 1936

Advertisement

Sailing regularly from Plymouth to New York, the SS Manhattan offers the last word in passenger comfort at excellent prices. Cross the Atlantic in speed and style! First-class dining, cabins, luxurious lounges and attentive staff. Fast and efficient. Only a few cabins remaining for the last crossing to New York before Christmas. Book your place now by contacting our agent Plymouth 467.

CHAPTER ONE

Kitty Bryant shivered and snuggled deeper into her fur coat. It was five o'clock in the morning and her feet were as cold as blocks of ice as she waited on the observation deck of the SS *Manhattan* for her first glimpse of New York. After seeing nothing but storm-tossed waves and grey skies for days, the sight of land could not come soon enough.

Matt had his arm around her waist as the pale rosy light of dawn lit the sky with pinkish-gold streaks. All around them the hubbub of their fellow passengers, who had also come to the deck, added a buzz of excitement to the approach.

'Not long to go now, darling,' Matt murmured in her ear.

Kitty managed a wan smile. Under other circumstances, she too would have been excited to be on deck looking for her first glimpse of New York and the famous giant Statue of Liberty, which had been gifted to America by France some fifty years earlier.

Her trip to the city, however, was not for pleasure. The unexpected arrival of a telegram summoning her to New York just over a week ago had sent her into a whirlwind of worry and panic. The message had said her father, Edgar Underhay, was gravely ill and advised her to travel immediately.

She had replied right away to say they would come at once, advising they were travelling on the SS *Manhattan*, an American-owned liner. It had been the only ship departing from Plymouth that had berths available and was leaving almost straight away. She had hastily made arrangements for their housekeeper, Mrs Smith, to care for their pets and to look after the house.

Since then they had heard nothing. No telegrams to the ship, no replies to their telephone calls to her father's number. Nothing. The mysterious N. Dangerfield, who had sent the original telegram, had also not sent any further message. Kitty had clung to the hope that this meant that at least her father could be no worse.

There was a shift in the crowds surrounding them as people jostled for a better view. The great statue was clearly visible now against the backdrop of the immensely tall buildings of the city. Many produced Box Brownie cameras to take pictures, recording the moment. Kitty had to admit it was an impressive sight as they sailed towards Brooklyn and the estuary of the East River, where the ship was to turn and dock.

The air was cold and biting and they had been warned by the crew that the city had snow. Kitty shivered again, despite her many layers of clothes. The ship started its manoeuvres ready to dock, and the crowd began to disperse.

Kitty and Matt made their way off the deck to return to their cabin.

'Our trunks have already been collected,' Matt said as he picked up Kitty's shagreen vanity box from the top of the compact, but elegant, dressing table. 'There should be a car waiting to take us straight to your father's apartment.'

Kitty knew her husband had made all the arrangements before leaving England.

'I have no idea what we shall discover when we get there. I don't know if he is at home or in hospital.' She paused and bit her lip. She didn't voice her worst fear, that he might even have succumbed to whatever illness he had before they had even arrived. The crossing had taken five long days.

Even the luxurious comfort of their cabin and the first-class staterooms had not been sufficient to take her mind off her worries about her father. Edgar Underhay had been missing for most of her life, having left England for America at the beginning of the Great War. She couldn't bear to think of losing him now, only a few years after they had reconnected.

Kitty had been raised mostly by her beloved grandmother at the Dolphin Hotel in Dartmouth, Devon, after her mother too had vanished when Kitty had been a child. It had been 1933 when Edgar had finally made a brief return to Devon.

Since then, she had been introduced to a branch of her family she had never known and had finally discovered what had happened to her mother all those years earlier in 1916. Edgar had visited her and Matt a couple of times since then. Kitty was fond of her father, but, on each occasion, it had seemed trouble had followed in his wake.

Kitty was under no illusions about her father. His own sister, her aunt Hortense, described him as a ne'er-do-well. Her uncle had rather fewer favourable words to describe him, as indeed did her grandmother.

She had no idea what she would find when they reached her father's apartment. All she could do was to hope for the best and that the sender of the telegram had been exaggerating her father's condition.

It was after nine thirty before they had disembarked, had their passports inspected and their luggage loaded into a large black limousine. Kitty was glad of Matt's calm, reassuring presence beside her as their uniformed driver negotiated the car out of the docks and headed towards the city.

Her father was renting an apartment in a small block of serviced flats in a building close to Central Park. It was an expensive neighbourhood and Kitty had wondered how he had managed to afford it. Whilst not completely down at heel, her father's fortunes were precarious to say the least, since they often depended on which horse finished first in a particular race.

He was also known to take on things which were not always entirely legal. Something which had landed him in hot water on more than one occasion. It was no surprise that her eminently respectable aunt and uncle despaired of him.

Matt gave her gloved hand a comforting squeeze as they drove along the crowded streets. Kitty thought the city resembled a large anthill teeming with human life. The buildings were much larger and taller than the ones she was used to seeing in England and everywhere she looked building work seemed to be happening.

The large department stores were all decorated ready for Christmas and snow lay on the sidewalks and heaped up in the gutters. The pristine whiteness of the small drifts now grey or turned black with dirt from the city.

The car turned off the main street away from the stores and headed into what was clearly a more residential area. Eventually they pulled to a stop outside a smart building. Twin Christmas trees decorated with red and gold ribbons stood in stone pots on either side of the large glass entrance door.

'Please stay here,' Matt instructed the driver. 'We'll be back down shortly.' He climbed out of the car and held the door for Kitty.

She was grateful for Matt's assistance as the pavement was slippery underfoot, despite what looked like attempts to clear the ice from in front of the entrance. Looking up, the building seemed incredibly tall. She knew from his letters that her father's apartment was on the floor below the penthouse, so she guessed he must have good views of the city.

They made their way into the building to find a uniformed concierge seated behind a desk in the lobby.

'Excuse me, we are looking for Mr Underhay's apartment. I believe it to be on the seventeenth floor?' Kitty said.

The man gave her a slightly curious look. 'Do you mean Mr Edgar Underhay? You from England, ma'am?'

'Yes, that's right. I'm his daughter. Do you know if he is at home?' Kitty's heart was in her mouth as she asked the question, but she thought the concierge would probably know if her father was still in his apartment or had been taken to hospital.

'I believe so, ma'am. The elevator is to your right and will take you straight up.' The man indicated the ornate ironwork door of the lift.

'Thank you.'

Matt followed her as she crossed the marble-tiled floor of the lobby and pressed the brass button to summon the elevator. A moment later they were ascending rapidly inside the shiny metal walled box.

The elevator stopped and they stepped out onto a wide landing. A carpet runner covered the centre of the marble-tiled floor. Potted plants stood on wooden stands and Kitty could see there were two apartments on this floor.

'I believe that one is your father's.' Matt nodded in the direction of the door to the left.

'I think you're right.' Kitty checked the number on the discreet brass plaque affixed to the wall above the bell push.

She pressed the button and waited for a response, her heart hammering in her chest with anxiety. Her father might be too unwell to answer the door. He might have had to employ a nurse. All kinds of scenarios raced through her mind as she waited on the doormat.

There was no answer to her ring, so she pulled off her

leather glove and rapped on the door. The sound of her knocking resounded loudly along the landing. She stood on tiptoe and applied her eye to the small glass spyhole in the door, hoping to see if anyone was at home.

'Can you see anything?' Matt asked.

'Nothing.' Kitty relaxed down onto her heels.

'Let me take a peek.' Matt stepped forward and took her place at the door as Kitty gave the bell one more push.

'Any luck?' Kitty asked. Her husband was much taller than her so hopefully could see a little better.

'I swear someone is inside. I'm sure I heard something.' Matt frowned as he spoke.

'Oh honestly, what is going on?' Kitty asked and thumped on the door once more. 'Papa, are you in there?'

This time there was the sound of a bolt being drawn and a chain being removed, before finally the door of the apartment cracked open and her father peered out through the slit.

'Kitty, my dearest girl, and Matthew, come in out of the cold.' Her father opened the door more widely to permit them to enter.

For a man who was alleged to have been at death's door little more than a week ago, Edgar Underhay appeared to have made an excellent recovery. Kitty's initial feelings of relief at discovering her father apparently safe and well were rapidly being replaced by ones of confusion and irritation.

'What has happened to you? We had a most worrying telegram implying you were seriously ill. Have you been in hospital?' Kitty asked after kissing her father on the cheek. She scrutinised his appearance with a keen eye.

'Ah, um, perhaps you and Matthew should come in and sit down, darling.' Her father led the way into a bright and airy sitting room furnished in the latest style.

'The driver is waiting downstairs with our luggage,' Matt said, stopping at the entrance to the sitting room.

'Oh, well get him to bring it up, dear boy. You are most welcome to stay with me. There is an excellent guest bedroom and I've had it all made ready. It's even got a separate bathroom, all the mod cons here,' Edgar said, walking over to stand by the marble fireplace.

Matt disappeared to go and deal with their luggage as Kitty undid her coat and prepared to tackle her father. He seemed to her to be perfectly fit and well. The dark-red silk smoking jacket he was wearing fit perfectly with no sign of him having lost any weight. His colour was good and he looked much as he had when she had last seen him a year before back in England.

'Well?' Kitty asked as she took a seat on the black leather sofa.

'I am so sorry for alarming you, darling. Honestly, it was the last thing on my mind, but Nora had sent the telegram to you before I could stop her,' her father said as he inserted a cigarette into a small ebony holder.

'Nora?' Kitty asked. She had the sinking feeling she and Matt had been inveigled into a trip to New York.

'A lovely woman, you'll meet her soon, I daresay. She has the penthouse apartment upstairs. Such a kind soul, you'll adore her. Well, I was rather unwell, a bad chest you know.' Her father gave a somewhat theatrical cough as he lit his cigarette.

Kitty raised her brows but said nothing as she waited for her father to continue his story.

'She had called in to visit me. Brought a basket of fruit and some rather fine port. Really was most generous of her. Well, she was alarmed at how ill I looked and the next thing I knew she'd sent for you.' Her father's gaze skittered away from hers.

'And you didn't think it was worthwhile to let me know you were feeling better? Answer your telephone or send another telegram? Message the ship?' Kitty asked.

Her father shifted a little uncomfortably. 'It was too late by then, darling. I had no voice to answer the telephone for a few days and by the time I could have sent a message, well you were on your way.'

Kitty was not amused. She had spent the last week and a half imagining her father lying in a hospital bed seriously ill and now he was as large as life telling her it was little more than a cold. She suspected there were other factors at play in this supposed illness. Her father's dodgy dealings and shady past made it more than likely that his illness was a convenient social disorder rather than a medical problem.

'Who were you avoiding?' Kitty could hear bumps out on the landing and suspected that Matt and the driver were unloading their trunks from the elevator.

'Really, darling!' Her father adopted an affronted expression at the bluntness of her question.

'Papa?' Kitty glared at him. She knew her instincts had been correct. His reluctance to open the door had been a giveaway for a start.

Edgar sighed. 'I may have had one or two minor financial issues. All resolved now, of course. A mere temporary problem.' He held up his hand to prevent her from interrupting. 'As I said, Nora, the dear soul, unfortunately summoned you here before I could prevent her. Still, now you and Matthew are here, we can have the most marvellous Christmas together. Nora is throwing a costume party tomorrow night. Casino themed. She will be thrilled to meet you both.' He looked hopefully at her. 'You're not too cross, are you, darling?'

Kitty swallowed a sigh of exasperation. If they had been in England, for two pins she would have cheerfully walked out and gone home. Cross was an understatement. Now, however, they would be unable to leave until the new year so it seemed she, and Matt, would have to make the best of things.

CHAPTER TWO

Matt tipped the driver and dismissed him once the two large trunks had been deposited in the guest bedroom of his father-in-law's apartment. He had heard Kitty's slightly raised voice during her conversation with her father. If he had to guess, they seemed to have been tricked into coming to America.

Edgar certainly appeared to be quite in the pink for a man alleged to be dying just a few days earlier. It was clear the old rogue had been up to something shady again. Still, they had no choice now but to try to enjoy their stay, no matter how annoying it might be. Matt set the trunks in place and wandered over to the window to gaze out at the view.

The apartment block was situated right next to Central Park and the guest bedroom suite afforded a nice outlook over the trees. They were mostly bare of their leaves now and the trunks made a stark black contrast against the snowy landscape of the parkland.

In the distance he could see the shape of what appeared to be a large tea room, twinkling with electric lights and people walking through the park with their dogs. Their passage to return to England was booked for the new year, so it seemed they would be spending Christmas with Edgar in New York.

He went back into the lounge to discover Kitty looking cross as she took off her fur coat. Edgar was just finishing his cigarette, stubbing it out in a large glass Lalique ashtray. A small number of gaily coloured Christmas cards stood on the mantelpiece. A tiny festive tree sporting multicoloured baubles was in a pot on a glass and chrome side table.

'The trunks are in the guest room ready to unpack,' Matt said as Kitty returned from the hall where she had gone to hang up her coat.

'Thank you, darling. Papa is apparently much recovered, and we are invited to a costume party tomorrow evening.' She shot a glance at her father, who ran a forefinger around the rim of his collar.

'That sounds delightful, if unexpected. I'm glad to see you looking so chipper, Edgar. Kitty and I were very worried,' Matt said.

'Yes, that's all most unfortunate. All a bit of a misunderstanding. I was just explaining what happened to Kitty,' Edgar said as he offered Matt a cigarette from his silver case.

Matt shook his head and declined the offer as Edgar popped the case back inside the pocket of his smoking jacket. There was a ring at the front door as he did so. One short ring and two longer ones.

Kitty looked at Matt. 'Shall I get it?' she asked her father.

'No need, my dear. I'll go. That will be Nora now. I know that she is longing to meet you both.' Edgar hurried off into the hall and opened the door.

It seemed plain to Matt that the style of the rings at the door was some kind of code that Kitty's father had arranged with his neighbour. All of which confirmed his belief that Edgar had been up to no good.

'Nora, my dear, come and meet my daughter, Mrs Kitty

Bryant, and her husband, Captain Matthew Bryant. They have just arrived and will be staying for a few days.' Edgar stood aside and introduced a glamorous-looking, expensively dressed, dark-haired woman in her mid-fifties. 'Kitty, darling, this is Mrs Nora Dangerfield, my upstairs neighbour. She was the lady who sent you the telegram when I was so ill.'

'Oh my, you are just a picture, Mrs Bryant. Edgar has shown me some photographs of your wedding, but they really don't do you justice.' Mrs Dangerfield embraced Kitty and kissed her cheek, before greeting Matt in a similar fashion. 'Captain Bryant, I'm thrilled to meet you at last. Edgar told me you were a private investigator in England. How fascinating. You must have so many stories.' Nora beamed toothily at them.

'We're delighted to meet you, Mrs Dangerfield,' Kitty said.

'Oh pish, call me Nora. We don't stand on formalities here, do we, Edgar, honey?' She gave Kitty's father a playful nudge with her silk-clad elbow.

'Of course not, my dear,' Edgar said, giving another of his artificial-sounding little coughs.

Matt caught Kitty rolling her eyes when Nora began fussing over Edgar. He had to stifle a chuckle.

'Your poor father was terribly sick. It's hard to think that now, but I was so worried when I laid eyes on him that I had to send a telegram. When you're ill, all you want is your family and it must be so hard, honey, with you living in England,' Nora said as she plumped up a cushion on one of the armchairs and insisted that Edgar take a seat.

'Oh yes indeed, absence takes quite a toll sometimes,' Kitty agreed. 'Do you have family close by, Nora?'

'I have the one daughter, Lorena. She's married, and she and her husband Rudolph live a couple of blocks away. You must meet her, I'm sure you'll get on like a house on fire. You will both come to my party tomorrow night, won't you?' The older woman looked first at Kitty and then at Matt.

'Edgar was just saying something about it when you arrived,' Matt said.

He was privately amused at Kitty's expressions when she thought Nora and her father weren't looking at her. It was clear that despite her relief at finding him well, she was both furious at Edgar and slightly baffled by the situation they found themselves in.

'It's a Christmas costume party, mainly, of course, just an excuse to dress up and wear masks, with a casino theme. I'm raising money for orphaned children in the city. It's a cause very close to my heart as my dear late husband was cared for there as a child. I hold one every year.' Nora pressed a bejewelled hand to her bosom.

'It sounds like a very worthy cause,' Kitty said.

'And it will be so lovely for your father to have you at his side. I'm certain he is still quite weak, although he puts on such a brave front. I swear he had pneumonia.' Nora rested one hand lightly on Edgar's shoulder as he attempted to live up to his neighbour's description. 'I'll have Peggy, my secretary, put you on the attendee list. It's held in my apartment, so at least your dear father doesn't have to go out in the cold.'

'That's very kind of you,' Matt said. 'Kitty and I would love to attend.'

'Oh, how splendid. I shall enjoy the evening all the more knowing that Edgar is being looked after.' Nora beamed at them. 'Well, I must get back. Peggy does require supervision over the little details and there is still such a lot to do.'

'I'll see you out, my dear.' Edgar rose and escorted his friend out of the apartment.

'I had better see to our trunks,' Kitty said and disappeared off to the guest bedroom to unpack.

. . .

Matt took a seat on the sofa and waited for his father-in-law to return. Edgar reappeared after a moment and resumed his own seat in the armchair near the fireplace.

'You have made a good recovery, Edgar. Kitty and I were unsure if you would be at home or in hospital,' Matt said.

A dull reddish colour tinged his father-in-law's cheeks. 'Well, you know how these things are, my boy. I was unwell but well, truth be told, I'd had a bit of bad luck on the old gee-gees, the horses you know, and I owed a few dollars here and there. I thought it best to lie low and let my fortunes recover. Dear Nora, bless her, is the soul of kindness and took it upon herself to send for you both when she heard I was ill. By that time, of course, I'd had a change of luck and was feeling much better, but you were already on your way by then.' Edgar gave a slight shrug of his shoulders. Matt wondered if he had given Kitty the same spiel.

'Well, we're both delighted to find you so well. I daresay Kitty will wish to let her aunt and uncle know you are recovered.' Matt hid a smile at the look of consternation that crossed Edgar's face as he realised that his sister had been informed of the telegram.

'Oh yes, of course. I do hope Hortense was not too worried?' Edgar asked in a nonchalant tone.

'Kitty's aunt and uncle are in Yorkshire at the moment with Lucy, Rupert and baby William, but I am sure they will be happy to have their minds put at rest.' Matt knew Kitty's relatives were spending Christmas with her cousin Lucy and the new baby.

'That sounds most delightful. And Kitty's grandmother, is she in good health?' Edgar appeared relieved that his sister and her husband had other things to occupy their minds.

'I believe so.' Matt knew there was no love lost between Edgar and his mother-in-law. 'This is the most splendid apartment. The view over the park is quite something,' Matt said.

He, like Kitty, had wondered for a while how her father had managed to acquire living accommodation in such a prestigious area given his poor financial decisions.

'Ah, well, I had a stroke of luck there, dear boy. My good luck, of course, not poor Cubby Pendleton-Weeks. He's the chap who really owns this place,' Edgar explained, waving his hand airily around at his surroundings.

'Oh?' Matt could see there was a story to be heard.

'Yes, poor Cubby, he's in the middle of some marital strife. Quite unpleasant, I shan't bore you with all the ins and outs. A bad decision involving a chorus girl. The dear boy needed to, erm, hide some assets for a while. Just until the divorce blows over, you understand, so he put this place in my name. I'm just the caretaker really but it's jolly nice,' Edgar said.

'I see.' Matt blinked. Like a cat, Kitty's father had a knack of landing on his feet, and it certainly seemed he had done so in the case of this apartment.

'Now then, I mustn't neglect my duties as a host.' Edgar jumped to his feet in quite a spritely manner. 'I have a small kitchenette just through here for making tea, coffee, that kind of jazz. May I offer you some refreshments?'

* * *

Kitty emerged from the guest bedroom as he spoke. 'A cup of tea would be most welcome, Papa.'

'Of course, my dear.' Edgar hesitated for a second as if half-expecting Kitty to offer to make it.

Instead, she took a seat next to Matt, leaving her father to disappear through a door on the other side of the room. She was familiar with the arrangements for serviced flats like Edgar's. The kitchenette permitted the making of hot drinks and the preparation of snacks. Dinner and more substantial meals were ordered from a menu and delivered to the apartment. Dirty crockery was collected and taken away, and cleaning provided by a maid. There was also an arrangement for laundry services, all run by the concierge who liaised with the tenants.

'I've unpacked our things. I'm so glad we had Alice's assistance to get everything ready in such a rush for this trip. Nothing would be fit to wear otherwise,' Kitty said.

Her friend, Alice, had been a chambermaid at the hotel Kitty and her grandmother owned in Dartmouth. Earlier in the year, however, Alice had left to set up her own dressmaking business in the nearby village of Paignton. Her skills with a needle were only matched by her talent for packing and folding.

'And now it seems we shall require eye masks to wear with our evening clothes for Nora's party,' Matt remarked with a smile.

'We have the ones from the ship when they did that masked ball. I suppose I can try and decorate them to make them a little better.' Kitty had kept the plain black masks the ship had provided for the first-class passengers for an event held on board.

She had not particularly been in the mood to attend but Matt had thought it might take her mind off worrying about her father. She glared at the closed door to the kitchenette. It seemed her concern had been for nothing, and her father had merely used illness as a cover for avoiding his debtors.

Kitty would need to send some telegrams to allay her aunt and uncle's fears and to let her grandmother know that all was well. She suspected both her aunt and her grandmother would have a few choice words to say when they discovered the extent of Edgar's latest shenanigans.

The telegrams were duly sent and dinner for three ordered for delivery to Edgar's apartment for that evening. Kitty and Matt settled in to enjoy their stay in New York. The weather had closed in and more snow began to fall so they decided to postpone exploring the city until the following day.

Kitty had to admit she was quite looking forward to visiting some of the large department stores. Especially as they had seemed crammed to the hilt with all kinds of festive delights as they had driven to the apartment.

'You must go and see the enormous Christmas tree outside the Rockefeller Center, my dear. The decorations are quite a sight to be seen,' Edgar informed them as they started to make their plans about where they would like to go.

'Alice and I saw a Pathé news film of the Macy's Christmas parade at the picture house, so I must visit the store so I can tell Alice all about it,' Kitty said.

'If you intend to visit Macy's, then you can call at the Empire State Building, it's not far away and you can view the city from the top,' Edgar suggested. 'If you are good with heights, of course.'

'That certainly sounds appealing,' Matt agreed.

'The ice skating is also open in Central Park, I believe, although I suspect shopping may be more to your taste, Kitty, my dear.' Her father smiled indulgently at her.

'I have never really tried ice skating. One doesn't often even get frosts in Dartmouth, and certainly I've never seen the river ice over,' Kitty said. She had often wondered if she would be able to even keep upright on a pair of ice skates.

'It might be interesting to see.' Matt smiled at her. 'And we can always take tea somewhere afterwards.'

'I suppose so,' Kitty agreed, her spirits rising. She was not overly fond of being cold and a nice tea somewhere sounded much more to her liking. It certainly sounded as if they would have a full agenda over Christmas.

CHAPTER THREE

By the following morning the snow had stopped falling and the view from their bedroom revealed a pristine white canvas in the park below. Kitty knew that would not last long once everyone started to get out and about.

Her father had offered to accompany them on their outing. Kitty suspected he was attempting to make some kind of amends for having lured them to New York in the first place. It would be helpful though to have someone accompanying them who knew their way about the city.

They decided Macy's should be their first stop since Kitty wanted to buy some gifts to take home with her. She also wanted to buy a few things to spruce up the masks from the ship that she and Matt intended to wear for Nora's casino party that evening.

The concierge summoned a taxi for them, and they set off for the stores. Once they were out of the cab, Kitty was glad of her fur coat and hat as the wind blowing along the streets between the buildings was bitterly cold. They spent a pleasant but tiring morning in a whirl of sightseeing and shopping. Lunch was taken in the restaurant of one of the stores and after the promised trip to the giddy heights of the Empire State Building with its fashionable art deco styling and stunning views of the city, Kitty declared herself exhausted.

'I think we should go back and rest for a while if we are partying this evening,' she suggested.

'Very wise, my dear.' Her father coughed as he spoke and Kitty gave him a sharp glance, unsure if he was unwell or if this was another of his tricks.

They returned to the apartment laden with shopping. Kitty was keen to apply some of the trimmings she had acquired to their masks so they would be dry for the evening's festivities.

They had to wait in the lobby for the elevator since there seemed to be a number of people taking various items to Nora's penthouse apartment ready for the party.

'Is Nora's apartment much larger than yours?' Kitty asked her father once they were finally able to enter the elevator cage to ascend upwards.

'Oh yes. Nora's place covers the whole of the top floor and has a roof terrace too. So it's more than double the size of my little pied-à-terre,' Edgar assured her. 'She's a very wealthy woman.'

The elevator stopped and they made their way inside Edgar's apartment. Kitty removed her coat, hat and gloves before kicking off her shoes with a thankful sigh. Matt took her parcels into their bedroom, while Edgar seated himself beside the fireplace and drew out his cigarettes.

'How long have you known Nora?' Kitty asked as she came to join him, perching herself on the end of the sofa.

'About two years now, I should say. We met in the lobby the one day. I was staying here with Cubby then, before his problems. She was giving Enrique, the day concierge, an earful about some kind of maintenance problem in her apartment. We got talking, as one does, and she is something of an anglophile. She's visited many times and we've been pally ever since.'

'She said she was a widow?' Kitty was very curious about her father's friendship with the attractive and wealthy Mrs Dangerfield.

Her father lit up his cigarette. 'Hmm, she lost her husband about eight years ago. They were devoted to one another. Her daughter Lorena is married. She only has the one child.'

Edgar caught sight of Kitty's expression. 'There is no romance there, if that is what you're thinking. Nora has other fish to fry in that direction, believe you me.'

'Oh?' Kitty wondered what her father was implying.

'It's a tad complicated. You'll see what I mean at the party tonight.' Edgar blew out a thin plume of smoke as Matt emerged from the guest room and made his way to the kitchenette. 'I say, do pop the kettle on, there's a good chap. I'm dying for a spot of tea.'

The subject was changed so Kitty's curiosity about Nora was forced to remain unsatisfied for the moment.

'This is not what I thought I should be doing on this trip?' Kitty remarked to Matt as she sat in front of the small French walnut dressing table to put on her ruby dropper earrings. Above them she could already hear music.

'No. I think we both envisaged it would be more bedside nursing or visits to a hospital,' Matt remarked drily as he adjusted his white tie.

'It's a good thing Alice insisted we pack more evening attire. She thought we should need it on board the liner.' Kitty frowned as she patted her short blonde curls into place.

'And now we are to don masks ready to gamble and dance the night away to raise funds for an orphanage.' Matt bent and dropped a kiss on top of her head.

'Terribly decadent. Father said there was poker and roulette. There is also a tombola and raffle apparently. I feel as if

I have been drafted into an American version of one of Mrs Craven's fundraisers,' Kitty said.

Matt laughed. 'Dear Mrs C. This would be right up her street.'

Mrs Craven was Kitty's grandmother's dearest friend. A former mayoress of Dartmouth, she knew everyone and was on every committee possible. She and Kitty had never seen eye to eye and since Kitty's marriage, Mrs Craven had seemed to make it her personal mission to try and rope Kitty into assisting her with her charity work.

Kitty stood and smoothed down the dark-red satin skirt of her evening gown. 'I hope we are not the only ones not in costume,' she said.

'Edgar said that it would be a mix of people in costume and others, like us, just in evening attire with masks,' Matt reassured her as he picked up the mask Kitty had trimmed with some sequins for him to wear.

'I hope so.' She collected her own mask and her small gold evening bag.

Her father was waiting for them in the lounge. To her surprise he was dressed in full costume with a ruffled shirt and black mask and carrying a small guitar.

'I'm a wandering minstrel, before you ask.' He fixed her with a stare through the eye holes of the mask which covered the top half of his face. 'I shall sing for my supper if required.'

Kitty smiled. 'Well, that will be a first for me. I don't recall hearing you sing before.'

Her father gave a deep bow and a flourish of his hand. 'I have a fine baritone, I'll have you know. Now, shall we go? Nora will be looking out for us.'

Since her father assured them that the elevator would probably be busy, they followed him along the landing past the front door of the second flat that shared the space and walked up a flight of stairs to the penthouse floor.

The strains of jazz music grew even louder before they even entered the generous square landing. The front door of the apartment was slightly ajar, so Edgar led the way and pushed it open.

An attractive, young, dark-haired woman of around Kitty's age was situated just inside in the hallway clutching a notepad and pen. She was dressed in a pale-pink satin costume as a Christmas fairy with a tinsel halo around her head. The girl also appeared to be quite flustered.

'What ho, Peggy, my dear. May I introduce my daughter, Mrs Kitty Bryant, and her husband, Matthew. This lady is Miss Peggy Marsh, Nora's right-hand woman.' Edgar performed the introductions and Kitty deduced this must be the assistant Nora had mentioned on her visit to Edgar's apartment.

'I'm delighted to make your acquaintance. Nora said you had come from England,' Peggy said.

'Yes, from Devon. It's very kind of Nora to invite us tonight,' Kitty said, smiling at the girl.

'I hope you'll enjoy it. Do go right on in. Nora is with her daughter, Lorena, and her son-in-law, Rudolph, in the salon.' Peggy marked their names off the list in front of her.

The salon appeared to be a large room, twice the size of the lounge in Edgar's apartment. The walls were hung with what appeared to be expensive artworks and there were several glass and mahogany bijouterie cabinets full of silver trinkets. A tall, thin, elderly black man dressed impeccably in a dinner suit came forward to offer them a glass of champagne from the silver tray he was carrying.

'I say, Horatio, it looks like a jolly good turnout tonight,' Edgar remarked to the manservant as he accepted a glass.

'I believe Miss Nora is very pleased, Mr Underhay,' the man replied.

It was clear that her father knew the man well so Kitty assumed he must be one of Mrs Dangerfield's permanent staff.

There was a small area set aside for dancing, which appeared quite crowded and popular. The tombola and raffle table were situated in the area where presumably Nora held her dinner parties. A small roulette wheel attended by a young lady wearing a feathered headband was in one corner and a card table was set up nearby.

Uniformed maids in black dresses with starched, white-frilled aprons and caps were circulating with plates of canapés. Guests were attired in either sparkling masks or various fancy-dress costumes. A blue fug of cigarette smoke hovered just below the crystal chandeliers and the lively sound of laughter and chatter mingled with the music.

A huge Christmas tree glittered and sparkled with tinsel and lights, and the edges of the dance space were surrounded with exotic red-leaved plants in gold-sprayed pots. The manservant had moved away once Matt and Kitty had also taken a glass of champagne.

The music was emanating from an adjoining room where a young woman of about Kitty's own age was singing, accompanied by a man playing the piano and another two gentlemen playing saxophone and trumpet. A few people were seated in the space enjoying drinks, canapés and music.

Nora was holding court dressed in a splendid dark-green satin gown, a bejewelled mask covered the top half of her face and small glittering wings were attached to the rear of her dress. Diamanté clips adorned her dark hair and expensive diamond jewellery sparkled around her neck and wrists. A well-dressed, silver-haired man in a matching green-satin suit was laughing heartily at something she had just said.

Standing next to them was a smaller, auburn-haired woman of a similar age dressed in crimson silk, also masked and sporting wings at the back of her dress. She, however, appeared to find Nora's comment less amusing, judging by the sour twist of her lips.

'Oh lawks,' Edgar muttered on seeing who was with their hostess. Since good manners dictated that they should speak to Nora they had no choice but to approach. Even though Kitty suspected her father would rather have avoided the group.

'Edgar, honey, there you are, and with Matt and Kitty too. Welcome to my party. Isn't it splendid?' Nora greeted them all with a kiss on the cheek and a bright smile. She seemed full of more than just the festive spirit and Kitty wondered how many glasses of champagne their hostess had imbibed.

'A veritable triumph, my dear,' Edgar agreed. 'Kitty, Matthew, may I present my neighbours from a couple of floors down? Mortimer and Titania Liggett.' Her father introduced them to the man and woman standing with Nora.

'Delighted to meet you, I'm sure,' Kitty murmured, shaking hands with Mortimer and Titania.

'Now, I simply must find where Lorena and Rudi have gone. I do so want them to meet you both.' Nora smiled at Kitty and Matt.

'Stay here, I'll go and find them for you, Nora, darling,' Mortimer Liggett offered, and slipped away into the crowd.

'So kind,' Nora said, before taking a sip of her champagne.

'Oh yeah, Morty is a regular angel to damsels in distress,' Titania observed sourly.

'Your costumes look marvellous,' Kitty observed, hoping to change the course of the conversation. It was clear to her that Titania was not a fan of Nora and there was an odd atmosphere between them.

'Why thank you, Kitty. I'm dressed as the spirit of Christmas.' Nora beamed at her, her diamond and emerald earrings gleaming in the light from the crystal chandeliers. 'What did you say you had come as again, Titania, honey?'

'Holly. See, green leaves and red berries.' Titania indicated the decorations on her crimson gown.

'And rather prickly,' Edgar muttered in Kitty's ear, making her suppress an unladylike snort of laughter.

'Ah, here is my daughter now.' Nora turned slightly as the crowd parted to permit Mortimer and another couple through to join their group. Lorena was a younger version of Nora, but dressed in a somewhat shapeless gown of pink satin and chiffon. Her husband, Rudolph, was a good-looking but rather vacuous-looking man. He wore neither a costume nor a mask.

Nora performed the introductions and Kitty was glad her mask was hiding some of her face when she noticed Lorena's husband unashamedly eyeing her up. She felt Matt stiffen at her side and knew her husband had also noticed.

'Kitty and Matthew came to New York to be with Edgar when he was ill. I'm happy you've recovered so well.' Nora glanced fondly at Kitty's father. 'At least you can all have a lovely family Christmas together now.'

Kitty murmured agreement while thinking about the Christmas they had been planning. Lunch at the Dolphin Hotel with her grandmother, then an afternoon walk by the sea. High tea and an evening of card games and music with friends popping in. A wave of homesickness swept through her and she wondered how her dog and cat were settling without them. She hoped they were behaving for her housekeeper, Mrs Smith.

'Delighted to meet you, I'm sure,' Lorena said. 'Have you come from London?'

'No, from Devon. We sailed from Plymouth,' Matt said.

Lorena and Rudi looked blank.

'We've been to London several times, haven't we, Rudi?' Lorena said. 'So quaint.'

'It was delightful,' Rudolph agreed.

'Now then, my darlings, let's go mingle and spend some dollars. I want tonight to be the best fundraiser I've ever held.' Nora shooed them all away.

Peggy, Nora's assistant, appeared to have finished her duties at the door and Kitty saw her talking hurriedly with Horatio as he circulated with his tray of glasses. She still looked anxious. Edgar had gravitated to the roulette wheel and Kitty hoped he would not get too carried away.

'Shall we try our luck at the tombola?' Matt asked.

'Why not, it's for a good cause,' Kitty agreed, and they edged through the room to the table where two uniformed maids appeared to be in charge of the drum and taking the money. The tombola had certainly seemed popular and many of the prizes had already been claimed. Kitty's tickets were blanks but Matt was more successful, winning a Kewpie doll which he promptly presented to Kitty.

'A nice little souvenir of the event,' Matt said.

'Thank you.' Kitty stowed the tiny doll, which was dressed in white satin with a marabou trim, inside her gold evening purse.

They also purchased some of the raffle tickets and then went to watch the roulette table, where Edgar appeared to have settled.

'How is it going?' Matt asked him.

'Not bad, old bean,' Edgar replied as a small pile of chips was sent his way by the croupier.

Kitty was relieved to see that he didn't appear to be losing and for once seemed to be placing moderate bets. Her mind more at ease, she happily accompanied Matt back into the other room so they could take a turn about the tiny floor in front of the band.

Titania was already on the dance floor but there was no sign of Mortimer. Instead, a rather portly older man was escorting her around the room and looking very pleased with himself.

As they danced Kitty caught glimpses of various people through the archway that led to the other room. Mortimer talking intimately with Nora. Lorena looking as if she were searching for someone. Then Peggy cosied into a corner near the Christmas tree with Rudolph.

Flushed from the warmth of the room and the exercise, Kitty was glad to find a vacant seat to enjoy a Manhattan cocktail and a few of the dainty sandwiches that had also started to be circulated. The tea they had enjoyed before dressing for the party seemed hours away now and her stomach had started to grumble.

They had not been seated for long though before she became aware of a disturbance in the other room.

CHAPTER FOUR

Matt moved quickly to make his way through the crowd to see what was happening. Kitty followed behind him. Nora looked flushed and angry as she held her cheek. Mortimer was at her side, his arm around her waist. Titania was in a sobbing, crumpled heap on a gilt chair in front of them.

'How dare you assault my mother!' Lorena was also present and rounded on Titania, leaning over her, her cheeks pink with anger. Edgar appeared at Lorena's side, placing a calming hand on her shoulder.

Matt realised that the outline of a hand was visible on Nora's cheek when his hostess moved.

'I think you should take your wife home, old boy. I think the champagne may have made her somewhat overwrought,' Edgar suggested, looking at Mortimer.

'I think that would be wise.' Nora's tone was icy as she looked at Titania.

'Disgraceful behaviour,' an elderly matron standing near Matt said. Her diamond dropper earrings quivered with indignation. 'No manners these young people.'

Mortimer, with Edgar's assistance, scooped his wife up and got her to her feet.

'I'm so sorry, Nora. I'll take Titania home.' He glared at his wife who clung on tightly to him, still sniffling incoherently. 'Thank you, Edgar.' Mortimer led his wife away and the small crowd dissipated to return to their previous amusements.

'Mother, are you all right? Where is Peggy? I'll get her to put a cold compress on your cheek.' Lorena fussed over her mother.

'I'll find Miss Peggy, for you, ma'am,' Horatio offered.

'Goodness me, trust Titania to make a fool of herself,' Nora muttered, brushing away Lorena's ministrations. 'Don't fuss so, honey, I'm perfectly all right.'

Peggy came rushing up to her mistress, her cheeks flushed. 'I didn't see what happened as I was sorting something out for a guest in the hallway. Are you hurt?'

'I've just told Lorena, I am perfectly fine,' Nora insisted. 'It was a fuss over nothing.'

'She needs a cold compress for her cheek,' Lorena said.

'Oh yes, oh my, of course.' Peggy darted off.

'I thought something like this would happen,' Edgar murmured in Matt's ear.

'Oh?' Matt looked at his father-in-law.

'Mortimer's dalliance with Nora is the worst kept secret in New York. I'm not at all surprised Titania slapped her,' Edgar said in a low voice, shaking his head ruefully. 'It's been brewing for a while.'

Matt assumed he meant Titania's assault on Nora. 'I see. Most awkward.' He glanced in Kitty's direction to see her peering at him, no doubt hoping he had discovered the cause of the contretemps.

'Yes, it's quite the scandal.' Edgar grinned and clapped Matt on the back. 'You'd better get back to Kitty, I expect she will be bursting to find out what's gone on.'

* * *

Kitty was indeed agog to discover what had happened in the other room. Her limited view of events had indicated that the argument had been between Titania and their hostess. From the comments she'd overheard from people around her, there had been some sympathy for Titania.

'Poor girl, he's made a fool of her for too long,' one society matriarch remarked to her friend with a meaningful nod.

'Absolutely. Nora can be such fun, but a little discretion goes a long way in these matters,' her friend agreed.

Matt returned to her side and picked up his abandoned cocktail.

'Well, what was that all about?' Kitty asked, once she was certain no one else was likely to overhear them. 'I couldn't get close enough to hear what they said.'

'It seems our hostess and Mortimer Liggett have been having an affair. Titania seems to have confronted Nora about it and slapped her.' Matt grinned as he spoke.

'Goodness, how dreadful. That must have been why Papa was alarmed when we got here and saw them together. New York society is certainly much more avant-garde than in Devon.' Kitty's eyes widened.

'Absolutely. Can you imagine what dear Mrs Craven would have had to say about such shenanigans?' Matt's smile grew even wider.

Kitty gave him a playful push. 'I think this may be one story we don't share when we get home. They will be more disparaging than ever about the kind of company Father keeps if this gets out.'

The incident seemed quickly forgotten and Kitty continued to enjoy the party with more dancing and champagne. At eleven thirty Horatio rang a small silver bell to attract the attention of the guests. Nora, seemingly fully recovered, announced the prize for best costume.

This went to a plump lady with blonde hair dressed in silver lamé with an enormous crimson bow about her waist who had apparently come as a Christmas parcel. Nora congratulated her and presented her with a huge heart-shaped box of chocolates.

The raffle prizes were drawn and announced. Kitty's eyes widened at the munificence of some of the prizes. Hotel stays and five-course dinners, a day on a yacht, lunch at a country club and a case of champagne were amongst the spoils.

She and Matt were not amongst the winners, but Edgar was the winner of a luxury wicker hamper which appeared to be full of all kinds of delights. With the prizes dispensed, a toast was proposed and drunk, followed by the band leading the guests in some Christmas songs before the party wrapped up.

Peggy was at the door to wish them all goodnight.

'Thank you all for coming. Nora is thrilled that you were able to attend and support her tonight,' Peggy said as Kitty wrapped her fur stole around her shoulders for the short walk down the stairs to the floor below.

Matt had been entrusted with carrying Edgar's raffle prize since her father was still carrying his minstrel's guitar.

'It was a wonderful party. We really appreciate her kindness at including us,' Kitty said.

Looking back over Peggy's shoulder she could see their hostess apparently having heated words with Horatio. He appeared to be attempting to reassure her and Kitty wondered what the manservant had done wrong. He had seemed to her to be the epitome of a well-trained staff member.

'You seem to have raised a good sum of money,' Matt remarked as he shifted the weight of the wicker hamper in his arms.

'I hope so. We have to tally up the final amounts, but it all looks promising.' Peggy gave a tight smile and Kitty guessed the girl was tired after such a long day.

'Good news for the orphanage then,' Matt responded cheerfully, and they made their way back down the stairs to Edgar's apartment.

Edgar whistled a cheerful tune as he unlocked the door and stood aside to allow Matt to pass through first with the heavy hamper.

'It's fortunate that you recovered so swiftly from your illness so that we could attend the party tonight,' Kitty remarked to her father as she drew off her satin evening gloves.

The whistle died on Edgar's lips, and he had the grace to look a little shamefaced. 'Well, I'm still not quite one hundred per cent you know, darling girl. I know I put on a good front, but these cold winters here do rather take it out of one.' He followed this with an affected cough.

Kitty rolled her eyes at his nonsense and went to assist Matt who was examining the contents of the hamper.

'There are some quite splendid things in here,' Matt said as he admired a vintage bottle of port which was tucked in amongst the straw that lined the basket.

'Nora is always very successful at getting people to pony up prizes for these things. She is herself a very generous woman. Incredibly wealthy. Those diamonds she was wearing this evening must be worth a king's ransom,' Edgar said as he lit up one of his cigarettes.

'That was quite a scene this evening with Titania Liggett,' Kitty said as she seated herself opposite her father and slipped off her gold evening shoes.

'The gossip amongst the ladies who lunch is that Nora is expecting Mortimer to leave his wife and marry her. From things Nora has said to me, I think that's probably true. I don't know if Titania is aware of this plan.' Edgar blew smoke rings up towards the ceiling.

'But she knew of the affair?' Matt asked, leaving the hamper on the table and coming to join them.

'Oh yes. I rather think she thought it was simply a brief indiscretion and she could just ignore it and let it blow over. It's not the first time this has happened. Titania is the one with money in that marriage. Mortimer hasn't a bean of his own,' Edgar said.

'So, Titania thought her position fairly safe I suppose, but if Nora is wealthy herself then Mortimer may jump ship,' Matt observed.

'Dear me, what a scandal.' Kitty placed a hand in front of her mouth to suppress a yawn. 'I really think I must go to bed. All the dancing and excitement has quite worn me out.'

She said goodnight to her father and she and Matt retired for the night.

Kitty woke the following morning to a crisp, bright day. A fresh sprinkling of snow once again covered the ground and sparkled enticingly in the morning sunlight. Kitty was filled with restless energy and the desire to get out and explore Central Park.

'Papa said there is a tea house in the park that serves breakfast,' Kitty said as she gave Matt a winning smile. 'Let's go and walk the cobwebs away and do a little exploring. Papa rarely rises before lunch anyway so we can leave him a note to say where we have gone.'

Matt laughed and agreed. She suspected he too wished to get out into the fresh air. Being cooped up inside never suited him. Kitty scribbled a note for her father and left it on the coffee table.

They wrapped up warmly and made their way to the lobby, where they asked for directions to the tea house in the park from the concierge. He seemed to be a different man from the one who had been there the previous day.

'Just go out of here, turn to the left and through the iron gates into the park. Follow the path where it rises and you'll see it right up ahead,' the man said.

They thanked him and set off. The streets were crowded already with Christmas shoppers looking for last-minute gifts and grocery items. It was only four days to Christmas and the air crackled with the energy Kitty had already come to associate with the city, and she was glad when they turned off and walked into the calm of the park.

The grey slush of the well-trodden city sidewalks gave way to the delicious crisp crunch of fresh snow. Only a few people appeared to have passed that way and the white cover on the path had few footprints.

Their breath hung in frozen clouds in front of them as they walked, and Kitty was glad of Matt's arm to prevent her slipping, despite her stout boots. Within a few minutes they had drawn level with the back of the apartment building they had just left.

'There seems to be a path there,' Kitty said, indicating with her sheepskin mittened hand. 'I wonder that the concierge didn't send us that way.'

They both looked at the short and well-used path leading from the rear of the apartment block between some snowy scrubby laurels. Footprints leading to and from the building were just visible under the fresh snow layer.

'Perhaps it is used mainly by the staff. A service entrance to the building. The kitchens are there so the cooks and delivery people may use it,' Matt suggested as he followed Kitty's gaze. 'Wait, there is something there.' He paused and frowned.

'What is it?' Kitty stopped to look, alerted by the urgent tone in Matt's voice.

There was something incongruously green and bright against the snow, half-hidden by the bushes. Kitty exchanged a worried glance with Matt and together they took a few steps forward to investigate. Her heart pounded in her chest.

'Surely, that can't be?' Kitty gasped as they drew closer to the mysterious bundle.

Nora Dangerfield lay dead amongst the bushes. The green satin of her evening gown was frosted and lightly sprinkled with snow. A startled expression was on her lips and the diamonds she had been wearing in her ears and around her neck and wrists were missing.

Her lips were blue and there were signs of bruising around her throat. She was indisputably dead. It looked as if she must have been killed sometime before judging by the snow on her dress.

'She's been strangled. How on earth did she get here?' Kitty looked around for clues.

Nora's mink sable fur throw was trapped under her body, implying she had slipped it on to step outside for a brief moment. The ground was trampled and there were no clear footprints thanks to the snowfall.

'I don't know but we must get the police.' Matt's mouth was set in a grim line. 'I can't believe she's not been missed before now.'

Kitty shivered. What could have happened after the end of the party for Nora to have finished up dead outside the apartment building?

Matt followed the narrow path leading to the rear of the building, where Kitty heard him knocking on what she assumed must be the rear door of the block. She heard male voices and various bumps and bangs.

While she waited for Matt to return or help to arrive, she carefully examined the body, being certain not to touch anything. All of Nora's jewels were missing. Her bracelet, rings, watch, earrings and necklace were gone. Her party mask lay on the floor beside her body. The elastic on the back was broken and her bejewelled hair clips lay beside it, possibly shaken off in a struggle.

Kitty bent to study Nora's hands to see if there might be a clue there. A fragment of cloth or some blood beneath the woman's beautifully manicured nails, but there was nothing.

Matt returned to join her. 'The police are on their way. There was a service door as we suspected. It leads to the kitchen the chef uses to make meals for the building.' He placed his arm around Kitty's waist. 'Are you all right, old thing?'

Kitty nodded. 'Yes, I'm just a little shaken.' She managed a wan smile. 'I should be used to this sort of thing by now. Everywhere we go it seems a body turns up.'

Matt returned her smile. 'It certainly feels that way. I told the concierge not to alert Nora's staff or her family until the police arrive.'

Kitty gave her husband a sharp look. 'You think she was killed by someone she knew?'

'I don't know for certain but whoever killed her knew about this entrance to the building. She must have trusted them to voluntarily come down here after the party. It may be a member of her staff, or a family member was involved. In any case, the less people trampling over a crime scene the better.'

Kitty nodded, she could see his logic. She also thought it wouldn't be very nice for Nora's loved ones to see her like this. Discarded in the shrubbery like a piece of rubbish.

There was the sound of the service door opening once more and two fresh-faced uniformed police officers came through the shrubbery. They were accompanied by an older man with dark hair dressed in street clothes. He wore a dark-brown homburg hat and a thick dark-brown overcoat.

'Captain and Mrs Bryant?' he asked as he approached.

'Yes, sir,' Matt replied and waited as the detective gave Nora's body a swift, assessing glance.

'You found this lady and you and Mrs Bryant know her?' he asked, whilst stooping over Nora.

'Yes, this is Mrs Nora Dangerfield. She occupies the penthouse apartment in this block,' Kitty answered.

She was quite cold now, she couldn't even feel her feet from where they had been standing in the snow.

'You live in this building too?' the detective asked as he glanced up at her.

'No, sir, we're visiting from England. My father lives in an apartment on the floor below Mrs Dangerfield. We're staying with him for Christmas,' Kitty answered.

The two constables had stationed themselves, one outside the service door and one on the public path just a few feet away. Kitty presumed it was to prevent anyone else from stumbling across the scene.

'Hmm, the lady is in evening wear.' The detective straightened up.

'There was a party here last night. A charity fundraiser hosted by Mrs Dangerfield for a local orphanage. All her jewellery is missing,' Kitty said.

The detective looked keenly at her. 'You and your husband were at this party?'

'Yes, sir. Mrs Dangerfield extended us an invitation when she knew we were staying with Edgar, my father-in-law,' Matt answered instead of Kitty, and she felt his arm squeeze her a little tighter around her waist.

'I see. Which apartment are you staying in?' the policeman asked.

Matt gave Edgar's address.

'If I can ask you and Mrs Bryant to return to that address, and I'll come along to speak to you both shortly.' The detective took a card from his pocket and gave it to Matt. 'It's mighty cold out here and, Mrs Bryant, you must have had a nasty shock finding this lady like this.'

'Thank you, sir.' Matt tucked the card inside his coat pocket, and they retraced their steps back the way they had come. Kitty was glad to be moving again to try and get the circulation going in her frozen feet.

The concierge looked up as soon as they entered the lobby, an eager expression on his face. 'What's happening out there, sir, ma'am? I've had both Peggy Marsh and Horatio Blackstock asking me if I've seen Mrs Dangerfield this morning.'

'The police will be in shortly. I'm certain they will speak to Mrs Dangerfield's staff and family once they've established what's happened to her,' Matt said.

'This is a very reputable building. We've never had any trouble here before.' The concierge looked pale and troubled, running his tongue across lips which seemed to have dried.

'It is most peculiar. Were you on duty late last night?' Kitty asked.

'No, ma'am. My shift started at six this morning and the guy I took over from didn't hand across anything out of the ordinary. He didn't say as Mrs Dangerfield was out.'

'You have a record of people entering and leaving the building?' Kitty asked.

'Yes, ma'am. Just the residents and any particular visitors they might be expecting or packages, that kind of thing.' The concierge looked bewildered.

'I take it that the service door is usually used just by staff?' Kitty could see there was a door behind the concierge's desk, and she assumed that must lead to the kitchens and the door to the outside.

'Yes, ma'am. A lady like Mrs Dangerfield would never have gone out that way,' the concierge asserted.

And yet, Kitty thought, she had done so last night.

CHAPTER FIVE

'Father is going to be dreadfully upset,' Kitty remarked as they ascended in the elevator to the apartment. 'He seemed to be very good chums with Nora. It's such a dreadful thing to have happened to her. She was in such good spirits at the party.'

'Yes, it's a horrid shock.' Matt gave Kitty a concerned look when she shivered. 'Are you all right, darling? I think some brandy might be in order when we get inside.'

Edgar was up, drinking coffee from an elegant white geometrically shaped porcelain cup when they let themselves into the apartment.

'You two are back jolly early,' he exclaimed in surprise, looking at the clock on the mantelpiece. 'Did they run out of maple syrup at the tea house?'

His jovial expression sobered when he caught sight of Kitty's face.

'Papa, there is no easy way to tell you this, but I'm afraid your friend, Nora Dangerfield, is dead, murdered. Matt and I have just found her outside the building.' Kitty sat down heavily on the sofa.

Edgar startled, slopping a little of his coffee into the saucer. 'What? When? How? Oh, my darling girl, that's awful.' He stared at Kitty.

'It looks as if she was strangled in the early hours of this morning. She was still in her evening dress from last night,' Matt said as he took off his overcoat and hat. 'I think Kitty could use a little brandy. It's been a ghastly shock.'

'Oh yes, of course.' Edgar set down his cup and saucer and jumped to his feet. He rummaged inside a small stylish cocktail cabinet and produced three crystal glasses and a brandy bottle.

'The police are downstairs now dealing with everything. They will be up shortly, I daresay, to speak to us,' Kitty said.

A look of alarm spread over her father's face as he poured a generous shot of brandy into each glass. 'Police?'

'Well, yes, obviously. They will need a statement from me and Kitty since we were the ones who found her. I expect they will want to ask us all questions about the party too.' Matt picked up a couple of glasses and passed one to Kitty.

Kitty took a sip and gasped as the heat from the spirit hit the back of her throat. A moment later, a warm sensation spread around her sternum, and she gave herself a mental shake.

'What was the name of the detective that we met downstairs? Is it on the card he gave us?' she asked, looking at Matt.

Her husband rummaged in the pocket of his recently discarded overcoat. 'A Lieutenant Tanfield,' he said, looking at the small, oblong card.

Her father gave a slight groan and Kitty looked at him. 'I take it you have encountered him before?' she asked. Somehow, knowing her father as she did, she was not unduly surprised.

'Our paths may have crossed once or twice,' Edgar admitted.

Kitty's heart sank and she took another sip of brandy before putting her glass down on the table and discarding her fur coat.

She dreaded to think how her father may have encountered the lieutenant, but she suspected it was not in a positive way.

'I can't believe it. And it was definitely murder, you say?' Her father shook his head. 'Who would want to harm Nora?'

'She seemed to be having words with a few people last night,' Kitty said.

'Titania, you mean? But surely you don't think Titania would have harmed her?' Edgar looked aghast.

'She did slap her,' Matt said.

'I know, dear boy, but that was in the heat of the moment. Too much champers. I mean murder, well...' Edgar's voice trailed off clearly appalled at the idea that Titania might be a suspect.

'It's no use speculating. I suppose we shall have to wait until the police arrive before we learn anything more,' Kitty said. She finished her brandy and was relieved to discover she was starting to feel better. The combination of the cold and the shock of discovering Nora's body had made her feel quite ill.

It was sometime later before there was knock on the apartment door.

'I think I might make myself scarce, just while you talk to Lieutenant Tanfield. Give you more privacy,' Edgar said as he made a bolt for his bedroom.

Kitty suppressed a sigh and went to open the door for the police officer.

'Do come in, Lieutenant.' She led the way to the sitting room, after hanging up the policeman's overcoat. 'May we offer you some tea, or perhaps coffee?' she suggested, belatedly recalling that America was not so fond of tea as the English.

'No, thank you, ma'am.' The detective took a seat on one of the armchairs and pulled a notebook from inside the top breast pocket of his jacket. 'Perhaps you'd both be so good as to run me through what happened earlier today. What time did you stumble upon Mrs Dangerfield?'

Kitty took a seat next to Matt. 'I think we set off from here just before ten o'clock. We had been told there was a tea house in the park which offered a good breakfast menu.'

The policeman nodded and made notes as Kitty outlined what had happened.

'Did you recognise her straight away?' the policeman asked.

Matt shook his head. 'No, we just saw something bright green amongst the bushes, and it struck us as odd. It wasn't until we got closer that we realised it was Nora.'

'And you recognised her gown as the one she was wearing for her party?' Lieutenant Tanfield said.

'Yes, she'd taken the wings off the back of her dress. I assume so she could wear her fur stole but her mask and the diamanté clips she'd had in her hair were lying next to her.' Kitty gave a little shudder at the memory.

The lieutenant raised an eyebrow at this as he made his notes. 'You seem to be very observant, Mrs Bryant.'

Matt pulled his silver card case from his pocket and offered the policeman one of their business cards. 'We are in a similar line of work to you back in England, Lieutenant.'

The detective studied the card before slipping it inside the front cover of his notebook. 'Private eyes, eh? You over here on business?'

'No, sir, as we said, we are here to visit my father. He's been very ill and Mrs Dangerfield had sent us a telegram urging us to come here,' Kitty said.

'Your father seems to have been very friendly with Mrs Dangerfield.' The policeman looked at Kitty.

'They were neighbours,' Kitty said. She thought it best not to enlarge on their friendship.

'Is your father at home now?' The detective glanced about the apartment.

'He's resting in his room at present. He was very shocked at the news of Nora's murder and he has been ill lately. I can see if he is awake.' Kitty rose from her seat and went along the hall to tap on her father's bedroom door.

Not hearing a reply, she opened the door and peeped inside to discover her father lounging on his bed studying the racing pages of the newspaper. 'The detective would like to speak to you,' she said.

'Drat.' Edgar cast the paper regretfully to one side. 'Very well, darling, tell him I'll be right out.'

Kitty nodded and went back to her seat in the sitting room to relay the message. Edgar joined them a moment later looking his usual dapper self. Lieutenant Tanfield gave him a nod, his eyes narrowing in recognition.

'I believe we have met before, haven't we, Mr, erm, Underhay?'

'Yes, I rather think we have had that pleasure,' Edgar agreed as he took his seat on the vacant armchair.

'Your daughter was telling me that Mrs Dangerfield telegrammed her to visit as you were very ill. I take it that would be about a week or so ago?' The policeman looked at Edgar's seemingly healthy pink complexion.

'Yes, that's right. I have a bit of a chest issue, causes problems from time to time. I was rather rough for a few days, and I think she panicked. Nora was such a dear lady and a good neighbour. I can't believe this has happened, I shall miss her.' Edgar looked regretful.

'You and Mrs Dangerfield were close?' The lieutenant's eyes narrowed again as he asked the question.

'Only as neighbours, dear boy. She would call in for afternoon tea occasionally and a bit of advice on the old gee-gees. That's horses to you Americans.' Edgar adjusted his shirt cuffs.

'I see. Did she confide in you at all during these visits? Talk about anyone she might have argued with?' the policeman asked.

'Well, there were a few things obviously, but all quite trivial in the scheme of things.' Edgar suddenly looked uncomfortable.

'Such as?' Lieutenant Tanfield asked.

'Well, she would argue with her daughter, Lorena, from time to time. Mother and daughter type things. Nora would offer advice and Lorena would ignore her. Nora paid for most of their bills though so Lorena would soon come around to her mother's way of thinking. There had a been a few issues lately, I think, about Lorena's husband, Rudolph,' Edgar said.

'What kind of issues?' The lieutenant's pen raced across the page.

'She was very vague about it, but he suddenly seemed to have fallen out of favour. Nora would blow hot and cold with people, so I didn't place much store on it. She was complaining a lot lately about Peggy too.'

'That's the assistant?' The policeman looked at Edgar to make sure he had the right person.

'Yes, that's the one. She said things were going missing, then turning up some place else. She said Peggy was careless.' Edgar gave a small shrug.

Kitty remembered how tired the girl had seemed the previous evening.

'I see. Did she mention Mr Blackstock to you at all?' Lieutenant Tanfield asked.

'Horatio?' Edgar's brow puckered as if he were trying to remember. 'Not really, only that she felt he was getting older, and he might wish to consider retiring,' Edgar said.

Kitty hadn't considered that the manservant might be of retirement age. She had thought him most spritely, efficient and well trained at the party.

'When did you and Mrs Bryant first meet Mrs Danger-field?' Lieutenant Tanfield switched his attention to Matt.

'I think it was the day we arrived. She called in for a brief visit on the afternoon. I believe the concierge downstairs had informed her of our arrival,' Matt said.

Kitty nodded in agreement. 'She popped in and kindly extended an invitation to her party to raise funds for the orphanage. She said it was a cause close to her heart. It was very kind of her.'

'Her late husband was an orphan, I believe. She held the party every year,' Edgar interjected.

Lieutenant Tanfield made a note. 'What time did you all leave Mrs Dangerfield's party?'

'We left just after midnight, I think. Everyone was going then. There were still a few people after us saying goodnight,' Kitty said.

'You all left together? None of you went back for anything? And you saw Mrs Dangerfield at that time?' the policeman asked.

Kitty nodded. 'Yes, we came away together. Papa won that hamper over there.' She indicated the large wicker basket which still stood on the side table. 'So Matt carried it down for him. We sat around here chatting for a few minutes, then we all went to bed. Nora was speaking to Horatio Blackstock as we left so she was in the apartment then.'

'None of us left the apartment here until Kitty and I went out for breakfast this morning. Edgar was still in bed when we left.' Matt picked up the note Kitty had scribbled which was still on the table to show the detective.

'Mrs Bryant, you seem to be very observant. Did you notice if Mrs Dangerfield was wearing her jewellery when you left?' Lieutenant Tanfield asked.

'Oh yes. She had a lovely diamond necklace, two bracelets, dropper earrings with emeralds and a gold evening watch. She also had a couple of diamond and emerald rings. I noticed she wasn't wearing them when we found her. I assume they are not in her jewel box?' Kitty said.

'No, ma'am. Her assistant says they are missing. She has searched the apartment and the safe has been checked,' the policeman said.

'And did they not notice Nora leave the apartment after the party? I mean, surely Peggy and Horatio would have been there clearing up even if the other staff had gone home,' Kitty said.

'Apparently Mrs Dangerfield would sometimes leave the apartment without telling anyone and would return a short time later.' The lieutenant appeared to be reading from his notes. A faint flush appeared on his cheeks and Kitty wondered if this might be due to the reasons for Nora's 'popping out'.

'Oh, when she would slip off to meet up with Mortimer Liggett, you mean.' Edgar had far less discretion.

'Mrs Dangerfield's assistant says that Mrs Liggett assaulted Mrs Dangerfield at the party.' The policeman looked round at them in turn.

'Titania slapped her. It was hardly an assault. Simply a combination of too much champagne and overwrought emotions, I'd say,' Edgar said.

'But Mrs Dangerfield and Mr Liggett were conducting an affair?' Lieutenant Tanfield asked.

'I don't see any point beating about the bush. It has to be the worst kept secret in New York. They were hardly discreet. I believe Nora expected Mortimer to divorce Titania and marry her.' Edgar ignored Kitty's slightly disapproving look.

'And Mrs Liggett was aware of the affair? Or did she only find out about it last night?' The policeman waited for Edgar's response.

'Oh, Titania knew but Mortimer is a bit of a dog. It wasn't his first foray outside the old matrimonial bedroom. I think she thought it would fizzle out. Titania has the money in that marriage. Usually, she just cuts off the old dollar supply and Mortimer comes home with his tail tucked between his legs.' Edgar gave a slight shrug.

'Except this time, Mrs Dangerfield also had lots of money so could woo Mr Liggett away.' The policeman added more notes.

Kitty could see the policeman mentally making a case against Titania Liggett and she couldn't really blame him.

CHAPTER SIX

Matt could also see the way the detective's mind was working. However, Titania had been a drink-sodden, emotional wreck, barely able to walk when Mortimer had removed her from the party. He couldn't see how she could have recovered sufficiently to lure Nora to her death a scant hour or couple of hours later. Let alone having the presence of mind or strength to strangle her love rival.

Mortimer Liggett could have persuaded Nora to meet him and then killed her, but surely he had more to gain from simply divorcing his wife and marrying Nora. Although if Titania had proved difficult and refused the divorce, then he could have framed Titania and inherited her money when she was convicted and executed. All of which sounded horribly cold blooded and complicated.

Then there was the mystery of the missing jewellery. Had whoever murdered Nora taken it or had it been stolen later by some opportunist stumbling across her body while she lay dead in the shrubbery?

'Thank you all for the information. I have to talk to Mrs Dangerfield's daughter and son-in-law now. Naturally, Mrs

Briggs is most upset about her mother's death.' Lieutenant Tanfield closed his notebook and tucked it away inside his pocket ready to depart.

'I expect she is. It's such a terrible thing to happen, especially after last night when everyone was so happy and enjoying themselves,' Kitty said.

'Please pass on our condolences to her and her husband,' Matt said as he rose from his seat to see the detective out.

'Sure thing, thanks again,' Lieutenant Tanfield said and left to go and talk to Lorena and Rudolph.

As soon as the detective was out of earshot, Kitty rounded on her father. 'Papa! What was that all about? It's not like you to discuss your friend's private affairs with the police in that way.'

Usually, her father would tell the police as little as possible when he was questioned over anything. Something she had witnessed for herself several times before, so his recent behaviour was out of character.

Edgar shifted uncomfortably in his seat but feigned an air of nonchalance. 'Darling, Lieutenant Tanfield had obviously heard about Titania, and he's bound to discover Nora and Mortimer's affair. It would look bad if I didn't tell him.'

Kitty thought he was probably right about that, but she still wasn't sure why he had been quite so forthcoming. 'Are you sure that's all it was?' She eyed him suspiciously.

'I didn't have a choice. You must have seen how he was trying to work me into the frame? The way he kept on about Nora and I being friends. I have no intention of being hauled off to clink in handcuffs again for something that is nothing to do with me,' Edgar protested.

Kitty drummed her fingers on the leather-padded arm of the sofa in frustration. 'You were telling the truth about not seeing

Nora again after we left the party? You didn't go back up there to her apartment for any reason?'

She hated feeling so suspicious of her own father but Edgar's relationship with the truth could sometimes be rather tenuous, which is why he'd landed in trouble before.

'On my honour. Cross my heart and hope to die.' Edgar made the sign of the cross on his chest and attempted to look virtuous.

Kitty was forced to believe him, but the element of doubt still lingered. Matt joined them, taking his place beside Kitty.

'Lieutenant Tanfield seems like a decent sort of a chap,' Matt said. 'You said you and he had crossed paths before?' He looked at his father-in-law.

'Only a couple of times. A few minor misunderstandings, nothing serious,' Edgar said.

'Such as?' Kitty asked, noticing her father suddenly looking quite shifty once again.

'A couple of years ago there was a spot of bother over some carousing and something about a fire hydrant being damaged. All quite innocent, I assure you. A celebration that got a little out of hand.' Edgar's gaze slid away from Kitty's.

'And the other time?' Matt asked.

'I was looking after a few things for a pal. Just helping a fellow out of a tight spot, as one does. Only it turned out that the things he left with me weren't actually his, and it got a bit sticky for a while.' Edgar ran his finger around the edge of his white shirt collar, easing it away from his neck. 'Gosh, it's gone rather warm in here, don't you think? Shall I turn the electric fire down?'

Kitty could see how handling stolen goods could be described as being more than a little sticky. It was no wonder her father had looked so uncomfortable when Lieutenant Tanfield had entered the apartment.

'I think the heat in here is about right,' Kitty remarked drily.

Her stomach growled, reminding her that they had missed their breakfast. She saw the corners of Matt's lips quirk upwards and guessed he had heard her.

'Shall we go out for a spot of lunch,' her husband suggested.

'Good idea, you two go and enjoy yourselves. You deserve it after what's happened. I think I'll stay here, it's all been a bit much for me,' Edgar offered, and Kitty guessed he would be glad to have them gone for a little while after the events of the morning.

Kitty was quite relieved to pull on her winter coat and hat again to venture back outside. It would be nice to get out of the apartment and to escape into the cold air.

'What a morning,' Kitty exclaimed as they entered the elevator.

'Quite. Let's go into the city and find somewhere nice to eat. It's a little late now for lunch so the first rush may have subsided,' Matt suggested as they stepped out into the lobby.

The concierge who had assisted them earlier was busy as they walked across the foyer, so they stepped outside and walked along until they reached a junction where they could hail a passing taxi.

'Where'd you wanna go?' the driver asked once they were inside the cab.

Kitty suddenly realised they didn't know the city well enough to have a particular destination in mind.

'We'd like a nice restaurant for lunch. Where do you recommend?' Matt asked.

'You got it, I know plenty of places. You wanna go to Ronni's? You like Italian food?' the driver asked as he pulled back out into the traffic.

'That sounds lovely,' Kitty agreed. She wasn't sure if she did like Italian food. She tried to recall what she had ever eaten that could be classed as Italian cuisine. She had tried French food, naturally, many times, still this would be an adventure.

They were soon dropped off outside a very nice-looking restaurant that was still fairly busy with diners. The restaurant had been decorated for Christmas with red, white and green ornaments and ribbons on the Christmas trees. The tables were dressed in crisp white linen and there was a pleasant buzz about the room.

'This looks rather lovely.' Kitty smiled approvingly at Matt once they were seated comfortably at a dining table. A leather-bound menu was placed in front of them and wine ordered from the attentive, smartly suited waiter.

'It's good to get away for a little while,' Matt agreed. 'Especially after this morning.'

'Can you believe the nerve of my father?' Kitty asked once the waiter had taken their order for lunch and left them to enjoy their wine.

'Unfortunately, yes.' Matt grinned at her. 'I mean, there's the fact that we're here in America having dashed across the Atlantic assuming he might be at death's door only to find him in the pink.'

'You know he was avoiding some people he owed money too? That he probably feigned being ill just to lie low in his apartment until he could get enough money to get them off his back.' Kitty took a sip of her white wine.

'I had rather gathered that.' Matt's eyes twinkled with amusement.

'It's not funny, Matt. And now there's this dreadful murder.' Kitty placed her glass back down carefully on the white linen tablecloth.

'Yes, I know.' Her husband's expression sobered.

The waiter returned and placed two bowls of butternut squash soup in front of them before withdrawing.

'Nora must have slipped away downstairs to meet someone

she knew. She would never have gone otherwise,' Kitty said, picking up her spoon. 'She must have made an arrangement and didn't want anyone to know about it.'

'I agree. It also had to be someone familiar with the building who knew she would know about the door. If the concierge took regular breaks at night she would know and could slip outside through the empty kitchens,' Matt said.

'Unless you think perhaps someone forced her to go down there?' Kitty suggested.

'It's possible, but she had taken off her wings and put on her fur stole, so she intended to step outside. She could have followed someone down I suppose, hoping to catch them in some kind of wrongdoing,' Matt mused picking up his bread roll.

'You mean like when Father said Nora had complained that things were going missing and she blamed Peggy, her assistant? There were a lot of very valuable things in that apartment.' Kitty finished her soup and placed her spoon down in the empty bowl.

'Peggy could have been stealing from Nora and passing things on to an accomplice. There was a lot of money there that night after the party from the stalls and the raffle.' Matt finished eating.

'And Nora spotted her sneaking out and followed her downstairs where she was attacked, and her jewellery stolen?' Kitty nodded slowly. She could see how that might be possible.

'We could make the same sort of case against Horatio Blackstock. We don't know how he felt about Nora suggesting he should retire. He may not have much money put aside and could have been taking things, then letting the blame fall on Peggy,' Matt said.

The waiter collected their empty dishes and returned within a few seconds with plates containing pasta in a creamy white sauce. Kitty sniffed appreciatively when the food was placed in front of her.

'That's very true. I saw Nora telling him off about something as we left,' she agreed once the waiter had departed after offering to add freshly ground pepper to their food.

Kitty took her first mouthful and was pleasantly surprised by the texture and creaminess of the dish. They remained quiet for some time as they both concentrated on the delicious food in front of them.

'Then we have Mortimer and Titania,' Matt said, wiping the corner of his mouth with his napkin. 'They live in the same apartment block so both of them know the building well. They would know about the back door and the kitchens. Nora has been in the habit of slipping out at night, presumably to meet Mortimer somewhere.'

'Yes, but Titania didn't look in any fit state to set up a meeting with Nora and I don't think Nora would have agreed to meet her somewhere clandestine anyway. Especially since Titania had just hit her,' Kitty said. She took another mouthful of her food, savouring the taste. It really was delicious. The taxi driver had made a good suggestion.

'She would have agreed to meet Mortimer, but then why would he want to kill Nora? Or steal her jewellery?' Matt said.

'Titania could have heard them planning to meet. She could have followed them and killed Nora and Mortimer could be covering it up?' Kitty suggested. She didn't think it sounded very plausible, but it was a possibility she supposed.

'I don't know if he would cover for her, but she could have bribed him I suppose. Then there is Lorena and Rudolph.' Matt set his knife and fork down on his now empty plate. 'Your father seemed to believe that Nora was unhappy with Rudolph for some reason, and we know Nora funded their lifestyle.'

'Well, we know they don't live too far away either. I suppose they would know the building since Nora had been living there for quite a while. I can't remember if they had already left before us or not.' Kitty crinkled her brow as she tried to recall when she had last seen Lorena and her husband at the party.

Matt frowned. 'I think they were still there. I seem to recall seeing Lorena near the Christmas tree when I picked up that hamper.'

'So, they both have to be considered I suppose, although Nora seemed very fond of her daughter.' Kitty set her own cutlery down with a satisfied sigh. Lunch was proving very nice indeed.

The waiter took their plates and they succumbed to the idea of dessert, persuaded by the appearance of the dishes being delivered to a neighbouring table.

'That is Bonet, madam. Chocolate and amoretti cake,' the waiter explained when Kitty enquired.

'We'll have two of those then, please.' Matt smiled at her, guessing she wanted to try it.

Once their desserts had arrived, Kitty tried a small piece with her spoon. 'Oh, this is quite delicious.' She sighed happily as she gazed around the restaurant. 'I can't believe we are here, enjoying our lunch after that ghastly journey all the way across the ocean worrying if my father would be alive when we arrived.' She shook her head in disbelief. 'And, now we find ourselves embroiled in a murder case.'

'I know. Although I am obviously delighted to find Edgar hale and hearty, it's not at all the Christmas we had planned,' Matt said.

'This probably is me being foolish, but you don't think my father had a point about this Lieutenant Tanfield suspecting him of being involved in Nora's murder?' Kitty asked as she spooned up the last morsel of her pudding.

The frown returned to Matt's face. 'I suppose he would have to consider the possibility, but your father and Nora appeared to be on excellent terms. He has no motive, and we were with him at the party and afterwards.'

'True, and Father's criminal record is not for anything violent. Just, well, bending the law usually.' Kitty gave a heavy sigh. That, and sticking to some things that were not technically his property.

'There seems little more that we can do. We are strangers here and we will have no insight into anything the police may discover.' Matt looked at her. Kitty guessed he already knew that she was thinking they could poke around a little and ask a few questions.

'I suppose so,' she agreed. Although, if they were to come across something, especially something that would ensure her father was completely out of the frame, then what harm could that do?

'Let's pay the bill and take ourselves shopping for an hour or two. Embrace the festive spirit. It'll be Christmas Day in four days' time,' Matt suggested as he drew his white linen napkin from his lap.

'Very well.' Kitty smiled back at him. After all they were in New York, and despite everything they should make the most of being there.

CHAPTER SEVEN

Matt was delighted to see that his suggestion had proved to be a good one. A trip to see several huge Christmas trees later, they arrived back at the apartment block laden with bags and boxes containing various gifts for friends and family back in Devon. Matt had also managed to acquire a rather pretty brooch as a surprise anniversary gift for Christmas Eve for Kitty.

Kitty shivered as Matt paid the taxi driver and picked up all their bags. The air was bitingly cold and he suspected it would probably start snowing again during the night. The street was already dark and the sidewalk was slippery underfoot.

They stamped the remnants of snow from their shoes on the mat inside the front door and said good evening to the concierge, who appeared to be busy decorating the lobby with more Christmas items.

Matt couldn't help wondering if this was an attempt to distract the residents from the murder that had taken place at the rear of the building. He guessed it would take more than a few sprigs of holly to succeed in that aim. The elevator came and they piled inside ready to ascend to Edgar's floor.

As they approached the stop Matt became aware of loud voices from somewhere on the floor above them. Kitty looked at him as they exited the elevator, and they paused outside Edgar's front door to listen. It sounded as if an argument was in full spate.

'I think that's Lorena's voice,' Kitty murmured. 'Whatever is going on up there?' She thrust her bags into Matt's already over-loaded arms and before he could stop her, she had disappeared up the staircase leading to the penthouse floor.

He sighed and resigned himself to waiting for her to return before carrying all the packages inside his father-in-law's apartment.

* * *

Kitty crept quietly up the stairwell aware that she was being nosey. The voices grew louder as she neared the top and she waited just below the top step to listen. She guessed the door of Nora's apartment must be open, which was why the sound of the quarrel was audible on the landing of the floor below.

'Please don't try to play the innocent with me!'

Kitty was sure that was Lorena's voice. She had noticed that the woman had a slight huskiness to her tone that was quite distinctive.

'I have no idea what you are talking about. I already told the police I said goodnight to your mother and went to bed. I have no idea what she did after that or where she went.'

A woman's voice, young and sounding frightened. That had to be Peggy Marsh.

'I know you're lying. Where is my mother's jewellery? And how do I know that all the money that was collected up from the party is still here?' Lorena demanded.

'I don't know where her jewels are. They aren't in the apartment so she must have been wearing them when she left. The money is all in the safe. Your mother watched us put it in there herself before I went to bed, along with the receipts. You can ask Horatio if you don't believe me.' Peggy sounded as if she were about to cry.

'Well, of course he'll cover for you. You could be in this together. Mother told me she was going to dismiss you for theft. She said her silver kept disappearing.'

Kitty's eyes widened at this. So, it was true, Nora had suspected Peggy of stealing some of the trinkets from her. Kitty flattened herself against the cold, cream painted wall of the stairwell and leaned forward to listen more closely.

'You're wrong. I would never steal anything. She never said anything to me at all,' Peggy countered.

'Miss Lorena, please. You are overwrought with shock.' The deeper, deferential male voice had to be Horatio, who seemed to have come to Peggy's assistance.

'And as for you, you're finished. I suggest you pack up your things and go. Mother said you were past retirement age.' Lorena, far from calming down, seemed to have taken her anger up a notch.

'Miss Lorena, please, it's Christmas, I have nowhere to go and surely it would be imprudent to leave the apartment unattended with so much to do.' There was a note of panic in the manservant's voice.

'Lorena, honey.' Another male voice joined the conversation and Kitty assumed it had to be Rudolph.

'Don't honey me,' Lorena said.

'I know you're upset but he does have a point. There are a lot of valuable things here that need to be taken care of. Let's not be too hasty,' Rudolph said.

'Very well, Horatio, you have until the new year and then I want you gone. Both of you,' Lorena snapped.

'Lorena, do be reasonable,' Rudolph pleaded.

'I think I am being more than reasonable. I want both Peggy and Horatio gone. You both have till January second.' The door banged and Kitty hurried back down the stairs to where Matt was waiting patiently outside Edgar's door.

'Quickly, open the door.' Kitty took some of the packages, while Matt found the spare key that Edgar had given them to the apartment.

They had scarcely made it inside when the elevator rumbled past on its way down from the penthouse. Kitty closed the front door with a sigh of relief.

'That was a narrow squeak,' she remarked cheerfully as Matt shook his head in despair at her antics.

He carried their packages into the sitting room and placed them on the table. Edgar was seated beside the fireplace. The cream silk-shaded standard lamp was on and he was listening to a play on the radio.

'I say, been doing a spot of shopping, eh? I hope you had a good lunch?' Edgar remarked when he saw the bags and boxes.

'We had a lovely lunch, thank you. These are just a few gifts for people at home,' Kitty said as she discarded her outdoor clothes and came to warm her hands in front of the fire.

'Spot of tea?' Edgar asked as Matt too discarded his heavy grey woollen overcoat and his hat, before collecting up the coats and hats to hang them up on the hooks in the hallway.

'Marvellous,' Kitty agreed.

Edgar looked at her expectantly for a second and when she didn't take his hint he got up with a sigh and headed into the small kitchenette.

'Did you learn anything for your eavesdropping?' Matt asked in a low tone once Edgar was out of the room.

'Oh, my goodness, yes. Lorena was in a high temper over something. She accused Peggy of being a thief and insinuated that Horatio was covering for her. Then she gave them both notice and said they were to be gone by January second.' Kitty sat down on the sofa and looked at her husband.

'Good heavens, she hasn't let the grass grow under her feet, has she? My word. How did Peggy and Horatio take it?' Matt asked as he sat down beside her.

'Not terribly well, as you might expect. Both Peggy and Horatio sounded upset. Rudolph, Lorena's husband, tried to intervene, but she was very short with him too.' Kitty wondered what had gone on to trigger Lorena's ire against the two servants. She knew the woman had to be distressed at her mother's murder, but her reaction seemed quite extreme.

She had also sounded as if she was angry with her husband too. Edgar carried a loaded tea tray into the room and Kitty hastily cleared a space on the table so he could set it down.

'Here we are. Did you go somewhere nice for lunch?' he asked as Kitty took over pouring and serving the tea.

'It was very nice. The taxi driver recommended an Italian restaurant called Ronni's, have you ever been there, Papa?' Kitty asked as she passed a cup of tea to Matt.

'Oh yes, several times. Excellent food and service,' her father said as he took his seat back beside the fire and switched off the radio.

'Has anyone telephoned about the murder?' Kitty asked as she helped herself to one of the biscuits her father had thoughtfully added to the tea tray. She had wondered if people might ring once word got out, since Edgar lived so close to Nora.

'I had a telephone call from Mortimer. He sounded dreadfully cut up. The police had only just left there, and he said they really upset Titania. I gather they must have been implying that she had a motive after slapping poor Nora at the party.' Edgar stirred his tea.

'Did he say why he called?' Kitty asked as she brushed

biscuit crumbs off the front of her pale-pink cashmere jumper. Titania did seem to have a strong motive, but Kitty wasn't sure if she could have strangled her former neighbour.

'Not really. I think he was just trying to find out who else the police had spoken to. To try and reassure Titania that they were talking to lots of people. I rather think that Lieutenant Tanfield may have said that you and Matt found Nora's body,' Edgar said.

'Oh dear, had he spoken to anyone else?' Kitty asked. She wondered what else Mortimer had said. He could have been trying to find out what had happened when Nora's body had been found, she supposed. She hoped it wouldn't become common knowledge that she and Matt had been the ones to discover Nora. Although she suspected it wouldn't stay secret for long.

'He said that Lorena had telephoned him as soon as she heard the news from the police. I think the poor girl was in shock. She and Rudolph were coming over straight away to Nora's apartment. He said Lorena was very distressed that her mother's jewellery was missing. I suppose she would want to check for herself and to make sure nothing else had gone.' Edgar set his spoon in his saucer before taking a sip of his tea.

'I suppose she would be worried. Nora was wearing some very expensive pieces at the party. Did she have a lot of jewellery, do you know?' Matt asked.

'Oh yes, her late husband travelled a lot and would buy her pieces from all over the place. Rubies from India, sapphires from Ceylon, emeralds from Brazil. You name it,' Edgar said.

'Did she keep them all in her apartment?' Kitty asked. Personally, she would have thought that would have been most unwise, even with a safe.

'No, most of them are in a vault at the bank, although she still had some rather nice objets d'art around the place that are worth a pretty penny. Bits of silver and some rather lovely snuff boxes her husband had collected. You probably noticed her display cases,' Edgar said.

'I take it some of those things were the items Nora had said had gone missing?' Matt asked.

Edgar took another drink of his tea before replying. 'Yes, although some of them seemed to have simply been moved. At first the girl that does the cleaning came under suspicion, but then a rather jolly little silver picture frame disappeared, and it was the week the cleaner was off. Her son had measles.'

'Did that turn up again?' Kitty asked. She thought she could see something of a pattern to this tale. A glance at Matt showed her that he too was thinking along similar lines as they had investigated cases like this before.

'Yes, actually, I rather think it did. It had been moved from the piano onto a bookshelf apparently.' Edgar placed his now empty cup back on its saucer.

'How well do you know Peggy Marsh and Horatio Black-stock?' Matt asked.

'Horatio, not terribly well. He keeps himself to himself. He's one of the old school servants. He's been with Nora forever, I think,' Edgar said.

'So, you wouldn't be surprised that she was thinking of asking him to retire?' Kitty was puzzled. Good servants who were loyal and honest were not easy to come by.

Edgar frowned. 'Well, he is rather long in the tooth but yes, I was a bit surprised. However, I don't think he approved of her dalliance with Mortimer. Horatio is a very religious man; he attends church every Sunday morning. Mortimer can't stand Horatio. I know he told Nora he felt as if he were judging him all the time. Perhaps it was Mortimer's idea that Nora let Horatio go.'

'What about Peggy?' Kitty asked.

'Peggy would often stop for a little chat. She's quite a sweet girl. Nora, of course, worked her to the bone, ordering her here, there and everywhere. She always seemed a bit lonely and somewhat out of her depth. So, I think she enjoyed having someone to talk to. She told me that she hadn't much family, just a brother I think she said. So, working for Nora gave her a place to live and the chance to see the world. She had accompanied Nora, Lorena and Rudolph on several trips.' Edgar put his cup and saucer down on the table.

Matt glanced at Kitty. 'These missing items, the ones that vanished and then reappeared, do you think either Peggy or Horatio could have been pawning them?'

Kitty's father seemed taken aback at the suggestion. 'I don't know. Well, now you say that, of course I suppose it would account for it.'

Kitty had been right about her husband thinking along the same lines that she had been thinking. This was exactly what had happened in a case they had investigated in Dartmouth. 'Do either of them ever seem as if they might be short of money for any reason?' she asked.

'Well, I don't think their wages are high, but they do have room and board.' Edgar's brow furrowed. 'Horatio obviously has never spoken to me on a personal level about his finances, but Peggy doesn't ever seem as if she is struggling. She rarely goes out and her expenses are paid for, and she doesn't seem to spend a lot on clothes.'

'It is all very peculiar. Lorena seemed very angry, and she was adamant about both of them being dismissed.' Kitty wondered if Lorena had realised what might have been happening with her mother's possessions. She had certainly accused both servants of dishonesty. 'I can see why she might dismiss Peggy. With Nora's death, Peggy has no role. She might remain until after the funeral to deal with the condolences and packing up various belongings. Horatio though, he must have known Lorena from when she was very young?'

'I believe he was with Nora since early in her marriage to

her late husband, so yes, Lorena's known him all her life.' Edgar raised his eyebrows. 'I see what you mean, darling. It seems jolly cold to turf someone out after all these years. Retirement or no retirement.'

Kitty's mind was busy while she finished her tea and cleared away the tray.

'Are there any pawnshops near here?' she asked as she took her seat again beside Matt.

'One or two. There's one a couple of blocks away, not far from Lorena and Rudolph's apartment, and there's one further over at the far end of the park near the intersection by the busi-ness...' Edgar tailed off and eyed Kitty.

She assumed an innocent expression and decided not to press her father on his intimate knowledge of where all the pawnshops were located. She knew he had probably made use of all of them at some point.

'Why are you asking?' Edgar said.

'Oh, I was just wondering where someone might have gone with those things of Nora's if we were right and they had been pawned,' Kitty said.

'Now, Kitty, you listen to me, my dear, these New York policemen are not like the policemen back at home. They will not be happy to have any kind of interference in their cases,' Edgar warned.

'I wouldn't dream of interfering,' Kitty demurred. 'I was simply curious.'

Matt looked at her over the top of the *New York Post* news-paper that he had borrowed from Edgar. 'I hate to say it, darling, but your father is right. We can't interfere with the investigation into Nora's death.'

'I wouldn't dream of suggesting we interfere,' Kitty said virtuously. 'But, perhaps a stroll in that direction tomorrow might be interesting.' She waited hopefully to see if Matt or Edgar would agree.

Surely anything they discovered might assist the police and help ensure that Edgar was not going to be somehow dragged into the investigation simply because of his somewhat shady past.

'We'll see what happens in the morning,' Matt said, and Kitty was compelled to accept this rather unsatisfactory reply.

CHAPTER EIGHT

Matt woke early the next morning unsure at first of what it was that had disturbed his sleep. He slid out from under the covers taking care not to wake Kitty. The air in the room was cold and he shivered as he tugged on his thick tartan fleece dressing gown and pushed his feet into leather slippers.

The room was dark as he made his way out of the bedroom, closing the door quietly behind him. He paused in the hallway to listen again to try and hear what had woken him. There was something definitely wrong. Above him he heard a series of muffled thumps and thuds as if something was being knocked over.

He listened for a second longer, then picked up the key to Edgar's apartment from the painted ceramic Chinese-style dish on the hallstand. Without pausing to think twice he let himself out of the apartment and headed across the landing to the stair-well that led up to the penthouse.

His first thought was that someone was burgling the apart-ment. He crept quietly and quickly up the stairs wondering if Peggy and Horatio were in the flat. Had they been attacked? Were they the ones stripping the place out?

He reached the top of the stairs and peered out onto the dark landing. The only light was from the window at the far end where dawn was breaking, offering him little more than moonlight to see by.

Everything looked normal. The door to Nora's apartment was closed and there was no sign of a forced entry. Matt listened again but heard nothing. He had just started to believe it was all a bad dream and he had imagined it, when he heard a noise again from inside the apartment.

It sounded like a muffled scream or moan of someone in pain.

Matt hammered on the door of the apartment. Someone inside was in desperate trouble, he was sure of it. He hoped if someone had somehow forced their way into the apartment that they wouldn't be armed.

After a moment he heard the sound of the bolt being drawn back and the chain released. He found himself face to face with a bleary-eyed and confused-looking pyjama-clad Horatio Blackstock.

'Captain Bryant?' the manservant asked in a bewildered tone.

'I apologise for disturbing you, but I've heard dreadful noises coming from inside the apartment, so I had to check that you were all right?' Matt could see the man was not properly awake and he guessed he must have been in such a deep sleep he hadn't heard the disturbance. Horatio opened the door a little wider and adjusted the belt on his dressing gown.

'I took medication to make me sleep. I haven't heard anything until you knocked the door,' the man said.

Just as he spoke there was another crash from along the hall behind him.

'That's Miss Peggy's room,' the man said, turning to head towards the girl's room. Matt followed in his wake as the manservant knocked on Peggy's bedroom door.

'Miss Peggy? Are you all right in there?' He tried the door handle when he got no reply. He jiggled it up and down futilely for a minute. 'It's locked.'

'Stand clear.' Matt urged the older man to stand back as he applied his weight to the door. On the third attempt the lock gave and the door opened. Horatio snapped on a light, and they looked in horror at the scene before them.

Everything from the top of Peggy's nightstand had been knocked onto the floor and the stand itself was tipped over. Her beside lamp lay broken, the glass shade smashed to pieces. A bottle of what looked like tonic medicine and a glass were among the debris. The bedclothes were strewn around the bed and Peggy herself was dead on top of the mattress.

Her eyes were wide and staring and her body contorted. Her dark-pink nightdress was wrapped tightly around her body. Horatio went as if to step forward to cover her up, but Matt extended a hand to prevent him.

'Go and telephone the police.'

'What's happened to her?' The manservant seemed unable to take his eyes from the horrific scene.

'I'm afraid it looks very much to me as if she has ingested poison.' If Matt had to make an informed guess, he would have said it was strychnine. The girl's end had been painful and unpleasant as she had convulsed and thrashed about wrecking her room as the poison had taken its effect.

Horatio gulped and scurried down the hall to the sitting room, presumably to make the call. Matt made the most of the servant's absence to take a good look at the scene. He was careful not to disturb anything, but he wanted to see if he could discover how Peggy had taken the poison.

The glass on the floor had obviously contained some kind of dark-brown fluid which he assumed must be the tonic that had spilled from the bottle, which was slowly dripping its viscous contents onto the Persian rug.

There were various papers and a book on the floor amongst the mess. The papers looked like letters and he peered more closely at them to see who they might be from. The spidery, copperplate handwriting indicated they were from an older person, and it seemed when he read part of one of the letters that he was right. The author appeared to be talking about an old neighbour of Peggy's and asking if she was likely to visit soon.

'The police are on their way, sir.' Horatio reappeared at the door of the bedroom.

'We had better wait in the sitting room for them. There is nothing we can do for Peggy now,' Matt said, straightening back up.

He accompanied the servant into the lounge where Horatio had switched on one of the Chinese-style silk-shaded lamps. Matt could see the older man was trembling as he took a seat.

'I don't understand. Why didn't I hear anything?' Horatio looked shaken.

'Where is your room?' Matt asked.

'Near the kitchenette, it's a box room. Miss Nora had a bell installed so she could call me if she wanted anything and I would be handy to make drinks or snacks for her,' the man said.

That meant the man was sleeping on the far side of the apartment away from Peggy's room.

'I think Peggy's room is directly above the guest room where Kitty and I are staying, so the thud of the nightstand toppling is probably what disturbed me. You are on the other side of the drawing room, and you said you had taken a sleeping draught.' Matt looked at the man.

'I don't use my medicine unless I'm unwell, but after Miss Nora's murder and Miss Lorena being so upset yesterday.' The man paused and shook his head in disbelief. 'My mind couldn't settle.'

'When did you last see Peggy?' Matt asked.

'Last night before we went to bed. I had been finishing off clearing up the apartment. The police had been going through various things and there was still some debris from the party. We had supper together, and then we had the radio on for a while.' Horatio's hands were still shaking, and he glanced towards Peggy's room as if reliving the horror of their discovery.

'What time was this?' Matt said.

The manservant frowned. 'I reckon it must have been about eleven when we turned in. Miss Lorena and Mr Rudolph had been over with the police earlier and then they stayed on a bit afterwards. Miss Lorena was very upset. After they had gone, Peggy and I had supper then she went out for a spell. Said she had to post some letters. She came back about eightish and we listened to the radio while we finished up some more tidying. She said she was tired, and I was too. It was a pretty rough day yesterday,' Horatio said.

'And then you went to bed?' Matt confirmed.

The man nodded. 'I said I was going to take a sleeping draught and Peggy said she hoped she would be able to sleep.'

'There was some tonic in a bottle beside Peggy's bed.' Matt phrased the words carefully.

'Yes, she had low iron, and she would usually take it at night. She wasn't the best at remembering it so she would take it whenever she thought about it.' The man looked at Matt, his eyes widening. 'You think she took it in her tonic?'

'Or someone poisoned her tonic,' Matt said grimly just as a loud knock on the partially open door of the apartment announced the arrival of the police.

Lieutenant Tanfield, looking slightly rumpled and sleepy-eyed, entered the room with two uniformed officers. He looked surprised to see Matt seated with Horatio.

'Miss Marsh is dead. I believe she has ingested strychnine,' Matt said succinctly as he and the servant rose to greet the officers.

The lieutenant's gaze sharpened. 'I see. Show me.'

Matt took the officers back along the hall to Peggy's room. Matt suspected Horatio was in no fit state to face the site of Peggy's demise again.

'We haven't touched anything. It was clear she was beyond help when we found her.' Matt stood back, and the police entered the room. He slipped away to leave them to their task, rejoining Horatio in the drawing room until they were needed.

'Perhaps the officers would welcome some coffee,' Matt suggested to the manservant. He could see the man was upset and restless. Perhaps going about some of his normal duties might help him to settle.

'That's a good idea, sir. I'll go and make a pot.' The man went off to the kitchenette.

By the time he returned bearing a tray with coffee, cups and saucers, more police had arrived, and the hall of the apartment was a hive of activity.

Lieutenant Tanfield came to join them and accepted Horatio's offer of coffee. 'Now, perhaps you two could shed some light on what's happened and how you came to discover Miss Marsh. I see the bedroom door lock has been busted off.'

Matt explained how he had come to the apartment after being woken by the strange noises and the actions he and Horatio had taken.

'I guess that explains the pyjamas,' the policeman said in a wry tone as he made his notes in between sips of coffee.

'I take it Peggy's death was due to strychnine?' Matt asked.

The lieutenant glanced sharply at him. 'Our doctor will confirm that but yes, I'd say you were on the money with that idea.'

'I didn't see a suicide note,' Matt said.

The policeman stopped writing and tapped his pen thoughtfully on the corner page of his notebook.

'I guess you didn't,' he said.

'Why would Peggy want to kill herself? And in such a terrible way? That doesn't make a lick of sense,' Horatio said. He seemed more alert since he had drunk some of the coffee.

'She didn't seem distressed or upset when you said good-night to her?' the lieutenant asked.

The servant shook his head. 'No, sir. She had been upset earlier when Miss Lorena gave us our notices, but she seemed to have calmed down. After she came back from the post, she seemed almost cheerful. I thought she must have been thinking about getting fixed up in a new situation. She was smart and pretty so she wouldn't have struggled for a new job,' Horatio said.

'Mrs Briggs gave you both notice?' the policeman asked.

'She was mighty upset about her mother's death. She wasn't thinking quite right so she said a few things which were uncalled for.' Horatio's tone had shifted slightly, and Matt could see the man was still angered by what had been said.

'And what sort of things did Mrs Briggs say?' Lieutenant Tanfield asked.

'She implied Peggy was dishonest and that I had colluded with her. Miss Nora had mislaid some things recently and she had told Miss Lorena some items were missing. With the party preparations though and all the entertaining Miss Nora did I'm sure there wasn't really a problem. Things would get moved around.' Horatio's voice rose slightly.

'I understand that Mrs Dangerfield had suggested you retire from her service?' the policeman said. 'I presume Mrs Briggs agreed with her mother?'

'She did suggest that, but I have worked for Miss Nora and her family for almost all my working life. I can't afford to retire, and I have no wish to do so. I had hoped Miss Lorena would keep me on.' Horatio stiffened.

'You were going to seek new employment if she didn't?' Matt asked. He wondered what the servant had done with the money he had earned over the years. He assumed the man had never married and his bed and board had always been provided. Even on a modest salary he must have some savings.

'That is correct, sir, yes,' Horatio said.

'I don't suppose you know who Miss Marsh's letters were written to?' the policeman asked.

'The ones she went to post? No, sir, she didn't say. She wrote to her brother pretty regular though.' Horatio appeared to have calmed down again.

'I see. Thank you. I'm afraid we shall be here for a while longer. Captain Bryant, thank you for your assistance. I expect you will want to return to your father-in-law's apartment. Your wife will wake up and wonder where the heck you've gone.' Lieutenant Tanfield returned his notebook to his pocket.

'I'm sure she will. Kitty is usually an early riser. She'll be very upset to hear about Miss Marsh, as indeed will my father-in-law.' Matt stood ready to leave.

The policeman accompanied him along the hall past the hustle and bustle inside Peggy's room. They paused out on the landing outside the front door of Nora's apartment. More light was coming through the window now and the sky between the buildings was streaked with pink and gold.

'Something did cross our minds yesterday afternoon, Lieutenant. Kitty and I had a case not long ago where items disappeared and were then returned. It turned out the son of the house gambled and would pawn items, retrieving them if he won and if he didn't, they stayed lost.' Matt spoke a little diffidently. He wasn't certain how the policeman would take his hint.

Lieutenant Tanfield scratched his chin. 'You think that may be what's happened here? This tale of pieces of silver going missing, then turning up someplace else later on?'

'I just thought I should mention it as a possibility. My father-in-law said there were a couple of pawnbrokers not far from here. It could be the items are linked to the murders,' Matt said.

The policeman eyed him with a keen gaze. 'I see you said murders, Captain Bryant. You don't buy suicide for Miss Marsh's death?'

'No, and I don't think you do either, Lieutenant. There was no note, no sign of her putting something in her tonic and why wait till the middle of the night to do such a thing? I think her tonic was tampered with. She woke for some reason, realised she had forgotten to take her medicine, took it and suffered the consequences,' Matt said.

'Hmm, that's a theory,' the policeman said. 'I'll bear it in mind and I'll be in touch later today if I have more questions.'

Matt nodded and shook the man's hand before heading back downstairs to Edgar's apartment.

He had scarcely let himself in and closed the front door when Kitty appeared in the hall. She had her dressing gown on and her blonde curls were ruffled from sleep.

'Where have you been? I was worried sick,' she said, her hands on her hips once she realised that on this occasion at least, he had not been sleepwalking.

CHAPTER NINE

Kitty had woken with a start and realised the space in the bed beside her was empty and cold. She had lain quietly for a moment, aware of strange, muffled noises in the apartment above them. For a second, she had panicked. Matt was prone to sleepwalking, a legacy from his time in the Great War.

He would suffer from dreadful nightmares and would often destroy things or roam around the house while still in a deep sleep. These incidents had gradually become less frequent, but times of stress or being in a strange place could trigger them. She sat bolt upright and shivered at the cold air in the room.

She hopped out of bed and tugged on her dressing gown. She needed to find Matt and make sure he was safe. He could have let himself out of the apartment without being aware of his surroundings. If that was the case, she needed to locate him quickly. She pushed her feet into her slippers and heard the sound of a key in the front door.

Opening the bedroom door, she peered out and saw Matt re-enter the apartment. From the sheepish and guilty look on her husband's face as he returned the apartment keys to the bowl on the hallstand, she realised this was not one of those events where he had been sleepwalking.

'Where have you been? What's going on?' She kept her voice low so as not to wake her father who preferred to rise later in the day. Overhead she could still hear strange noises coming from Nora's apartment.

'Let's get some tea, and I'll tell you,' Matt suggested.

Kitty followed him into the drawing room and he disappeared to go and make some tea, while Kitty turned on the fire to take the chill off the room. Once he had returned, he took a seat on the sofa next to her.

'Peggy Marsh is dead from strychnine poisoning,' Matt said as she poured them both a drink.

'What happened?' Kitty asked.

She listened horrified as Matt explained what had gone on and why he had headed up to the penthouse apartment.

'Good heavens, how terrible!' Kitty stared at him. 'I can't believe it. Poor Peggy. Poor Mr Blackstock too. He must have been dreadfully upset to find you banging on the front door. Then to discover Peggy in such an awful way.' She could scarcely believe her ears. She was even more annoyed that she had slept through the whole thing.

Matt told her what he had learned from the scene in the bedroom and from his conversation with Horatio.

'Well, I did overhear what Lorena said to them both yesterday.' Kitty frowned. 'It was quite nasty and must have been awfully upsetting for both of them.'

'Indeed. Horatio was quite frank with the police about what Lorena had said. I shared with the lieutenant our thoughts on the pawnshop theory. I felt I should since it might have some relevance on the case,' Matt said.

'Yes, I would have done the same. Horatio Blackstock is bound to come under more suspicion now though, isn't he?'

Kitty's frown deepened. 'He'll be seen to have means and opportunity, I suppose, for killing both Nora and Peggy.'

'Yes, although the motive part is rather weak. He could have been angry at Nora for wishing him to take retirement and he told Lieutenant Tanfield he couldn't afford to retire. He could possibly have been the one taking the items,' Matt said.

'And Nora found out, followed him downstairs and he strangled her. Then Peggy guessed it had to be him and he killed her too?' Kitty suggested.

'It's a possibility, but Horatio definitely looked to me like a man who had been in a deep sleep when he opened the door. I could perhaps see him committing a murder in the heat of the moment but to tamper with Peggy's tonic and then calmly take a sleeping draught himself and go to bed...' Matt paused and looked at Kitty.

'Yes, that would be quite something, wouldn't it?' she agreed. 'I suppose anyone who knew Peggy might know of her habit regarding her medicine. The strychnine could have been added to the bottle at any point by anyone who had access to it. It could even have been done during the party.' Kitty shivered at the thought.

'That's very true. I can't see Peggy's death being suicide. She would have left a note and chosen something that was less unpleasant, surely, if that was the case. No, this has all the hallmarks of murder,' Matt said.

'It's a very worrying idea,' Kitty agreed.

Matt finished his tea and put his cup down on the tray before raising his hand in an attempt to stifle a yawn.

'Perhaps you should go back to bed for a while. Try and catch up on your sleep for an hour or too,' Kitty suggested.

'I think I might,' he said, getting up from his seat. He dropped an affectionate kiss on her head and went back to the bedroom.

Kitty tidied up their cups and carried them off to the kitchenette to wash them up. She felt too restless to join Matt in catching an extra forty winks. The noises from the penthouse apartment seemed to have stopped and Kitty assumed that the police must probably be finishing their work in Peggy's bedroom.

From Matt's description it sounded as if the poor girl had suffered a horrific and painful death. As she dried the cups on a linen teacloth she tried to recall anything from the party that had seemed unusual or out of place. Anything at all that might indicate who could have wanted Nora and Peggy dead.

There had been one moment when she had glimpsed Peggy with Lorena's husband, Rudolph, looking quite intimate together, partly concealed by the giant Christmas tree. Was there something there? Was that why Lorena was so eager to dismiss Peggy? The story of the missing items could be a smoke-screen. Lorena could have been the one behind it to get her mother to dismiss Peggy.

Kitty thought Rudolph had certainly seemed to have a bit of a wandering eye for the ladies. He had made her feel a little uncomfortable when Nora had made the introductions.

She put the clean, dry cups back ready on the tray and rinsed out the teapot so it would be ready for use when Matt and her father roused themselves. Then there was this business of Mortimer and Nora's affair.

Mortimer and Titania lived a couple of floors below Edgar's apartment. Mortimer had likely been a frequent visitor to the penthouse apartment. He would probably know about Peggy's habits with her medication, and by default it was likely his wife would know that too. Either of them could also be responsible for Nora's murder. And also, she supposed, for Peggy's too.

If Peggy had discovered that Mortimer or Titania had killed Nora, or if they thought she might have noticed something, then it would have been fairly easy for them to place strychnine in Peggy's tonic.

She had no doubt that the tonic was the most likely source of the poison. Matt had said there was no other glass or cup on the fallen nightstand. The taste of the tonic would also have concealed any taste of the strychnine.

Kitty wandered back into the sitting room and turned up the electric fire to try and dispel some more of the chill from the room. It still felt cool, and the heating had not yet come on. She had grown cold dawdling over the washing-up in the kitchenette.

She amused herself by picking up and reading some of the Christmas cards her father had received and placed on display on the mantelpiece. An expensive-looking personalised card from Nora, a foiled card from Mortimer and Titania, a simple card from Lorena and Rudolph, and various others which Kitty assumed were from friends and neighbours.

There was one from her aunt and uncle and Kitty and Matt's own card, which had obviously preceded their arrival in New York. It was not many days now until Christmas and she wondered if the lieutenant would have caught the murderer before the celebrations.

She settled herself back down in her father's favourite chair near the fire and enjoyed the feel of the heat on her legs. She was careful to keep her night attire well clear of the bars on the fire. She had seen too many reports in the newspapers of people who had been badly burnt or killed by being too close to coal or electric fires.

'Good morning, darling. Up early?' Her father appeared in the doorway dressed in his pyjamas and dark-red silk mono-grammed dressing gown.

'Good morning, you're an early riser too today. Shall I make some tea and toast?' Kitty asked.

'That would be marvellous. I say, are you all right, dear girl, you look a little pale this morning?' Her father peered at her with a concerned expression.

'I'm afraid I have some more rather shocking news,' Kitty said and told him about Matt going up to the penthouse and the horrific discovery of Peggy's death.

'Oh, I say, that's dreadful.' Her father sank down onto the end of the sofa, his face betraying his shock at the unexpected news.

'Matt thinks Peggy's death is murder rather than suicide. He suspects her medicine had been tampered with,' Kitty said.

'You mean that ghastly tonic stuff she took for her anaemia?' Edgar said.

'You know about Peggy's medicine?' Kitty asked in surprise.

'Oh yes, I think most people knew she took medication for her iron levels. She was prone to fainting if her iron dropped too low and she was awful at remembering to take the wretched tonic. So, whenever she would get light-headed Nora would scold her and make her take her tonic,' Edgar explained.

'I see.' Kitty thought that answered her question about who might know of Peggy's habits with her tonic. From what her father had just said it appeared half of New York society knew.

'I can't believe it, poor Peggy. Who would wish to harm her?' Edgar asked.

'I don't know. Was she generally well liked?' Kitty asked as she rose to go and put the kettle on.

'I think so. She was a very inoffensive girl,' Edgar called after her as she went inside the kitchenette.

'No recent arguments you know of with anyone other than Lorena?' Kitty stepped back into the room while she waited for the kettle to boil.

'Obviously Lorena must have believed Nora's tale of suspecting Peggy of stealing some of her things, but most of those things reappeared.' Edgar looked baffled.

'You don't think that perhaps it was Lorena herself moving things to try to get her mother to dismiss Peggy?' Kitty suggested. She thought she might as well try her theory out on her father. He knew the people involved much better than she did.

Edgar's eyes widened. 'No, well actually, I suppose she could have, but why would she do something like that?'

Kitty ducked back inside the kitchenette as she heard the kettle start to whistle. She emerged a moment later bearing the tea tray.

'I just wondered. Lorena's husband seemed to be very attentive towards Peggy at the party when they thought they were unobserved,' Kitty said as she set down the tray.

'Really, I wouldn't have thought Rudolph would have been so foolish to try his luck so close to home.' Edgar waited for Kitty to stir the tea in the pot before she set the metal strainer on top of the cup.

'He seemed to have a wandering eye I thought, when we first met him at the party.' Kitty replaced the lid of the teapot and poured the tea through the strainer.

'Yes, you're quite right there. Lorena keeps him on a short leash. Still, the fella knows which side his bread is buttered. I don't know that he would ever risk upsetting Lorena and, more importantly, Nora. Nora funded his and Lorena's lifestyle. Dear Rudolph doesn't have a penny to bless himself with. Even less than Mortimer,' Edgar said as he spooned sugar into his tea.

'Really, so if Rudolph were having a bit of a fling with Peggy, then presumably he would be in big trouble if Nora found out?' Kitty said.

'I suppose so. I know he's strayed before. Lorena, I think, knew but she was careful not to let her mother find out. Lorena adores Rudolph and will do anything to keep him happy, even overlooking his, um, dalliances.' Edgar stirred his drink and rested the spoon on his saucer.

'Did Nora ever find out about any of his flings?' Kitty asked, settling back in her chair while balancing her own cup of tea in her hand.

'Oh yes, there was one huge blow up about, let me think, yes, August time. Nora told me about it when they came back to town. It was while they were away on holiday in Hawaii. It was a bit of a scandal as the girl, I can't recall her name, contacted Nora and said she was pregnant. Rudolph denied everything, of course, and Lorena swore black and blue that it was all a ploy to get money from the family.' Edgar took a sip of tea.

'What happened in the end?' Kitty asked. She wondered if this meant there was someone else out there that they didn't know about who may have had a grudge against Nora.

'I'm not quite certain but I rather think Nora got her lawyers involved and I believe the girl was paid off.' Edgar looked at Kitty. 'After that Lorena has kept a closer eye on her husband, the whole business upset her dreadfully. Nora, I think, would have urged Lorena to dump him like day old soup if he even stepped a toe out of line again. She would do anything for Lorena to keep her happy. That was the only reason she put up with Rudolph's nonsense. Losing him would devastate Lorena.'

'Hmm.' Kitty drank her tea and mulled over this new information.

'I guess now Nora is dead Lorena will be a wealthy woman,' Edgar said.

'And her husband? Does he get any of the money?' Kitty asked. She was aware that in most couples the man held the purse strings regardless of who had brought the money into the marriage. However, she also knew of several wealthy women who had taken steps to ensure they would keep their money safe if the marriage didn't work out.

'I don't think so. Nora and her husband were very shrewd people. I know Nora mentioned to me before that she had taken steps to secure Lorena's fortune. She opposed the marriage but Lorena eloped, and since she was of age Nora was forced to accept it.' Edgar finished his tea and set his cup down on the tray.

'What about in a divorce?' Kitty asked.

'Same thing, I assume. She told me when they came back after that disastrous holiday that if Rudolph were to leave Lorena, he wouldn't see a single cent,' Edgar said.

Kitty decided that from what her father had just told her, it sounded as if both Lorena and Rudolph might have motives for murdering Peggy and Nora. Lorena to stop her mother from insisting she divorce Rudolph, and then getting rid of Peggy to ensure Rudolph was no longer tempted to stray.

Rudolph could have killed his mother-in-law if she had discovered his fling with Peggy and he wouldn't want to lose his comfortable lifestyle. Peggy may have been a fly in the ointment, so by getting rid of her, no one would be any the wiser about his affair. It would seem as if he too had a motive for murder.

Matt strolled into the room, shaved and dressed for the day. 'Any tea left in the pot?' he asked after greeting his wife and father-in-law.

'I'll make some more.' Kitty took the pot into the kitchen as Edgar started to ask Matt about Peggy.

She wasn't sure if she was much further forward with trying to work out who could have killed Nora and Peggy and why. There seemed to be quite a few people who might all have motives and the opportunity. However, she was determined her father's name would be cleared of any suspicion.

CHAPTER TEN

Kitty left her father and her husband to enjoy their tea while she went to her bedroom to dress for the day. She chose a pale-blue cashmere twinset and a heavy heather-coloured tweed skirt from her wardrobe, along with some thick stockings.

Outside the window the sky was ominously grey, and it seemed that even more snow was likely. She had just finished patting her short blonde curls in place when someone pounded on the front door of the apartment.

She opened the bedroom door in time to see Matt letting a distraught-looking Mortimer Liggett into the apartment hallway.

'Is it true? Enrique, the concierge, just told me that Peggy Marsh is dead. I'd gone downstairs to ask if a parcel I was expecting had arrived and the police were outside the building again. What's happened? Do you know?' Mortimer looked at Matt, then at Edgar who had followed Matt into the hall.

'I'm afraid it is true, old boy. Come through into the lounge. It's been the most dreadful shock for everybody,' Edgar answered, leading the group back into the cosy comfort of the sitting room. Kitty followed along behind them.

Mortimer sank down on the end of the black leather sofa, his head in his hands. 'I can't believe it. Peggy? Do you know what happened?' He raised his head and looked up as Matt approached him with a tot of brandy in a crystal balloon glass.

'Here, you look as if you need a drink,' Matt suggested in a firm but kindly tone.

Mortimer took the glass obediently and took a sip. 'Thank you. I just couldn't believe what he said. It's dreadful, especially so soon after our dear Nora. What is happening? Was it an accident? Or suicide?'

'I know, we were horribly upset by it too.' Edgar looked at Matt. 'My son-in-law and Horatio were the ones who found her.'

Mortimer stared at Matt. 'You and Horatio? How? When? Where?' He looked bewildered.

Matt explained the circumstances which had taken him to the penthouse apartment a few hours earlier. Kitty watched as a series of expressions crossed Mortimer's pleasant but nondescript face. From astonishment, horror, and then concern.

'Poison?' Mortimer squeaked before taking another, slightly larger, gulp of brandy.

'I'm afraid so, my dear chap. Matt and Kitty are very experienced in these matters. They work as private investigators back home in Devon.' Edgar leaned back in his seat and looked at his friend.

'Was it suicide? Did Peggy harm Nora and then take her own life?' Mortimer looked around at them all.

'No doubt someone will hope that is believed to be what happened, but no, I rather fear that Peggy too has been murdered,' Matt said.

'Good heavens.' It took a moment for the implications of what Matt had just said to seemingly sink in for Mortimer.

'Two murders in just over twenty-four hours. Didn't

Horatio see or hear anything? Is he under arrest? I mean surely he must be involved?' Mortimer asked.

'The police are investigating I assume, but I doubt they have any reason to think Horatio is involved in either death. At least, he is probably no more a suspect than anyone else. In fact, he may even be at risk himself from whoever did this,' Matt suggested.

This thought had crossed Kitty's mind too while she had been dressing. With Nora and Peggy both dead, Horatio might be next if the killer thought he posed a risk.

Mortimer startled at this suggestion, his eyes agog. 'Oh my, yes, I see what you mean. But why Peggy? Did she see something or suspect someone of murdering my dear Nora?'

To Kitty's slight alarm, the man's voice wobbled and he appeared to be dangerously on the brink of tears. She could understand that he and Nora had been conducting an affair, but the man was still married to Titania. Kitty decided she must be getting old; she was turning into Mrs Craven. She could hear the older woman's voice in her head as she looked at Mortimer. '*Deplorable behaviour.*'

'I don't know. That will be a matter for Lieutenant Tanfield, I expect,' Matt said.

'Tanfield? He's the one who came to see me and Titania after, well, after Nora was killed.' Mortimer paused and looked at Matt. 'You found Nora too, didn't you?' There was a hint of suspicion in his voice.

'Yes, it's not been the nicest of starts to our holiday,' Kitty said in a crisp tone.

'No, I suppose not,' Mortimer mumbled, abashed at Kitty's response. 'Tanfield was very harsh towards Titania when he came to our apartment. He virtually accused her of killing Nora,' Mortimer said.

'Well, she did slug her at the party, dear boy. Everyone saw what happened so she could hardly claim they were the best of chums,' Edgar pointed out.

'Titania had had a little too much champagne. She was overwrought and not thinking straight. You know how she can be,' Mortimer said in a huffy tone.

Kitty longed to say, *and whose fault was that*? But bit her tongue instead.

'I expect the police will wish to see you again now Peggy is dead,' Matt said.

Mortimer stared at him. 'Whatever for? Why would we know anything about Peggy's death?'

'It's standard procedure usually. You know, to find out where everyone was when she died. If you knew about her medication and had access to the penthouse,' Kitty said.

A dark-plum colour mounted in Mortimer's cheeks and he opened and closed his mouth like a goldfish gasping for air. 'We were both asleep. Titania had taken a sleeping draught. She was so upset after Tanfield's questions I had to call a doctor in to see her.'

'The poison could have been put in her tonic during the party I suppose, or just afterwards,' Matt mused.

'The poison was in Peggy's medicine?' Mortimer asked. 'I know she took some kind of iron tonic. Nora used to have to remind her to take it. Everyone knows that.'

Kitty exchanged a glance with Matt. 'And obviously you and Titania are familiar with the layout of Nora's apartment,' she said.

Mortimer swallowed the last of his brandy and placed his empty glass on the table. 'Now, I do hope you're not implying that either I or Titania had anything to do with Peggy's death.'

Kitty raised her hands in a gesture of defence. 'I wouldn't dream of such a thing. But obviously the police will ask these kinds of questions.'

Mortimer blinked. 'Oh, of course, I... Yes, I see, you're right. No, Titania will be dreadfully upset when she hears about Peggy.' The bluster had died from his voice.

'Was Titania close to Peggy?' Kitty asked.

'Well, they would talk you know, whenever Nora organised a dinner or something. Girlish gossip,' Mortimer said.

Kitty thought his answer was unsatisfyingly vague.

'Do you think the police will have let Lorena know about Peggy?' Mortimer asked. 'It's her mother's apartment after all and she is still in Lorena's employ now, I suppose.'

'I expect they will want to talk to her and to her husband,' Matt said.

'Especially after Lorena dismissed Horatio and Peggy yesterday,' Edgar added.

Mortimer goggled at Edgar. 'Lorena fired Peggy? I mean, I know Nora had said Horatio needed to retire, which I wholeheartedly supported, but I would have thought Lorena would have kept Peggy on to deal with things for a while at least.'

'Did Nora ever say anything to you about suspecting either Peggy or Horatio of being dishonest?' Kitty asked.

'Well, she told me some things had been moved and others had gone missing. Nora had a lot of little fancy knick-knacks, silver snuffboxes and things. She would move them herself for parties and dinners or events. I didn't take too much notice. She did mention she thought Peggy had become careless,' Mortimer said. 'It had really started to bug her.'

'And Horatio?' Matt asked.

'He was past it really. I mean he'd been with Nora for ages. I always feel like he doesn't approve of me; he was a leftover from her marriage. Always snooping about and quite obsequious, if you know what I mean.' Mortimer gave Matt a meaningful look. 'Nora was going to let him go anyway in the new year.'

The clock on the mantelpiece struck the hour and Mortimer jumped to his feet. 'I had better get back to Titania. She will wonder where I've been and there'll be another row if she thinks I've been out someplace without her. I do hope that Lieutenant Tanfield won't be round upsetting her again. She's going to be distressed enough when I tell her about Peggy.'

Edgar accompanied his unexpected guest from the room. 'I'll see you out, dear boy. Do give our best to Titania. I'm sure the police will have this all wrapped up in the shake of a lamb's tail.'

'I wish I were as confident about the police capturing this killer as your father is,' Matt murmured in a low voice once Edgar and Mortimer were in the hall out of earshot.

'I know. The more we learn the more horribly complicated it all seems. So many of them seem to have motives for killing Nora and Peggy,' Kitty said.

The front door closed, and Edgar sauntered back into the room. 'Old Mortimer has the wind up, doesn't he? Still, Nora's death has hit him pretty hard. He just told me that he had asked Titania for a divorce right before they came to the party. Had a huge fight in the elevator about it.'

'But they still came to the party together? Held by the woman he was having the affair with?' Kitty stared at her father in astonishment.

'He said Titania seemed to think he was bluffing. They had already committed to being there and he intended to go without her, but she insisted she attend. She can be a scary woman,' Edgar said.

'No wonder Titania slapped Nora, in that case.' Kitty couldn't believe her ears. 'She must have been so embarrassed by his behaviour, and everyone there knowing about what was going on.'

'It was rather awkward. I had a feeling there was going to be trouble when we arrived. I could tell by the look on Titania's face. As I said, she's quite fiery.' Edgar swapped his slippers for a pair of brogues and prepared to go downstairs to collect his newspaper.

He let himself out of the apartment and Kitty wondered if he would learn anything else about the murders while he was in the lobby.

The snow had started to fall once again outside the apartment and great white snowflakes spattered against the windows blurring out the view.

'I don't think we shall be going very far today,' Matt said as he looked at the weather.

'No, I think perhaps a quiet day after all the drama of this morning,' Kitty agreed.

Edgar returned after a few minutes with his paper but no fresh information. They passed the day quietly. Kitty read a book and did a jigsaw puzzle with Matt, while her father read his paper and listened to the news on the wireless. By late afternoon the snow was still falling, and it was dark outside.

Kitty drew the dark-green brocade curtains and switched on more lamps. They had been forced to turn some of them on just before dinner since the cloud cover outside was so dense.

There was another knock at the apartment door just as Kitty was thinking of setting the small circular oak table ready for dinner. They had chosen their meals from the daily menu and the trolley would be sent up at seven.

Edgar went to answer the door.

'My dear Lieutenant Tanfield, this is an unexpected pleasure. Allow me to take your hat and coat. Do go on through.'

Kitty heard her father greet the policeman and she hastily tidied up the papers and books that were strewn about the furniture.

'Captain Bryant, Mrs Bryant, I thought I ought to call in

and see you all.' The policeman took a seat on one of the armchairs and waited for Edgar to rejoin them.

'Do you have news, Lieutenant?' Kitty asked once Edgar was resettled in his armchair.

'The doc has confirmed that your husband's suspicions were correct. Peggy Marsh was killed with strychnine. It was in her tonic which several people have told us she would often forget to take regularly. Apparently, it was not unknown for her to suddenly remember and then just pour a dose and take it,' the policeman said.

'So, we can assume something woke her, or she was unable to sleep, and suddenly remembered she had forgotten her tonic,' Matt said.

'I think so, yes. We have also checked in with the pawn-shops you mentioned to me. Mr Blackstock identified a couple of items which Nora Briggs had said were still missing so I sent an officer out to enquire.' Lieutenant Tanfield paused and looked at Matt.

Kitty waited for the detective to say more. Had she and Matt been right about their suspicions that someone had been taking Nora's things and pawning them?

'Did you discover anything?' Matt asked.

'We did indeed. The first shop, the one closest to Mr and Mrs Briggs's apartment, drew a blank. No record of anything fitting the items that Mr Blackstock thought were still missing. However, the other shop was a different story.' Again the detective paused for a moment before continuing.

'Were the items there?' Kitty asked. She was impatient to know if they had been right.

The lieutenant turned his gaze to Kitty. 'Yes, both the missing items were there.' He made a show of consulting his notebook. 'An engraved silver snuffbox, English with a Chester hallmark and a silver figure of a swan, two inches tall with a Birmingham hallmark. Quite distinctive items.'

'I know that swan figure. Nora was very fond of it. She told me once that it was a memento from her honeymoon. They travelled around Europe and her husband bought it for her after they had seen *Swan Lake* at the ballet. A very touching tale,' Edgar said.

Kitty looked at her father, who suddenly seemed to realise he may have been better saying nothing at this point.

'Did anyone at the shop have information on who had brought the silver in?' Kitty asked.

She knew in England, usually a ticket was issued so the items could be redeemed and the details entered in a ledger. This was often helpful should anything be proved stolen later on. Although, the address and name given were often false.

'The shop records were unhelpful. Whoever pawned the items used a fake name and address. However, the assistant remembered the items being brought in,' Lieutenant Tanfield said.

'Did the description fit anyone we know?' Kitty was impatient to discover if there might be a connection between the missing items and the murders. Knowing who had taken the silver from Nora's apartment could provide them with a vital lead.

'The description the assistant gave was of a young woman, mid-twenties, well-spoken, pleasant appearance and nicely dressed. Light-brown hair, wearing a dark-grey lambskin coat and matching hat,' the detective said reading from his notes.

'That sounds like Peggy. She had a coat like that.' Edgar looked puzzled.

'He said the young lady had been in several times before. On each occasion she had different items, all small and silver. Usually, she redeemed them after a week or so but a couple of times she let them slip. He assumed that she was on her uppers and needed the money for rent and bills and when her pay came in she fetched back whatever she could afford.' Lieutenant Tanfield glanced up from his notes.

'It was Peggy who was taking the silver then, but why?' Kitty asked. The whole case was becoming more baffling by the minute.

CHAPTER ELEVEN

'That's a very good question,' Matt agreed.

'Well, I'm no expert in these matters obviously, but it sounds to me as if she may have had a bit of a gambling problem. I mean, I know of people who rely on borrowing a few bob from old Johnny Pawnbroker if they have a run of bad luck. Then they go and get the bally things back when a gee-gee or a dog trots home.' Edgar attempted to maintain an innocent expression as Kitty gave him a hard stare.

'Interesting.' Lieutenant Tanfield scribbled something in his notebook.

'Is there any evidence of something of that nature with Peggy?' Kitty asked.

'We are still making enquiries, this is all at an early stage in our investigation, Mrs Bryant,' the policeman said.

'I suppose the other reason could be if she were taking drugs of some kind,' Matt suggested. 'Cocaine, perhaps, and needed money before she was paid. It can be a real problem in some places.'

Lieutenant Tanfield nodded. 'There was nothing found amongst her possessions to indicate either drug problems or gambling. The autopsy has only revealed evidence of strychnine, although some blood results are still to come in.'

'There is one other possibility I thought of. That perhaps she might have been doing this for someone else's benefit. Someone she loved, perhaps, who might need money urgently from time to time. A boyfriend or lover, or a family member?' Kitty suggested.

'Mr Blackstock didn't know of any boyfriends, but Peggy does have an older brother, James, who lives in New York. My officers have been out to see him to break the news of his sister's death,' Lieutenant Tanfield confirmed.

Kitty found this quite interesting. So, Horatio had not suspected that perhaps Peggy and Rudolph may have been romantically involved. Perhaps she had been mistaken in what she had observed at the party. Then there was this new development of a brother. Could he have been the person Peggy was supplying with money?

Times were hard and she had seen articles in her father's newspaper about how many people were struggling to stay in their homes and get enough food. She and Matt had been donating money to various charities when they had been out and about in the city.

'Does he live far away from here?' Kitty asked. New York was a big city, and she had not yet managed to sort out the geography of the place in her head. Despite the straight lines of many of the streets and the concept of the layout, it still seemed very alien compared to the villages she was more familiar with at home.

'A mile or so away across town. He works as a car mechanic,' the lieutenant said.

'I see.' Kitty wondered how well-off Peggy's brother was. She presumed being a car mechanic must pay reasonably well. It was a skilled job and since there were more motor vehicles on the streets now and less horses, he must be in demand. At least it seemed he was in employment.

Lieutenant Tanfield stood and tucked his little black note-book away again inside the breast pocket of his jacket. 'If you should think of anything further which may be helpful or discover anything new, please give me a call. You have my card.'

'Of course,' Matt assured him and walked out with the policeman to the hall to find his overcoat and hat.

Kitty waited until the lieutenant was out of earshot before rounding on her father. 'Honestly, Papa, are you determined to make yourself a suspect? You knew all about the location of the pawnshops and then you hinted at why Peggy might have used them. Lieutenant Tanfield might start to think she was stealing the silver and pawning it for your benefit. Especially after your recent shenanigans.'

Her father chuckled and then sobered at the serious expression on her face. 'Darling girl, really, I don't think so. It's a bit of a stretch, don't you think?'

'You're the one who said not to get involved in the case and to be careful around these New York policemen,' Kitty pointed out as she folded her arms.

Matt walked back into the sitting room. 'That was good of the lieutenant to let us know what he'd discovered.' He glanced at Kitty.

'It was very good of him,' Kitty agreed. She glared at her father, determined not to let him off the hook quite so easily.

He really had been behaving very badly even before they had arrived in New York. He could have sent another telegram to prevent them from a wasted journey or answered his tele-phone to put her mind at ease.

Then, ever since they had arrived, and she had discovered the real reason he had been pretending to be at death's door, he had seemed to treat everything as a lark. Even Nora's murder and Peggy's death, once he had recovered from the immediate shock and distress. Now he had somehow managed to entangle himself in the crimes in such a way the police were bound to keep him on their suspect list.

Edgar coughed gently. 'I must admit, the lieutenant does seem to be a very thorough fellow. I knew she had a brother, but I wasn't aware that Peggy had any family actually in town.'

'The letters I saw in her room seemed to be from an old neighbour, but I am certain the address was in Maine. Peggy's brother must have moved to New York when Peggy moved,' Matt said.

'Lieutenant Tanfield said that he was older than Peggy. He may have moved here first and then Peggy may have got the job with Nora and followed him. The Depression has forced a good many people to come to the city to seek work from what I've read in the newspapers,' Kitty said.

'Perhaps he was the person she was writing to the night she died,' Matt suggested.

Kitty frowned. 'Possibly, but I would have thought a car mechanic would have had a telephone at his workplace. She could have telephoned him instead. Surely she would want to let him know that her employer had been murdered and she needed to urgently find a new position.'

'We also don't know if they were on good terms,' Edgar pointed out. 'They might not get on.'

Kitty caught her father's eye as he spoke, and she sensed this was a subtle reminder at her reproof to him a moment earlier.

'Yes, you have a point. It's so annoying that we have no access to any of these people to find out more information,' Matt said.

'Even though we are definitely *not* investigating this case.' The corners of Kitty's lips curved up into a slight smile.

'No, most definitely not. We are here on holiday and it's almost Christmas.' Matt smiled back at her as he spoke.

She knew that her husband was as keen to investigate as she was, despite his words.

'Speaking of Christmas. After supper, there is a carol concert at St Patrick's Cathedral this evening. It's just off Fifth Avenue and I think you would enjoy it,' Edgar suggested. 'You know, get us all back in the old festive mood a bit.'

Matt looked at Kitty. 'What do you think? It would be nice to do something Christmassy.'

'The church is quite impressive and it's worth a visit just to see it,' Edgar added.

'Why not?' Kitty agreed, resigning herself to a night-time trip out into the snowy city. Still, it did sound rather fun, and they might as well make the most of their stay.

* * *

Matt could see that Kitty was still a little out of humour when they climbed into the back of the taxi ready to set off for the cathedral. She was wrapped up in her furs and the end of her nose and cheeks were pink with cold.

The snow had stopped falling but the roads and sidewalks were treacherous and there were less people about. Edgar was his usual cheerful self and had taken a seat in the front of the taxi. He was busy chatting with the driver about the weather, and if he thought the sporting fixtures would be affected.

The taxi dropped them off on Fifth Avenue, right outside the huge arched entrance to the cathedral.

'Well, it's certainly impressive.' Kitty looked up, admiring the two huge spires at the front end of the stone building.

'I thought you'd like it,' Edgar said in a smug tone.

There were several people already making their way inside the cathedral, so Matt offered his arm to Kitty, and they followed them through the open doorway.

Many of the seats on the polished wooden pews that filled

the vast interior were already taken. A huge Christmas tree stood at the end of the aisle and the nativity set was in place. Matt, Kitty and Edgar took a seat on the end of a pew and gazed about the building.

Matt could see it had been modelled in a gothic revival style with arches and vaults similar to the much older European cathedrals they were used to seeing. Someone was playing the organ and the music drifted around, mingling with the chatter and occasional cough of the congregation.

After a few minutes, the choir in their red and white robes filed along the central aisle accompanied by the priest. The air was scented with incense from the burners as the procession passed by and after a few words of welcome and a prayer, the concert began.

After a few minutes, Matt could see that Kitty had begun to relax and enjoy herself. He knew she had always loved Christmas. Since they had been married on Christmas Eve it was a special time of year for both of them.

She turned her head towards him and smiled. He gave her mittened hand a gentle squeeze. Even his father-in-law appeared to be enjoying the festive music. Although why Edgar hadn't spontaneously combusted when he'd set foot inside a church Matt wasn't certain. He had been a little surprised when Edgar had suggested the outing, but he suspected that his father-in-law wished to make amends to Kitty.

The carol concert was a delight with singing from the choir and participation pieces for the congregation. The concert ended with a moving version of 'O Little Town of Bethlehem' and a blessing. Kitty took Matt's arm once more and they made their way out of the cathedral, with Edgar following behind them.

'It will be tricky to get a taxi from here, with this crowd. Follow me,' Edgar said, taking the lead.

They followed him carefully along the street until he

turned off into a small nondescript looking doorway. Kitty hesitated and Matt could understand her reluctance to go after him.
One never knew with his father-in-law quite where you were
likely to end up.

Edgar popped back out again when they didn't follow him
inside. 'Do come in, Kitty. I promise even that ghastly Craven
woman would approve of this place.'

With that somewhat dubious reassurance they followed him
inside the entrance of what turned out to be a discreet,
upmarket bar.

'Now then, I say we have a quick round of drinks in here, let
the crowd die down and my chum, Johnny, will call us a cab,'
Edgar suggested, raising his hand in greeting to the large,
smartly dressed bartender.

Matt could see the sense in Edgar's suggestion. At least they
would be warm, dry and comfortable. It was better than
standing in the dark on a crowded, icy street trying to get the
attention of a passing taxi, along with all the other concert
attendees.

'Very well,' Kitty agreed as she drew off her mittens and
stowed them inside her black leather handbag.

The bar was fairly quiet, with just a few patrons present
and a pianist playing popular tunes. The air was slightly hazy
with cigarette smoke and a small Christmas tree stood in one
corner.

'Not seen you for a while, Edgar,' the bartender said as
Kitty's father ordered their drinks.

'No, I was, um, unwell.' Edgar gave a theatrical little cough.
'This is my daughter, Kitty, and her husband, Matthew. They
are here for Christmas from England.' Edgar introduced them
to his friend, Johnny.

While Johnny poured them a whisky and soda it transpired
it had been Johnny who had mentioned the concert at the
cathedral to Edgar some weeks earlier.

'I used to be an altar boy there, see,' Johnny informed them with great pride as he set out the drinks. 'Wasn't sure if your pop would want to go as he's on the other side.'

It took Matt a moment to realise that Johnny was referring to Edgar not being Catholic.

'It's a splendid building and the carols were lovely.' Kitty accepted her drink and smiled at the bartender. 'Thank you for suggesting it to my father. I think we all feel rather more festive now.'

'You're welcome,' Johnny informed her and returned her smile.

Edgar stayed at the bar, but Matt and Kitty seated themselves at a small round table close by. Matt could see his father-in-law conversing in low tones with Johnny, followed by a discreet exchange of dollar bills. He guessed that Johnny was one of the people who would place bets for his father-in-law and he hoped Kitty hadn't noticed the transaction.

'Johnny will telephone for a taxi for us in about fifteen minutes. Just enough time to enjoy our drinks, eh. Bottoms up!' Edgar said as he took his place at the table, before chinking his whisky glass against theirs.

Edgar's plan worked perfectly and some thirty minutes later they were back outside their apartment building having passed a convivial fifteen minutes or so at Johnny's bar. It was freezing now, and snow had started to fall once more as they made their way into the lobby.

Matt was somewhat surprised to see the concierge desk was empty with a note saying the attendant would return shortly. He saw Kitty had noticed it too and guessed that her thoughts mirrored his own. Had the concierge been away from his desk on the night Nora had been murdered? Perhaps that was why no one had seen Nora come down in the elevator and slip out through the service door at the rear of the building.

Edgar pushed the brass button to summon the elevator and

far above them Matt heard the clank and rumble of the cage beginning its descent. The brass arrow above the doors indicating it was returning from the top of the building. When the elevator arrived, it was occupied by Rudolph Briggs who was carrying two large, brown-leather valises.

'Rudi, dear boy, Lorena not with you? Still, it's a ghastly night to be out and about. We were so sorry to hear about poor Peggy. Must have been the most frightful shock coming so soon after what happened to Nora,' Edgar said as he opened the iron fretwork cage so Rudolph and his bags could exit the elevator.

'Yes, it was a horrid shock. Lorena is most distressed by the whole business as you can imagine,' Rudolph said as he stepped out into the lobby.

'My word, those look heavy,' Edgar said as the other man hefted one of the bags to adjust his grip on the handle.

'Lorena and I were concerned that Nora had a lot of very valuable items in her apartment. With things going missing and the police telling us that some items had been retrieved from a pawnshop, well, Lorena felt it would be best if we got the most expensive things and took them to our apartment for safekeeping,' Rudolph said.

'Oh, I quite agree, old chum. The responsibility for poor Horatio otherwise would be most worrying,' Edgar said in a cheerful tone.

'Yes, I suppose so.' Rudolph sounded less positive, and Matt guessed that Lorena had been more concerned that Horatio too might help himself to some items knowing that Peggy would probably be held responsible.

It seemed very untrusting of someone who the family had employed for many years. He was certain they had never had cause to question Horatio's honesty before, or the man would have been dismissed years ago.

'Have you arranged for a cab to pick you up?' Edgar asked.

'Yes, it should be along any minute now.' Rudolph started to edge towards the plate glass and brass entrance doors of the lobby.

'Do you want us to stay with you until it arrives, dear boy?' Edgar asked. 'I mean, two murders in one building and you carrying all those valuables. I'd hate for you to be mugged.'

Matt could tell that Rudolph was a little irked by Edgar's concern for his well-being, but clearly felt compelled to agree since the concierge was still absent from his post.

'I take it the police informed you of their discoveries at the pawnshop then?' Matt asked as Rudolph peered through the glass looking for his cab.

'Yes, they did. Lorena confirmed the swan, and the other piece belonged to Nora,' Rudolph said.

'At least you got those back,' Kitty remarked. 'Edgar told us how much that little silver swan meant to Nora, and I suppose it must have a great deal of sentimental value to Lorena too. I can't think why Peggy would have done such a thing. Do you think she had a gambling or drug problem?' She blinked her wide, blue-grey eyes at Rudolph.

'I, erm, well, no, not that any of us knew,' Rudolph said.

'Or anyone who might have asked her to get money for them. Like a boyfriend or family member?' Kitty continued.

Rudolph shifted uncomfortably. 'No, I don't know. I mean, Lorena might know more about Peggy in that way, I suppose.'

'Oh, you didn't know Peggy that well then?' Kitty persisted.

As she spoke a black cab drew up in front of the building. Its headlamps illuminating the semi-dark street.

'I'm afraid not. Well, this looks like my cab. Thanks for your help.' Rudolph made a bolt for it through the doors towards the waiting taxi. The bags clanked as he hoisted them out and into the back of the taxi next to him.

'Extraordinary fellow,' Edgar mused as they regrouped once more at the elevator doors.

CHAPTER TWELVE

Kitty awoke with a shiver the following morning to discover the city had been coated with a fresh layer of crisp, white snow overnight. She washed and dressed quickly before scampering through to the lounge to turn on the fire. Although the flat had heating, she had been unable to discover how the thermostat was regulated and suspected it was probably set for the same temperature throughout the building.

While Matt was dressing and shaving Kitty made a pot of tea and set the table for breakfast. As she placed the plates and bowls on the table, she glanced at the mantelpiece to check the time. The sight of the cards reminded her that they hadn't checked with the concierge yesterday to see if any post had arrived.

She could hear Matt whistling cheerily as he got ready for the day and decided she had time to nip downstairs to collect any mail and pick up Edgar's morning copy of the newspaper.

Kitty pulled on her coat and took the keys from the Chinese bowl on the hallstand, before heading down to the lobby in the elevator.

'Good morning, ma'am,' Enrique greeted her as she approached the desk.

'I thought I would see if there was any post for my father and pick up his morning paper,' Kitty said after returning the man's greetings.

'Sure thing, ma'am.' Enrique picked up a slim bundle of post and took a neatly folded newspaper to add to the pile.

'Oh dear,' Kitty said as she caught sight of the front page. 'It seems Nora and Peggy's deaths have made the newspaper.'

'They seem to have caught onto the poisoning. With Miss Peggy being young and pretty and all.' Enrique's tone was sad.

'Did you know Peggy well? I suppose she must have come down here quite often running errands for Nora,' Kitty asked.

'Pretty well, ma'am. Peggy was a nice lady, very kind and thoughtful. She would always stop and ask how my mother was or would sometimes bring me a doughnut from the stand down the street. She was good that way, ya know,' Enrique said.

'The police said she had an older brother here in the city, James, a motor car mechanic. Did she ever talk much about her family?' Kitty asked.

'She would say she missed her old home but that she couldn't stay there. There was no employment and she wanted to see the world. She did say she had a brother. Peggy was real proud of him. She would get excited if he dropped her a note. She wrote to him a lot, but he wasn't much of a writer, I guess.' Enrique gave a slight shrug.

Kitty collected up the post and the newspaper. 'I noticed there was no one on the desk last night when we returned from the carol concert. Mr Rudolph Briggs was here too taking some things from Nora's apartment, so we waited with him until his cab came.'

'Zavier was on duty last night, so I figure he was probably fixing himself a hot drink in the kitchen or maybe was in the bathroom. He's conscientious so I expect he just stepped out for a few minutes. Sometimes we get called to apartments too if something goes wrong.' Enrique started to tidy his desk.

'Was he on duty the night Nora was killed?' Kitty asked as she prepared to head back upstairs.

Enrique nodded. 'He sure was. He was real upset by what happened. I know he spoke with Lieutenant Tanfield about it. He told me that he'd no idea that Mrs Dangerfield had come down and gone out back.'

Kitty nodded. 'I'm sure he must feel terrible. It was dreadful for all of us.'

She walked the few feet across the marble floor to the elevator and pressed the call button. While she was waiting for the car to return, the front doors to the lobby opened and a stocky, brown-haired man in his mid-thirties entered. He was dressed in navy workman's overalls, a heavy dark-blue peacoat and a twill cap and woollen muffler.

He stamped the snow from his boots on the entrance mat and approached the desk.

'I've come to collect my sister's things. Miss Peggy Marsh.'

'Oh, you must be James? Peggy's brother? Kitty Bryant, my father, Edgar Underhay, knew your sister quite well. He was her neighbour. I'm so very sorry for your loss.' Kitty had turned and approached the man as soon as she had heard his query.

She held out her hand for the man to shake, aware that she sounded very English.

'Thank you, yes, ma'am, Peggy's death has been an awful shock.' The man removed his woollen gloves, shoving them into his coat pockets before shaking her hand. She noticed the palm was rough and calloused and there was a faint rim of black engine oil under his fingernails.

'I can take Mr Marsh up to the penthouse, Enrique,' Kitty suggested to the concierge. 'If you could let Mr Blackstock know that we are on our way up.'

'Sure thing, Mrs Bryant,' Enrique agreed and picked up the telephone receiver to call up to Nora's apartment.

Kitty stepped back over to the elevator where the cage was now waiting for them. Peggy's brother opened the gate so she could enter first.

'Thank you,' Kitty said as he followed her inside.

He looked tired, with dark circles under his eyes. She couldn't imagine how awful he must be feeling.

'Mr Blackstock was Mrs Dangerfield's manservant. He worked closely with your sister, as I'm sure you know,' Kitty said as the elevator glided slowly upwards.

'Yeah, she wrote some in her letters. She liked a letter, did Peg.' James rubbed his hand across his face.

'When did you last hear from her?' Kitty asked as she saw from the dial that they were approaching the top floor.

'A week ago. She wrote every week mostly about where she'd been and what events she was organising. I'm not much of a writer myself so I didn't always get to reply. She knew I liked her letters though,' James said as they came to a halt outside the front door of Nora's apartment.

James opened the door of the elevator and went to step out.

'Mr Marsh, I hope you won't consider this an imposition, but would you like my assistance with dealing with your sister's things? It's just that I know the task will be distressing for you and Mr Blackstock and well, there may be feminine items.' Kitty phrased her question delicately.

Her offer was borne from both a desire to genuinely assist, and also her inbuilt need to snoop.

James looked a little surprised at first, before slowly nodding his head. 'Thank you, Mrs Bryant. Yes, if you wouldn't mind, I think Peggy would have well appreciated that.'

Kitty followed him from the elevator, and they knocked on the door of the penthouse apartment. Horatio opened it immediately.

'Mr Marsh, come in. Please accept my condolences on your loss. Peggy was a lovely young woman and a valued colleague.' Horatio looked slightly surprised when Kitty followed James inside the apartment after Peggy's brother had acknowledged Horatio's words.

'I have offered to assist Mr Marsh with packing up some of Peggy's most personal items,' Kitty explained as they followed Horatio into the large sitting room.

Kitty could see that Rudolph had done a thorough job the night before stripping the apartment of valuables. The lovely bijouterie cabinets were now empty, and the silver-framed family photographs were also gone.

'A very generous thought. May I offer you coffee, Mr Marsh, Mrs Bryant?' Horatio asked.

Kitty thought the manservant had aged overnight. Before she hadn't thought that he particularly looked to be retiring age but now there were lines around his eyes and mouth. His shoulders were slumped and there was an air of dignified defeat about his person.

'Thank you, sir,' James said. 'I set off early this morning and had to take two buses to get here and it's mighty cold outside.'

'Shall I go and make a start, while you warm up? I can pack her clothing and shoes and place any papers and personal items you may need separately,' Kitty offered as she shook her head to decline Horatio's offer of coffee.

'Thank you, Mrs Bryant. I truly appreciate your kindness.' James Marsh sat gingerly on the edge of one of the couches at Horatio's invitation.

Kitty sucked in a breath to brace herself for the task ahead and went back along the hall to Peggy's room. Someone, Horatio, she guessed had straightened the place up. The nightstand had been put back beside the bed and all the broken items had been cleared away.

She opened the small rosewood wardrobe to find a large

carpet bag on the top shelf, so she took that down ready to place Peggy's belongings inside. The bag was empty, and Kitty guessed it was probably the bag the girl had used when she had first moved into the apartment.

At the bottom of the wardrobe were three pairs of shoes, winter ones, summer sandals and evening shoes. She placed them in the bag first. There were two handbags. One a daytime cream leatherette and the other a small silver-beaded evening purse. The evening purse was empty.

Kitty turned her attention to Peggy's handbag. Out in the drawing room she could hear the faint murmur of male conversation so guessed Horatio and James were discussing Peggy and what had happened to her.

The bag held the usual things. A worn-looking leather purse with a few coins and dollar bills. She set that aside for James. There was a lipstick in pale rose, a cotton handkerchief, a comb and a cheap gilt compact. In the silk lining of the bag Kitty found two pawn tickets. These had to be for the items the police had recovered. She removed them to pass to Lieutenant Tanfield. There was also another slip of paper tucked inside that crackled as she removed the tickets.

Kitty dug down and pulled out a piece of good quality writing paper. Opening it up she discovered it was a note.

Can't get away tonight but I'll make it up to you soonest.

Rather annoyingly, it was unsigned and undated. Kitty quickly tucked it in amongst the post and the paper she had carried with her from downstairs, before continuing with her task. She folded up the meagre supply of clothes in the wardrobe, taking care to check any pockets as she did so. With those packed she turned to the small chest of drawers in the corner of the room beside the washstand.

These yielded nothing except stockings and undergarments, all of which Kitty carefully packed in the carpet bag. On top of the wardrobe were two hat boxes. Kitty had to drag the dressing table stool across to fetch them down. They both contained inexpensive straw summer hats. She placed those on the bed next to the carpet bag.

Kitty wondered what James would do with the things. Perhaps he had a wife or girlfriend who might make use of some of them. The dressing table drawers held a paperback novel and some toiletries. Kitty added those and the dressing set to the contents of the carpet bag, along with a small cosmetics bag.

The final piece of furniture was the nightstand itself. It had been obvious to Kitty that the contents of the cupboards had already been searched. She presumed by the police looking for either a suicide note, or something to give a clue to the murderer.

There was a chip and several scratches on the nightstand, probably from where Peggy had turned it over when the spasms from the strychnine had kicked in. It was a flimsy, cheap piece of furniture and didn't match the other pieces in the room. Kitty could only assume that like so many wealthy people, Nora had furnished the servants' rooms with odd pieces from other places.

The contents of the drawer were higgledy-piggledy from being knocked over. There was a small, black leather-bound Bible that looked worn and well used. Kitty looked inside the cover and saw it was inscribed to a Sarah Marsh. She wondered if it had belonged to Peggy and James's mother. There were a few strands of beads and a cheap costume brooch and bangle. A jar of cold cream and some hair grips. The letter from her former neighbour that Matt had seen was also stuffed in the drawer.

Nothing that indicated anything about Peggy's personal life.

No photographs of her parents or of her brother. Nothing at all that revealed much of who Peggy had been as a person. Her likes and dislikes, her love life or her past. It wasn't much to show for a life, she thought.

Kitty took a last quick glance around the room. There wasn't even an ornament that was personal to Peggy. She wondered if the police may have taken anything but thought it unlikely. She collected up her own bundle of post and the newspaper and returned to join Horatio and James who were sitting sipping coffee together.

'Everything is packed ready for you. I've left her purse out next to the bag of her things and the hat boxes. I am truly sorry for your loss,' Kitty said.

'Thank you, Mrs Bryant. I truly appreciate your help. I was dreading this task as I travelled here this morning. Peggy was all I had in the world since our mother passed away. I was expecting to get a letter this week and maybe see her at Christmas for an hour or two. This whole ordeal has been like a bad dream ever since I got the news.' James's eyes filled with tears, and he blinked fiercely to keep them at bay.

'It's terrible,' Horatio agreed, gazing mournfully about the ransacked apartment. 'I can't believe that this room was full of people and gaiety just a few days ago. Everybody excited for Christmas and the New Year, and now this.'

'I couldn't believe it when the police said it was murder. Why in the world would anyone want to kill Peggy? She had no money, she never hurt anyone. She was the kindest soul anyone could ever meet.' James looked bewildered.

'I don't know. Unless, whoever killed Nora thought that Peggy might know who they were,' Kitty suggested. She wondered if he knew about Peggy pawning Nora's things.

Horatio shivered. 'It's made me feel very uneasy being here alone. Tell the truth, I was relieved when Mr Rudolph took all the silver out of the apartment last night. I'd been thinking, what if someone broke in? Or if maybe I would be next on the list. I don't mind saying I'm sleeping with a baseball bat under my bed.'

'Times are hard right now,' James agreed. 'It's why I came to the city. I'm lucky to have my job and a room.'

'It must be very worrying.' Kitty understood their concerns. 'Have you had the chance to think about where you might go in the new year?' She looked at Horatio.

The servant shook his head. 'Not many positions going to be advertised until January I don't expect. I've a little money to rent a room and hope I can get a job then.'

'You have no pension?' Kitty asked.

The man shook his head. 'No, ma'am. I haven't much savings neither. My sister has been ill for a long time, and I send every spare dime I get back home to pay for her medical bills.'

'I'm sorry. I hope things work out for you.' Kitty thought that at least explained why Horatio had no money after working for Nora for so long. She couldn't help feeling angry with Lorena for being so heartless, dismissing a long-standing elderly servant so close to Christmas.

It was certainly something she and her grandmother would never have done to an employee of theirs at the Dolphin Hotel. They always treated their staff well and paid generously. The reward had been returned in loyalty and low turnover with many of their employees being like family.

She said goodbye to James Marsh and let herself out of the apartment, insisting that Horatio sit and finish his coffee with James. She took the flight of stairs back down to her father's flat and let herself in with the key.

After removing her coat, she went through to the sitting room to find Matt seated at the dining table spreading butter on a slice of toast.

'The tea is cold now, darling. Where on earth have you

been? I was getting worried.' Matt jumped up ready to go make a fresh pot.

Kitty dropped the bundle of post on the table and extricated the note she'd found in Peggy's handbag, placing it on top of the newspaper.

'Doing a spot of sleuthing,' she said.

CHAPTER THIRTEEN

Matt set the almost empty teapot down and picked up the slip of paper. 'No signature, or date, that's a pity. Where did you find this?' He looked at Kitty who appeared very pleased with herself.

'Go and make us a fresh pot of tea and I promise I'll tell you everything.' She smiled beguilingly at him as she slipped into the empty seat at the breakfast table.

Matt chuckled and went to the kitchenette. When he returned a few minutes later armed with a hot pot of tea and some freshly cut bread he settled down to listen to Kitty's adventures.

'What did you think of Peggy's brother? Do you think she was pawning those things on his behalf?' Matt asked once Kitty had told him everything she had learned.

'He appeared quite shy, very upset over his sister's death, as you'd expect. He seemed like a normal working man. He has a job and a room. From the way he spoke it didn't seem as if he needed anything from his sister. I don't think he had seen her for a while. He said Peggy wrote once a week to him,' Kitty said.

'Did he say when he last heard from her? He could be one

of the intended recipients of the letters she said she had needed to post.' Matt watched as Kitty carefully spread butter in a thick layer over her bread.

'He said he was expecting to hear from her as she wrote regularly, and he had hoped to see her over Christmas. He set out very early this morning from his lodgings as he had to take two buses to get to this side of the city. His post will probably be waiting for him when he returns to his lodgings,' Kitty said, before crunching into her breakfast.

'You say this note was inside Peggy's handbag?' Matt looked at the creamy coloured slip of paper.

'Yes, tucked in a pocket in the lining with the pawn tickets for those items the police retrieved. Those are there too.' Kitty moved the note revealing the receipts from the pawnbrokers.

'It's interesting they were all found together. There's nothing distinguishable on this note either to track where it could have come from.' Matt glared at the offending item.

'I know, it's so tantalising. It sounds like something a married man might send to his lover, don't you think?' Kitty mused.

'I don't know, that seems rather a stretch to me. There are no kisses or signs of affection. To me it sounds more businesslike,' Matt said. 'We shall have to hand all of these over to Lieutenant Tanfield.'

Kitty finished eating her last bite of bread. 'I suppose so,' she agreed and wiped her mouth and fingers on the pale-blue linen napkin before pouring tea into her cup.

'At least we also know now why Horatio needs to continue working,' Matt said.

'Yes, it's quite awful of Lorena though to treat him this way after being with the family for so long. He did say he felt better that Rudolph had taken most of the valuables from the apartment. He was worried in case anyone tried to break in. It was a big responsibility knowing they didn't trust him.'

Matt shook his head when Kitty offered him more tea. 'It must be very uncomfortable for him, especially as he is aware he will be homeless and unemployed as soon as Christmas is over after years of loyal service to Nora's family.'

Kitty frowned. 'Doesn't it strike you as odd? I mean Nora seemed like quite a kind person when we met her. She took the time to send for us when Pa was ill, and she was raising money for the orphanage. She had to know that Horatio didn't want to retire and had worries about his finances.'

'Perhaps she considered she was doing him a favour,' Matt said. 'She may not have realised he had so little in his savings and thought after a lifetime of work he deserved to relax.'

'Hmm.' Kitty didn't sound convinced. 'I wonder if Nora left him anything in her will? It would be interesting to know exactly what is in her will. I suppose Lorena will inherit everything unless she left donations to charity.'

'You're thinking financial gain may be a motive for Nora's death?' Matt leaned back in his chair. 'It often is, I suppose. We already know from Edgar that Lorena and Rudolph's lifestyle was funded by Nora. I wonder if that would have changed if Mortimer had left Titania and married Nora. After all, if she was prepared to dismiss Horatio possibly because of Mortimer, then perhaps the gravy train would have left the tracks for Lorena too.'

'There is still the matter of the missing jewellery,' Kitty said. 'There was presumably no sign of that in the pawnshops. I suppose whoever took it could have tried selling it to a jeweller.'

'I would hope that the police would have alerted all of the reputable jewellery stores. I know that doesn't prevent a criminal from taking it somewhere less scrupulous but even so, the stones would be bound to come to light even if they broke up the set, I'd have thought,' Matt said.

Kitty finished her tea and set the cup back on its saucer.

'Then there is the strychnine used to kill Peggy. Where did it come from?'

Matt gave a wry smile. 'I hate to say it, darling, but I think it's pretty common knowledge that you can get it from rat poison. Every cheap crime novella or gory news story seems to have used that at some point in the plot.'

Kitty gave a heavy sigh. 'True, Alice and I have seen it in quite a few of the films at the cinema. Still, where did it come from in this case? Has the building had a pest problem?'

'I see what you mean. Yes, it must have come from somewhere and been close to hand if we are to believe that Peggy's death was a consequence of Nora's murder.' Matt could see what Kitty was driving at. Since Nora was killed first, they had assumed that Peggy's death was probably down to something she knew that could identify the murderer.

'But Peggy could have been the intended victim all along and Nora died before she could warn Peggy or prevent her death,' Kitty said.

'That theory could work.' A cold shiver ran down Matt's spine. He hadn't thought of the murders that way round. 'But why kill Peggy?'

'I would love to know what the police have discovered.' Kitty sounded mournful.

'Well, we can telephone the police station and let Lieutenant Tanfield know you have the pawn tickets and this cryptic little note,' Matt suggested as Kitty started to clear away the breakfast things.

She brightened at this suggestion, and he found the policeman's card from his pocket and went to make the call. There was a lot of noise on the other end of the line when he was finally connected to the right department.

Matt was informed that Lieutenant Tanfield was out, and the message would be passed to him on his return. He was forced to be content with this somewhat unsatisfactory answer and replaced the black telephone receiver in its cradle as Edgar sauntered into the room.

'You've missed breakfast, unless you just want some cereal,' Kitty said.

'Oh, nothing like that for me, dear girl. I don't suppose you could make some coffee, could you? Got a bit of a headache this morning,' Edgar said as he sank down in his favourite armchair.

Matt handed his father-in-law the post and the newspaper that Kitty had collected from the lobby. Kitty glared at her father, then went off to put the kettle on once more. Edgar leafed through the envelopes and slit them open with a small pearl-handled paperknife that he kept on a side table next to his chair.

'More festive good wishes,' he said as he extracted the Christmas cards and placed them ready to add to the collection on the mantelpiece. He caught sight of the front of the newspaper. 'Good heavens, it seems we are headline news.'

Matt hadn't taken much notice of the newspaper headlines. He had been focused on the note and the tickets which Kitty had placed carefully inside her own handbag now for safe keeping.

Edgar shook the paper open and took a pair of gold wire-framed spectacles from his breast pocket. Once they were perched firmly on the bridge of his nose he peered at the small print. Matt leaned over his shoulder, and they read the report together in silence.

* * *

Kitty carried in a small round, enamelled tray with a cafetière of coffee, and a jug of steamed milk. She placed it down carefully in front of her father.

'What does the newspaper have to say about Nora and Peggy's deaths?' she asked.

'Nothing that we don't already know. Except, of course, it's all highly sensationalised,' Edgar said as he rested the paper down on his knees and removed his glasses. 'Thank you for the coffee, darling girl.' He poured himself a drink and added sugar.

Kitty perched herself on the chair opposite her father and told him of her meeting with Peggy's brother.

'That must have been dreadfully upsetting for him.' Edgar shook his head. 'I still can't quite believe it.'

A sudden hammering on the front door of the apartment startled all of them. Kitty jumped to her feet and Edgar spilled some of his coffee in his saucer, while Matt rushed to answer the door.

A moment later, a somewhat tearful and distressed-looking Titania was in the drawing room. Her auburn hair was in disarray and the kohl around her eyes was smudged from crying, giving her a clownish appearance.

'I didn't know what to do or where to go. Oh, Edgar, I am relying on you as my only true friend.' Titania looked at Kitty's father and burst into a chorus of noisy sobs.

'Oh, my dear, whatever has happened?' Kitty soothed, seeing the look of horror on her father's face at the distraught woman's words. 'Here, do sit down.' She guided Titania onto the chair that she herself had just vacated.

Kitty wrinkled her nose discreetly at the stale odour of whisky emanating from their unexpected guest.

'It's Morty!' Titania wailed. 'Oh, Edgar, he's gone. He's left me and I don't know what to do. I'm sure the police think I killed Nora and then I'll be arrested and then who knows what will happen to me.' She pulled out a sodden scrap of lace-edged cotton and blew her nose noisily.

Matt looked at Kitty and inclined his head towards the drinks cabinet asking a silent question. Kitty gave a faint nod.

Perhaps a tot of brandy might help calm Titania down. Matt poured a small amount of liquor into a crystal glass and passed it to Kitty.

'Here, now have a sip of this and tell us what has happened to distress you so.' Kitty pressed the drink into Titania's shaking hands.

'Thank you.' Titania accepted it gratefully and downed the contents in one gulp. Matt's eyes widened in surprise.

'You said your husband had gone?' Matt asked.

'He's left me. He said he was still going to go ahead with a divorce even though Nora was dead,' Titania wailed. 'We had an argument, and he stormed out and now the police will arrest me, and I don't know what to do.'

'Why would the police arrest you?' Kitty asked. She was starting to think she should have given Titania some of Edgar's coffee instead of more alcohol.

Titania wiped her eyes, smearing more of the kohl onto her cheeks. 'Because he was going to marry Nora and I slapped her at the party. Now they think I killed her and poisoned Peggy.' She looked at the newspaper on Edgar's lap. 'It'll be in the news. I'll be ruined. I'll have to go to Mexico or Paris or somewhere.' Her gaze slipped away from Kitty's, and she wondered what Titania was concealing.

'Have the police said that they suspect you?' Matt asked.

'They told me not to leave town and I have a cruise booked in January.' Titania's volume increased. 'I want my Morty back. He always sorts things out for me.'

'Where has Mortimer gone?' Edgar asked with a bewildered air.

'I don't know! I thought you would know. You're a man, he talks to you.' Titania turned her bleary gaze on Edgar.

'I suppose he may be at his club,' Edgar muttered, looking severely discomfited.

Kitty raised an eyebrow. 'Perhaps you could telephone, Pa, just to put Titania's mind at ease,' she suggested.

Titania sniffled and held her hands up in an imploring gesture. 'Oh, Edgar, honey, please, would you? I just want him to come home so we can talk things out.' Her lower lip wobbled. 'He can't be serious about leaving me.'

Edgar sighed and set aside his paper and his coffee to pick up the telephone receiver. After being connected he conducted a brief conversation and ascertained that Mortimer was not at the club.

Titania's face crumpled as Edgar replaced the receiver in the cradle. 'Where can he be? I hope he doesn't do anything foolish.'

'Did he pack a bag? Take anything with him?' Matt asked.

Titania shook her head. 'No, he just slammed out of the apartment and said he wasn't coming back.' She looked at Edgar with pleading eyes. 'You must know of some other places he might be.'

'I'd have to think, dear girl. It might be better if you give him time to cool off. I'm certain he will come home, especially if, as you say, he didn't take a bag with him,' Edgar pointed out.

'Do you really think so?' Titania's expression brightened momentarily as she dabbed at the end of her nose with her sodden handkerchief.

'Absolutely,' Edgar assured her.

Kitty eyed her father cynically. She suspected he just wanted to get rid of Titania.

'Everything has been so crazy since Nora's party,' Titania said, giving her nose another dab.

'It's dreadful, first Nora and then poor Peggy,' Kitty agreed. 'What happened the night of the party? After Mortimer took you home?'

Again, Titania's gaze slid away from Kitty's. 'I don't know. I mean, I had drunk a lot of champagne, and my nerves were all on edge. I felt so humiliated and angry with Nora and with Mortimer. I mean, she wasn't the first little fling he'd had.' She paused to wipe her eyes again before continuing. 'I just thought it would fizzle out, you know, like the others. When he asked me for a divorce that night, I was shocked.'

'Why did you still go to the party together?' Kitty asked.

'Because it would have looked strange for me to be missing and I wanted the satisfaction of making them feel uncomfortable. I don't know. I suppose I thought I could warn Nora off, tell her I was refusing a divorce. I wasn't thinking straight. Then all night she looked so smug and self-satisfied, giving me these little pitying glances when she thought I wasn't looking.' Titania's hands balled into fists, squeezing her handkerchief.

'That was when you slapped her?' Edgar asked.

'Anything to wipe that look off her stupid face. Then Morty took me home. He shouted at me.' Titania covered her face with her hands. 'He said I was a lush and I'd embarrassed him. It was no wonder he wanted to leave me.'

'What happened after that? Did Mortimer stay with you? I don't recall seeing him again later on.' Kitty tried her best to sound soothing and sympathetic.

Again, there was that curious sense of evasiveness. 'I don't know. I went to bed with some water and an aspirin. I don't know what Morty did after that. I told that lieutenant that I wasn't sure about anything.'

Kitty was pretty certain that Titania was sure but didn't want to say, and she knew there could only be one reason for the older woman refusing to speak. Either Mortimer or Titania or both of them had left the apartment again that night at some point.

'When did Mortimer go out again? Was it after the party was supposed to have finished?' Kitty asked in a nonchalant tone.

Titania turned frightened eyes on her. 'I don't know what

you mean. I told you, I went to bed. I don't know what Morty did.'

'Oh really, Titania, darling, you are among pals here. Of course Mortimer went back out. I expect he went to see Nora to smooth things over,' Edgar said.

Titania's eyes widened and she opened and closed her mouth a few times like a goldfish gulping for air.

'I suppose you followed him,' Matt suggested.

'I... I...' Titania's gaze flickered from one person to another before landing back on Kitty. 'What would you have done in my position?' she pleaded. 'I was lying on my bed. I hadn't changed out of my frock. I'd just taken off my wings and my jewellery and slipped on my robe over the top of my dress. I heard the door of the apartment open, and I shot straight up.' She blinked a few times as if reliving the events of the evening.

'What happened then?' Kitty urged encouragingly.

'I opened the door of our bedroom and peeked out. The apartment was quiet. and I just knew he had gone to see her, the rotten cheating snake. I grabbed the keys to the front door from my bag and followed him. He had gone up the stairs. I could hear his footsteps going up from the landing.' Titania paused once more to blow her nose again.

'Did you follow him up the stairs?' Kitty asked.

Titania shook her head slowly. 'No, not right away, my head was a bit swimmy so I thought I'd wait a while. Give him a chance to get up there. He's not so fit anymore and there's a lot of stairs between our place and Nora's swanky penthouse.' Her tone was bitter.

'How long did you wait?' Matt asked.

'Only a minute or so. I wanted to confront them. Then as I was about to start up the stairs, I heard the elevator rumble.' A fearful look darted across Titania's face.

'Was it going up or down?' Kitty glanced at Matt.

Titania swallowed. 'I moved to the shadows and peeked out. It was going down. I couldn't see who was in it and I didn't hear any voices.'

Kitty sucked in a breath. Could the elevator have been taking Nora to her death? And if so, was Mortimer the killer?

CHAPTER FOURTEEN

'I didn't know what to do then. I thought perhaps it was the staff leaving, or maybe the last of the guests. I decided to creep up the stairs to see if I could see or hear anything. I thought he had to have made it up there by then.' Titania gave another sniff.

'Did you see anyone?' Matt asked.

The woman shook her head, making her untidy auburn curls waggle about. 'No, by the time I got up to the top floor everything was quiet. I thought I'd heard the elevator again when I was on the stairwell, so figured it must have gone back up.'

'What did you see on the landing outside Nora's penthouse?' Matt asked.

Kitty guessed he wanted to be absolutely certain that the woman hadn't missed anything and was telling them the truth.

Titania shrugged. 'The front door was closed. The landing was dark, and I listened for a minute or two as I thought about banging on the door to try to get them to open up.'

'But you didn't?' Kitty wondered why the woman hadn't made a fuss after going to so much trouble.

Titania's shoulders drooped. 'The booze was kicking in

good by then. I was cold and I looked down at my housecoat and thought to myself: *Titania, what do you think you're doing?* So, I turned around and went back down the stairs.'

'Did you see Mortimer again that evening?' Matt asked.

'I didn't look for him when I let myself back in the apartment. Everything was quiet and I just went straight to bed. He was in the apartment when I woke up the next day. He told me he'd slept in the spare room.'

'Did you believe him?' Edgar asked.

Titania looked bewildered. 'At the time, yes. We didn't know about what had happened to Nora until later when we heard from Lorena.'

Mortimer had certainly appeared very distressed, Kitty recalled, when he had knocked on their door the morning after the party. Was he Nora's murderer? Was he the last person to have seen her alive? So many questions were racing through her mind.

'Well, my dear, I think the best thing you can do is go home and freshen up. I'll try and track down your errant hubby and send him back to you,' Edgar suggested, looking at Titania.

'Yes, I expect Lieutenant Tanfield will probably be calling on everyone again,' Matt said. 'You need to tell him what you've just told us about what happened that night,' he advised Titania as she rose from her seat ready to leave.

'Oh no, I couldn't. It makes me sound so bad. Morty too.' She gave Matt a distressed look. 'They'll be more convinced than ever that I killed her.'

'Nonsense, Titania, darling. It shows your honesty. He'll only find out from somewhere else. They always do, and then it would look bad for you. He'd think you were hiding information from him on purpose,' Edgar advised in a fatherly tone.

Titania appeared unconvinced. 'I don't know.'

'Trust me, I've had many dealings with the police. Honesty

is the best policy,' Edgar declared virtuously, ignoring Kitty's shocked expression.

Matt escorted Titania to the door, before returning to the sitting room once she had departed.

Edgar eyeballed Titania's empty brandy glass. 'I know it's before noon but after hearing all of that I think I could use a bit of a stiffener,' he remarked.

'I rather think Titania had already imbibed before coming here,' Kitty said.

'That was all quite concerning. It may be that Mortimer was the last person to see Nora alive.' Matt looked at his father-in-law. 'Do you know where he might be?'

Edgar scratched his head. 'Well, if he's not at his club, there are one or two drinking dens where he may have holed up,' he said.

'Do you think he was in the elevator going down with Nora that night? The one Titania said she heard when she was going up the stairwell?' Kitty asked.

'It's possible, but it could have been anyone. Someone going home, Nora by herself, Mortimer by himself, both of them together, we just don't know.' Matt's expression was troubled, and Kitty could see he was deeply concerned.

'Peggy could have seen him with Nora after he left the party to take Titania home,' Kitty said. 'If Horatio had already retired for the night, his room is on the other side of the apartment. Peggy was the only person then who would know Mortimer had called back to see Nora.'

'She would have told the lieutenant that surely when he questioned her. I mean he was bound to have asked about Titania slapping Nora. And why would Nora have left the apartment with Morty? Why go outside to be together when they had her apartment? She wouldn't have traipsed outside in the cold to the back of the block.' Edgar picked up his news-paper again.

'Papa, are you going to try and find Mortimer?' Kitty asked before he could disappear back behind the newsprint. 'I think we really should try to speak to him.'

Her father sighed and set his paper aside once more. 'What do I say if I track him down? Go home, your wife is hysterical and, by the by, did you murder Nora or Peggy?'

'We need to talk to him.' Kitty looked at Matt for support. 'At the very least we need to know his state of mind. It doesn't sound as if he's thinking rationally.'

'If he's left Titania then believe me, he is doing the most rational thing I've ever known him do,' Edgar muttered as he flicked open his silver card case and began to look out for various telephone numbers.

'What should we do if Lieutenant Tanfield drops by to see us? We left him that message about the note and the tickets, remember?' Kitty said as Edgar began calling some of the places where he suspected his friend may have gone.

'I see, thank you, yes, we're on our way. We'll pick him up, don't worry.' Edgar set the receiver down. 'I've found him. He's at the Silver Rose, roaring drunk apparently. I told them we'd come and get him,' Edgar said.

'Right ho, we had better go then,' Matt said.

Edgar looked hopefully at his discarded newspaper, ignoring Kitty's glare.

'You need to go with Matt, Papa. Mortimer doesn't know us very well and you are his friend. He is much more likely to agree to accompany you. I suppose I should stay here in case the lieutenant calls.' Kitty made the offer grudgingly. She would much rather have gone with them to collect Mortimer from the bar. However, she could see that three people turning up to collect an inebriated Mortimer might not go well.

Matt nodded his agreement. 'I think that's a sensible suggestion. We'll bring him back here if he doesn't want to see Titania.'

Edgar finally gave up on his newspaper and rose from his seat. 'Very well. The Silver Rose is not the most salubrious of establishments, so I think you remaining here to man the fort is a wise choice, Kitty, darling.'

Kitty started to clear away her father's coffee tray and tried not to feel too disappointed at not being in the thick of the action.

Matt gave her a knowing smile and a quick kiss. 'We'll be back soon, hopefully with Mortimer, and we can find out what he wasn't telling us the day we found Nora's body.'

* * *

Matt knew Kitty was disappointed at not joining them on the trip to collect Mortimer from the Silver Rose. Edgar was surprisingly silent on the way to the bar as they passed the tall buildings in the centre of the city. Beyond telling Kitty before they had departed that the place was not very nice, he had made no further comments.

Matt wasn't sure what kind of state they would find Mortimer in when they arrived. Clearly the bartender had been happy that they were agreeable to collecting Mortimer so he must be causing some kind of nuisance.

The Silver Rose was in a part of the city that Matt and Kitty had not previously visited. This was an area with few signs of Christmas. There were blocks of tenement buildings, all of which appeared to be slightly run-down and there was litter amongst the piles of dirty snow. No one had made any attempt to clear the sidewalk and everywhere seemed grimy. Tattered posters advertising closing down sales and compulsory purchase notices were on nearby buildings.

The bar itself was a small, dingy door set in a blank brick

wall with a hand-painted sign above it. Matt guessed that many of these places had been established during the prohibition period and still retained a discreet, word of mouth presence.

Matt paid the cab and asked the driver to wait while he and Edgar entered the bar. The inside of the bar was as gloomy and dank as the outside. They soon spotted Mortimer sitting at a corner table with several empty glasses in front of him. A couple of other patrons were playing at the pool table and two more men were seated on stools at the bar.

The bartender nodded to Edgar as they entered. He clearly knew him well and Matt wondered what his father-in-law had been up to that he was frequenting places like the Silver Rose.

'Mortimer, my dear fellow, time for us to go,' Edgar said.

Mortimer looked at him with bleary eyes. 'I've left Titania. Nora is dead. I've nowhere to go.' He stank of stale liquor. His shirt was crumpled and dirty and his collar and tie lay askew.

'You can come home with me. The taxi is outside waiting for us, and Matthew here will help us along.' Edgar indicated Matt.

'Better to leave me alone. Save yourself,' Mortimer groaned. 'I need another drink.' His speech slurred as he spoke.

'I rather think you've had enough for now, old chap. Come along with us.' Edgar signalled to Matt to assist him in prising the reluctant and inebriated Mortimer from his seat to get him outside to the waiting taxi.

'I don't want to go home,' Mortimer wailed as Matt took one arm and Edgar attempted to take his other side.

'I told you, we're going to my apartment,' Edgar soothed.

Mortimer wobbled to his feet before attempting to escape their clutches. Matt caught hold of him just in time to prevent him from upsetting the table before him.

'The car is waiting. We have to go,' Edgar insisted as Mortimer threw one arm around his shoulders dislodging his hat.

'You're a good friend, Eddie,' Mortimer slurred. 'One of the best.'

Between them they managed to walk Mortimer out of the Silver Rose onto the sidewalk. Once there, the icy air seemed to hit the inebriated man with the force of a cold bucket of water in the face.

'Where we going?' He blinked at Edgar, as Matt attempted to keep Mortimer upright and open the taxi door at the same time. Not an easy task on the icy pavement.

'To my apartment, where you are going to drink some coffee and work out what you're going to do next,' Edgar gasped as Matt bundled Mortimer into the back of the cab.

Matt clambered in alongside him while Edgar got in the front beside the driver.

'Back to my address and for heaven's sake don't swing him about too much,' Edgar instructed with a nervous backward glance at his friend.

Mortimer sat slumped in the corner of the cab, his eyes closed. Matt hoped he would stay like that until they reached their destination.

* * *

Kitty tidied up the flat while Matt and Edgar were gone. She hoped they might get some information from Mortimer when he arrived. Although if he was too inebriated, she didn't hold out much hope of success.

The men had not been gone long when the doorbell buzzed. Kitty hurried to answer, hoping it might be the lieutenant so she could at least give him the items she had discovered in Peggy's handbag.

Instead, as she peeped out through the spyhole, she saw Lorena Briggs tapping her toes impatiently on the mat.

'Lorena, what a surprise. Do come in.' Kitty opened the

door and stood aside as the other woman swept past her with a swish of expensive fur and perfume.

'I'm afraid my father has had to go out for a short time. Is there anything I can help you with?' Kitty offered as she followed Lorena into the drawing room. 'May I get you some coffee or tea?'

Lorena took off her coat and handed it to Kitty as if she were the maid. 'A coffee would be very welcome.'

Kitty raised her eyebrows at this offhand treatment but hung up the coat and went to put on the kettle.

'Will your father be long?' Lorena asked as Kitty re-entered the room.

'No, I don't think so.' Kitty wondered what the woman wanted with her father. 'I'm so very sorry about the loss of your mother.'

Lorena bowed her head in acknowledgement of Kitty's condolences. 'It has been the most ghastly time. The police told me that you and your husband found her.'

'We did. We were on our way to get breakfast. It was awful,' Kitty said, before going to take the kettle from the hob to make a pot of coffee.

'I can imagine,' Lorena continued when Kitty returned a minute or two later with a tray. 'We still haven't discovered what became of her jewellery, you know. Everything was missing, her engagement and wedding rings even, and a dress ring my father gave her just before he died.' Lorena took a cigarette from a silver case and inserted it in a small, carved ivory holder. She offered the case to Kitty, who declined politely with a shake of her head.

'Her jewels were missing when we found her,' Kitty said as Lorena lit her cigarette and blew a small plume of smoke into the air.

'We hoped she'd taken them off and put them in her safe or that they were somewhere in the apartment, but there's no sign of them anywhere. We searched the apartment from top to bottom. The police have notified all of the jewellery stores,' Lorena said.

Kitty poured coffee for both of them. 'Oh dear, that's terrible. I do hope you get them back.'

'When all of that business about Peggy came out, I thought that perhaps she had taken them.' Lorena tapped some ash from the end of her cigarette into the glass Lalique ashtray that Kitty had placed next to her. 'You've heard about the business with her pawning my mom's silver, I suppose?'

'Yes, that was another dreadful shock. She seemed such a nice girl. She was so young and she suffered such a terrible death.' Kitty shuddered at the thought.

'Quite.' Lorena's nose crinkled as if she had suddenly detected a bad smell. 'I still believe it was suicide. The police were going to arrest her, you know, for Mom's murder. I believe Mom caught her stealing. I think she took something else from the apartment the night Mom was killed. Mom must have followed her downstairs and caught her passing it to her fence and they strangled her and stole her jewels.' Lorena's eyes narrowed as she looked at Kitty, as if determining if she believed her.

'I suppose that's possible,' Kitty agreed, 'but surely then she would have just packed her bags and disappeared with this mysterious accomplice. Why wait around to be arrested? Or take her own life? There was a lot of money in the safe and she knew the combination, I believe.'

Lorena shrugged her expensively cashmere-clad shoulders. 'Remorse, perhaps. She may not have been thinking clearly or her accomplice abandoned her. Peggy was terribly gullible you know. Mom always said she didn't have enough brain power to light a candle let alone a room. Perhaps someone was using her.'

'That does sound more plausible,' Kitty agreed, before taking a sip of her coffee.

'I did wonder if Peggy was in cahoots with Horatio for a while. They always had their heads together.' Lorena stubbed out her cigarette and removed it from its holder. 'Well, he can stop complaining about having no money now. I've just come from Mom's attorney for the reading of her will.'

'Oh?' Kitty peered over the brim of her coffee cup eager to hear whatever Lorena had to say on the matter.

'Mom left him a bequest in her will. Ten thousand dollars. He should be able to make himself scarce quite quickly with that.' Lorena's lip curled in distaste.

'I understand from my father that he's been in your family's employ for a very long time,' Kitty remarked mildly.

While she was sympathetic to Lorena's recent loss, she really didn't like the woman.

'Too long, if you ask me. Always snooping about and telling tales to Mom.' Lorena added sugar and more cream to her coffee.

'Papa said that Mortimer disliked him,' Kitty said.

'Mortimer hates that Horatio felt it necessary to voice his disapproval of his affair with my mom. Horatio is always preaching, given half a chance, and he was devoted to my father. Honestly, everyone knew that Mortimer and Titania were not suited to one another. It was only a matter of time before they divorced,' Lorena said.

'You approved though of your mother and Mortimer's relationship?' Kitty was taken aback by Lorena's comments but did her best not to show it.

'Why not? He was a good lapdog for Mom. Her money was locked down tight so if he amused her and made her happy then good for them. It gave her less time to poke her nose into my business,' Lorena declared with a sniff.

Kitty thought they were now coming to the crux of Lorena's dislike of Horatio and her eagerness to have him gone. If the manservant was in the habit of passing information to Nora and some of that news was unfavourable to Lorena, she would be eager to see him leave. She wondered if the same could be said of Mortimer. Was that his reason for wanting Horatio to retire too, rather than just the servant's distaste for the affair?

'Mothers can be difficult, I suppose, no matter how much we love them.' Kitty forbore to say that she had lost her own mother when she had been a child.

'Mom's problem was that she always had to be right about everything. She liked to choose my friends, my clothes, my décor.' Lorena paused to drink her coffee.

'Your husband?' Kitty suggested.

Lorena set her cup down on the saucer and gave Kitty a sharp look. 'Yes, including my husband. We had huge fights about my marriage. Mom didn't approve, even though we are very happy together.'

Kitty thought Lorena emphasised the last part of her statement just a touch too much.

'I suppose that's parents for you,' Kitty agreed in a mild tone.

Lorena glanced at the clock on the mantelpiece. 'My, I really need to get gone. Please tell your father I called to see him. Mom has left him a small bequest in her will. Tell him he'll know what it is. It was something of a joke between them.' Lorena stood and smoothed her skirt.

'Of course. I'll get your coat.' Kitty fetched Lorena's fur.

'Tell him to collect it from the apartment. Horatio knows it's his,' Lorena remarked mysteriously and left without thanking Kitty for the coffee.

'Well, really!' Kitty said as the door closed behind her guest.

CHAPTER FIFTEEN

Lorena had only been gone for about five minutes when Kitty heard the scrape of the key in the lock. She jumped up to find Edgar and Matt bearing what appeared to be a very inebriated Mortimer between them.

'I'll make more coffee,' Kitty said as Matt and Edgar deposited Mortimer in one of the armchairs. She was starting to feel like a waitress in a tea room with the number of times she had boiled the kettle.

Edgar collapsed thankfully onto his favourite armchair beside the fire. 'I thought we saw Lorena as we were arriving?'

'You did, she's just gone. She popped in here with a message for you,' Kitty called over her shoulder as she headed into the kitchenette once more.

'Oh, really, what did she want?' Edgar asked when Kitty returned after filling the kettle.

'She had just come from an appointment with her mother's lawyer. She had been to sort out her mother's estate and her affairs. It seems that you've been left a bequest in Nora's will,' Kitty said.

Edgar immediately perked up and looked interested, while

Mortimer merely groaned in his seat as Matt hung up their overcoats in the hallway.

'What kind of bequest?' Edgar asked.

Kitty shrugged. 'She didn't say exactly. She said something about it had been an item that was the nature of a joke between the two of you. She said that you could collect it from the apartment. Horatio knows all about it apparently.'

A broad smile spread across her father's face. 'Oh, I have a feeling I know what this is. She always said she would leave it to me. How very splendid of her.' He didn't elaborate any further and Kitty was forced to have her curiosity unsatisfied.

Once the kettle was boiled and the coffee pot replenished, they started to try and sober Mortimer up enough to get some information from him.

'Now then, dear boy, let's get some coffee into you.' Edgar placed a cup and saucer in front of his friend.

'What's the point? You should have just left me at the Silver Rose,' Mortimer sniffled, clearly feeling very sorry for himself.

'Nonsense, Nora would have hated seeing you like this,' Edgar declared robustly.

'There's no point to anything now she's gone.' Mortimer's tone was mournful as he picked up the coffee cup with a shaky hand.

'You can't just dive into a whisky bottle, dear boy, and stay there. Titania was here earlier looking for you. She's dreadfully upset about everything.' Edgar watched as his friend took a restorative sip of the inky-black sweetened liquid inside the porcelain cup.

'Titania, be blowed. I've told her it's over between us. I can't go on with her any longer. If I can't be with Nora, then I don't want to be with anyone.' Mortimer waved the cup around, spilling a few drops of coffee on the front of his already grubby shirt.

'Dearie me,' Edgar observed sorrowfully as Mortimer subsided and took some more sips of coffee.

'When did you last see Nora? Was it after the party?' Kitty asked in a kindly tone.

Mortimer turned his bloodshot gaze on her. 'I tried to see her. To make sure she was all right. I had to take Titania home after she slapped Nora.' His chin wobbled as he spoke. 'Disgraceful behaviour. I took Titania back to our apartment. She was making a scene as usual. I'd told her I wanted a divorce before we went to Nora's.'

'I have to say, my dear chap, that seems like bally bad timing on your part. Why on earth did you tell her right before the party? You know how hot-headed she is, especially when she's had a drink,' Edgar said.

Mortimer bridled at the criticism. 'She goaded me into it. Always bossing me around and holding her money over me. She was telling me all these ridiculous plans she had. Waffling on about a cruise in the new year. I knew it was simply a way to get me away from Nora.'

Kitty looked at Matt as Mortimer gulped some more coffee.

'You didn't go back up to Nora's apartment later to see her, after the party ended?' Kitty asked.

Mortimer clattered his cup back down on the saucer so violently Kitty thought at first that he had broken it. He stared, wild-eyed at her as if suddenly realising what she had been asking him. 'Who told you that? I never saw Nora again after I took Titania home.'

'But you did leave your apartment and go back up to the penthouse as the party ended to try to see Nora,' Matt said.

'Well, I was concerned about her, like I said. Titania had slapped her pretty hard. She left an imprint of her hand on Nora's cheek.' Mortimer's hands were shaking, and he clasped them together in his lap to stop the tremors.

'So once Titania had gone to bed, you let yourself out of the apartment and went upstairs to see Nora,' Matt pressed the question again.

'Yes, all right.' Mortimer groaned and placed his head in his hands. 'I admit, I did go upstairs but she wasn't there. At least I didn't see her.'

'Did you see anyone else?' Kitty asked.

'Peggy. I knocked on the door and she said Nora had retired for the evening and she closed it in my face. She didn't offer to go and tell Nora I was there or anything,' Mortimer said.

Kitty thought it was convenient that the one person who could have confirmed this was also now dead. Had Peggy told Lieutenant Tanfield about Mortimer's return visit? He certainly hadn't said anything to them about this.

'What did you do then?' Matt asked.

'I hung about for a bit on the landing, hoping that Nora might have heard the door and would come out but she didn't, so I went and took the elevator back to my apartment,' Mortimer said.

'Did you check on Titania when you got back?' Edgar asked.

Mortimer snorted. 'Do you go poking a sleeping bear? No, I went to the guest room and made myself comfortable in there. The next thing I knew was later that morning when the telephone rang and Lorena told me Nora was dead and the police wanted to talk to me.' Mortimer leaned his head back against the armchair. His face now chalky white against the black leather.

'You didn't see or hear anyone else while you were going to the penthouse apartment or on the way back?' Matt asked.

'Think carefully, dear boy, before you answer,' Edgar urged. 'It could be very important.'

Mortimer had his eyes closed and his brow furrowed as he thought. 'I heard the elevator when I was on the stairs but other than that nope, nothing at all,' he said eventually.

It seemed they were at a temporary impasse. Kitty hoped her father had some kind of plan to persuade Mortimer to go home now he was a little more sober. Her stomach growled, reminding her that it was lunchtime. They had their evening meal already ordered from the kitchen downstairs, but had made no firm plans for lunch.

The doorbell rang once more, and Matt went to answer it. Mortimer appeared to have slipped into a kind of slumber, emitting snoring sounds from the corner of his mouth.

Lieutenant Tanfield followed Matt into the sitting room, the shoulders of his dark-brown overcoat were damp, and Kitty realised that it must be snowing once more. The policeman raised a surprised dark eyebrow at the sight of a rather dishevelled Mortimer asleep in the armchair.

Matt took the detective's coat and hung it up, while the lieutenant seated himself on the opposite end of the sofa from Kitty.

'I had a message at the precinct that you had some information for me?' he said.

'Yes, that's correct.' Kitty collected her handbag and passed the pawn tickets and the note she'd found to the lieutenant.

'Where did you find these, ma'am?' he asked.

Kitty explained about assisting Peggy's brother to pack her belongings and the discovery in her handbag.

The policeman tucked them safely away in his notebook. 'Pity there's no date or signature on this note.' He didn't look too pleased with her discovery, but that might well have been because he was embarrassed that his colleagues had not been the ones to find them when they searched through Peggy's things.

Kitty refrained from saying that had been what she and Matt had both thought too.

'Was there anything more, that you wanted me to know?' Lieutenant Tanfield glanced around at them all.

'Well...' Kitty gave her father an apologetic look and told the policeman everything that Titania and Mortimer had said.

The policeman listened with a grave face and the occasional glance at Mortimer who was now dribbling from the corner of his lips.

'It seems I need to speak to both Mr and Mrs Liggett again,' the lieutenant said.

'I don't know if any of this is relevant too.' Kitty told him what Lorena had said, regarding the large legacy for Horatio. This was also new information for Matt and her father since she hadn't had a chance to tell them what Lorena had said when they had arrived with Mortimer.

'Thank you, Mrs Bryant. Yes, I am aware of the contents of Mrs Dangerfield's will. In fact, I think you have a small bequest in there too, sir.' The lieutenant looked at Edgar.

'So my daughter told me. Lorena dropped in to let me know. It's just a token thing, not worth a great deal in monetary terms, merely sentimental value.' Edgar waved a careless hand.

Kitty was a little irked that the policeman knew about the will and its contents already. 'I presume the bulk of Nora's estate was left to Lorena,' she said.

'Yes, Mrs Dangerfield left her money sewn up in such a way that only her daughter can touch it and obviously any future children she might have would also benefit,' Lieutenant Tanfield said.

Kitty hadn't thought about Lorena and Rudolph having children. She wasn't sure how long they had been married. She would have guessed that Lorena was at least ten years older than her, however.

'Were there any other large bequests, other than the one to Horatio?' Matt asked.

'Just some charitable donations to the orphanage that Mrs Dangerfield and her husband supported and, of course, to various art trusts and museums. The bequest to Mr Blackstock would not have been relevant if he had left her employment before she passed away,' Lieutenant Tanfield said.

Kitty's eyes widened at this. Ten thousand dollars to an impoverished man was a huge motive for murder. Especially if he wouldn't have received a single cent after he had been retired from her service. Had Horatio known about the contents of the will, Kitty wondered.

'Mrs Dangerfield's attorney did say that she had made an appointment for the new year to review the contents of her will,' Lieutenant Tanfield said as he tucked his notebook safely back inside his pocket.

'Did he know what her intentions were?' Matt asked.

'I believe she was considering reducing her bequest to her daughter to make provision for Mr Liggett. She had said something to him about a future marriage.' Lieutenant Tanfield looked at the sleeping man.

Mortimer let out a rippling snore and snuffled deeper into the armchair.

'How much has he had to drink?' the policeman asked.

Edgar gave an eloquent shrug. 'I have no idea. I was told when we tracked him down that he was hammering on the bar door just before they opened and then kept them coming once he got inside.'

'Have you had any sense out of him since you went and got him?' Lieutenant Tanfield asked.

'Only what we've just told you,' Matt said. 'I have to say that Titania Liggett wasn't in much better shape when she came looking for him earlier.'

'Hmm, in vino veritas, isn't that what you English say?' Lieutenant Tanfield stood and placed his hand on Mortimer's shoulder and gave him a shake.

Kitty was impressed by the policeman's quote and watched as Mortimer started in response to the agitation. His eyes opened and a look of panic spread across his face when he realised who had disturbed him.

'Mr Liggett, I think you and I need to have a chat. Perhaps with your wife present too,' the policeman suggested.

Mortimer's pale complexion turned slightly puce. 'Oh dear lord, not with Titania.'

'Perhaps if we go down to your apartment?' Lieutenant Tanfield nodded at Matt, and he went to the hall to collect both the policeman's and Mortimer's overcoats.

'Is it really necessary? I think I've told you everything I know already,' Mortimer protested when he realised the policeman was serious.

'Then it won't take very long,' Lieutenant Tanfield assured him. 'Now then, up you come.' He and Matt levered Mortimer from the chair.

Lieutenant Tanfield put on his coat, while Matt assisted Mortimer with his. 'Thank you for the things, Mrs Bryant, ma'am. Please, though, no more investigating.'

'Very well,' Kitty said as the policeman chivvied Mortimer out of the lounge and into the hallway. She was rather irked that her helpfulness had been rewarded with a rebuke.

'Well, that's rather a relief now Morty's gone,' Edgar said as the door closed behind them. 'Righty ho, I think perhaps a spot of lunch is in order and then I'll go and collect my bequest.'

CHAPTER SIXTEEN

Matt thought Kitty looked rather deflated now their visitors had departed. He was not surprised after the lieutenant's warning to stop any further investigating. Edgar's Christmas tree and his cards were providing the only spots of upcoming festive cheer in the apartment. Christmas was now only two days away but with the drama of recent events the sparkle had fizzled from the festive season.

'Good idea, let's go out for lunch,' he suggested. He turned to his father-in-law. 'Edgar, you must know some good restaurants?'

'Of course, everywhere might be a tad busy with the time of year,' Edgar mused. 'Let me see if I can snag us a reservation.' He picked up the telephone receiver and began to dial.

'Come on, Kitty, old thing, get your glad rags on. Let's go out and enjoy the city, get a bit of Christmas spirit back,' Matt suggested.

She looked a little doubtful for a second, but her stomach gave an audible low growl. 'You're right, we need to do something nice and as you can hear, I'm starving.' With that she kissed his cheek affectionately and went to refresh her lipstick and prepare for going out.

'I've managed to get us a table at a rather nice little spot I know,' Edgar said as he ended the call and started to dial again. 'I'll ask Enrique to get us a cab and we'll head off.'

Snow was falling once again when they stepped outside the building and into the taxi. Edgar gave the address of the restaurant which Matt assumed was not too far away. Kitty looked out of the window with interest at the crowded streets blurred by the large whirling white flakes of snow.

The stores were decorated for Christmas and shoppers laden with parcels mingled with people who were obviously city workers. They passed the Flatiron Building with its distinct triangular shape, something she had only seen before in a magazine article. Tomorrow was Christmas Eve and time was running out for people to get their shopping completed. The restaurant Edgar had secured a reservation at was situated a couple of blocks away in a high-end row of shops.

They entered through polished brass and oak doors into a world of glittering, hushed opulence. It was a far cry from the Silver Rose where Edgar had taken him a few hours earlier. There were no signs of the Depression here. A smartly dressed maître d' checked their reservation and showed them to a table situated discreetly in a quieter part of the busy restaurant.

They gave their coats to the staff and settled themselves at the white-clothed table to consider the menu and to look around at their fellow diners. The room was decorated for Christmas in red and silver, with a Christmas tree either side of the door where they had come in and a much larger one near the waiters' station.

'This all looks rather splendid.' Kitty smiled happily at her father as she opened the red leather-bound menu.

'This was one of Nora's favourite watering holes. We've had

many a convivial luncheon here,' her father answered a touch sadly as he too looked at the dishes on offer.

'It all looks wonderful, and there is so much choice.' Kitty studied the courses.

A waiter came for their drinks order and Edgar invited Matt to choose the wine. Once that was settled, they concentrated on selecting their meals and gave that order to their server. Once the business part was done, Kitty settled happily in her seat. Matt was pleased to see her starting to relax again.

She had been so worried about Edgar when they had left England. Then discovering that, as usual, he had been less than honest about his situation when they had arrived had been distressing. Add in two murders in quick succession and it was no wonder they were not feeling very festive.

It also seemed that despite their first intentions of not getting embroiled in investigating Nora and Peggy's deaths, they had been doing exactly that. Apart from the carol concert and a spot of Christmas shopping it had hardly been a holiday. Tomorrow was their wedding anniversary and Matt hoped that perhaps Kitty might heed the policeman's warning to leave the murder investigation to him. It didn't seem that Edgar was in the frame after all.

The waiter returned with their first course of clam chowder. The soup smelled delicious as it was set in front of them, and Matt realised he was as hungry as Kitty. Once they had finished and the empty dishes had been cleared ready for the next course, Edgar picked up his wine glass.

'I wonder if I could propose a little toast, for old times' sake. I think I am becoming increasingly sentimental as I grow older, but I should like us to raise our glasses in memory of Nora. She was a good neighbour and a dear friend. I shall miss her.'

Kitty gave her father an understanding smile. 'Of course.' She picked up her own glass and Matt followed suit.

'To Nora,' Edgar said, and they chinked their glasses together.

Matt followed his father-in-law's toast with one to Kitty ahead of their upcoming anniversary as a way of boosting all their spirits.

The restaurant seemed busier than ever as they tucked into the next course. Kitty had chosen fish, while Matt and Edgar had both selected the escalope of beef. Matt noticed several of the tables changing over as parties of diners left and new groups arrived.

Kitty too was taking a keen interest in her surroundings. 'I'm sure that woman over there in that darling hat is that film star who Alice is so keen on. We saw a film together just before we came away and she was the star.' Kitty discreetly indicated a table near the centre of the room.

'Alice would absolutely love this,' Matt agreed. He knew Kitty's friend adored her films and avidly read every magazine she could get that discussed their lives, homes and clothes.

Edgar finished his meal and placed his cutlery neatly on his plate. 'It's a very popular spot with stars when they are in town, so I expect you're right.'

The table Kitty had indicated was certainly attracting attention and a couple of people approached the woman seemingly seeking autographs.

'How very exciting,' Kitty said.

'Aren't you going to try and get her signature for Alice?' Edgar asked.

Kitty blushed and shook her head. 'Oh no, it would be a dreadful imposition. I think the poor woman should be allowed to enjoy the rest of her meal in peace. Alice might love an autograph but she wouldn't want me to upset anyone by doing so.'

Matt chuckled. He suspected Kitty was right. The star certainly looked as if she would prefer to eat her meal rather than smile and sign autographs for people. Kitty continued to gaze around the room. Suddenly, Matt saw her smile fade on her lips as she peered intently towards a table for two partly hidden by the Christmas tree.

'What is it, darling?' he asked.

'I could swear that's Rudolph over there in the far corner, but if it is him, that girl is most definitely not Lorena,' Kitty said.

Matt leaned slightly to the side to take a better look. 'I think you're right.'

The woman seated opposite Rudolph looked very young, probably nineteen or twenty. She had soft blonde short hair and big blue eyes. Rudolph appeared to be holding her hand as the girl hung on to his every word.

'Rudolph? Where?' Edgar turned his head to try and see where Matt and Kitty were looking.

'Shh, Papa, be discreet,' Kitty urged as the waiter returned to clear their table ready for dessert.

Edgar turned back to sit straight in his seat. 'It does look like Rudolph,' he agreed and looked at the waiter. 'I say, the fellow over there with the young lady, is that Mr Briggs?'

The waiter paused in his stacking of the plates. Matt guessed he must be one of the regular staff from the way Edgar had asked the question.

'I believe so, sir,' the man answered discreetly and hurried away with the crockery before anyone could ask anything else.

'The staff here all know Rudolph well, he used to come with Lorena and Nora. It's mighty bold of him to be here with another woman right after Nora's death,' Edgar mused.

'I wondered why he hadn't been with Lorena this morning to visit her mother's attorney for the will reading,' Kitty said.

'I don't suppose he would have been invited,' Edgar said, before taking another sip of wine.

'Really, why ever not?' Kitty asked.

'Well, because he would know that Nora wouldn't have left him anything. It would all go to Lorena and knowing Lorena, she wouldn't want him to have any idea of the exact figures involved. She spends enough on him already. Nora didn't really approve at all of Rudolph, so she cut down Lorena's allowance after the business in Hawaii,' Edgar explained with a shrug.

Matt saw Kitty's brow crinkle into a frown. 'Then why is he here, behaving like a single man? Surely, he'd be making nice with Lorena now the financial shackles are off presumably, and he can get her to give him whatever he wants.'

The waiter returned once more to set their desserts in front of them. Kitty had a meringue nest with winter fruits, while Edgar and Matt had both opted for New York cheesecake with cream.

'Perhaps Lorena hasn't been very willing to play ball. He might be trying to make her jealous. You know, make her think she could be losing him, so she'll splash out,' Edgar suggested as he dug his spoon into his dessert.

Matt thought Edgar might have a point, but he could tell from the way Kitty was attacking her meringue that she didn't think much of the idea.

Rudolph and his mysterious lady friend were just receiving their desserts when their waiter brought the coffees to Edgar's table.

'That was a lovely meal.' Kitty dabbed her linen napkin at the corners of her mouth with a satisfied look on her face. Matt noticed she kept glancing in Rudolph's direction as she sipped her drink and he guessed that she longed to know what was going on at the other table.

Rudolph signalled to the waiter to pay his tab, and it was clear that he and his companion were ready to leave. After glancing around at Kitty and Edgar, Matt could see they were all finished as well. He called their waiter so they could also pay their bill.

'I'll be back in just a minute.' Kitty sprang to her feet as the waiter approached. She gathered her handbag and hurried away towards the ladies' restroom.

Matt suppressed a grin when he realised that Rudolph's lady friend had also gone in the same direction.

* * *

Kitty was pleased to see that the restroom was quiet when she entered. The bathroom was as elegant as the restaurant with dark-green tiles, ornate gold-framed mirrors and fresh flowers on the countertops beside the sinks.

Rudolph's friend had entered a stall, so Kitty stationed herself by the mirrors and took out her lipstick. At the very least, she wanted to get a good look at the girl. Hopefully she could engage her in conversation.

After a minute the girl emerged and came to the sink beside Kitty to wash her hands. Kitty saw that her first impressions were correct. The girl was young and wearing rather more make-up than Kitty would have thought appropriate for daytime. Her clothes were stylish but clearly inexpensive.

She gave Kitty a friendly smile as she took a silver compact studded with jewels from her bag and started to powder her nose. Kitty carefully reapplied her own pale-rose lipstick.

'I say, that's a really sweet little compact,' Kitty said conversationally. The compact the girl was using looked expensive.

The girl blushed with pride. 'Thanks, it was a gift from my boyfriend. He often gives me little surprises like that.' She had a broad New York accent.

'Lucky girl. Was that the handsome man you were with earlier?' Kitty asked as she replaced the lid on her lipstick.

'Yes, lunch today was another treat as it's my birthday. Rudi is so generous.' The girl beamed at Kitty.

'How lovely, many happy returns of the day,' Kitty said as she fluffed up her own blonde locks in front of the mirror.

'Your accent is just the cutest thing. Are you from England?' the girl asked.

'Yes, I'm here visiting family for Christmas,' Kitty said.

'You certainly picked the winter weather. They say more snow is on the way. Looks like it'll be a white Christmas.' The girl gave a theatrical shiver as she popped her compact back inside her cheap imitation leather bag.

'Oh dear, it's already very cold. Are you from New York?' Kitty asked.

'Born and bred,' the girl confirmed. 'I hope you enjoy your stay.' She smiled at Kitty and left.

Kitty waited a couple of minutes before rejoining Matt and Edgar. She didn't want her new friend to point her out to Rudolph.

'The maître d' is arranging a taxi to save us from waiting outside in the cold,' Matt informed her when she arrived back at the table.

'Wonderful.' Kitty quickly told them what the girl had said.

Her father's eyebrows rose in surprise. 'Rudolph had better hope that Lorena doesn't find out that her husband is treating other women with her money.'

'Quite. It sounds as if Rudolph has known her for some time,' Kitty agreed as she accepted assistance with donning her fur coat ready to venture back out into the snowy New York streets.

'I suppose I had better collect my inheritance from Nora's apartment when we get back,' Kitty's father said as they climbed into the taxi.

Kitty gave him a sharp look. She didn't trust his innocent expression or his reluctance to enlarge on what this bequest was supposed to be. Her father was often fond of teasing her, however, and she had no intention of playing his game by asking questions.

'I suppose so. Lorena certainly appeared very keen that you should collect it,' Kitty said.

'Dear Nora, such a kind and generous soul.' A sad expression settled on her father's face, so Kitty didn't press him any further. She suspected he was rather enjoying teasing her about this unexpected legacy.

While they had been inside the restaurant eating lunch, the snow had continued to fall and the streets were less busy than before. The electric lights illuminating the stores cast eerie yellow reflections of the Christmas displays onto the slush-covered sidewalks.

Snow in shades of grey, black and white lay heaped up in the gutters and against the walls of the buildings. Shoppers battled with umbrellas and packages as they slithered and slipped their way along. The taxi took a different route and this time they passed one of the museums that Kitty hoped to visit before they were due to return to England.

The car pulled up outside their building and Kitty shivered as Matt assisted her out onto the slippery pavement.

'Shall we accompany you to Nora's apartment?' Matt asked Edgar as they stamped the snow from their boots onto the mat in the lobby.

Kitty's father smiled. 'Why not, let's go right on up. No time like the present, eh?'

They entered the elevator and Matt closed the cage before Edgar pressed the button to begin their ascent. Kitty knew her husband was just as curious as she was to learn more about Nora's bequest.

Edgar pressed the doorbell at Nora's apartment once they were all out of the elevator.

Horatio Blackstock opened the door. 'Good afternoon, Mr Underhay,' he greeted Edgar cordially, before saying hello to Kitty and Matt.

'Is it convenient to collect the item Nora left to me?' Edgar asked. 'Mrs Briggs said that you would be expecting me to pick it up.'

Horatio inclined his head solemnly. 'Yes, sir, please come inside. Miss Lorena is keen to get everything squared away. She and Mr Rudolph will be moving in here in a few weeks' time.'

Kitty followed Matt and her father inside the apartment. Horatio appeared to have wasted no time in following Lorena's instructions. Nora was barely cold and there were large packing boxes everywhere. All signs of Christmas were gone.

'Good heavens, you have been busy,' Edgar remarked as they entered the drawing room.

'Miss Lorena's instructions,' Horatio said as he gazed sadly around the elegant room, now untidy and denuded of most of its treasures.

'I take it the picture is still hanging in place at present?' Edgar asked.

'Yes, Mr Underhay. I've not yet had the heart to begin packing up Miss Nora's personal possessions,' Horatio said.

'May I go through?' Edgar asked politely.

'Of course, sir. Please help yourself. If you require assistance, I am happy to oblige,' Horatio offered.

Edgar disappeared off towards what Kitty assumed was Nora's boudoir. She took a seat on the edge of one of Nora's elegant chairs.

'I imagine that discovering Nora had thought of you in her will must have been a surprise,' Kitty said to the manservant. 'Lorena told me that her mother had left you a substantial sum.'

'Yes. I never thought for one moment that she would remember me and be so generous,' Horatio said.

'Will your plans change now that you will receive more money?' Matt asked.

'It means I shall be able to retire as Miss Nora suggested. I can travel back to my family and perhaps purchase a small home there. I don't mind admitting the news of the bequest and the size of it has come as a welcome relief,' Horatio said.

Kitty could see that despite his sadness, the heavy load the elderly man had appeared to be carrying seemed to have slipped from his shoulders. She wondered if he had known about Nora's will and the legacy she had left him. Ten thousand dollars was a lot of money and a sizeable motive.

Edgar popped back into the drawing room. 'I say, Horatio, old bean, I don't suppose you have a bit of sacking or something to wrap the picture up?'

'Of course, sir.' The manservant went to the kitchen and returned with a clean flour sack. 'I believe this might suffice, Mr Underhay.'

Edgar thanked him and returned to Nora's room.

Matt exchanged a glance with her, and she guessed that he too wondered what this picture was that Nora had been keen to give to her father.

'I don't suppose there has been any more news on Nora's missing jewels?' Kitty mused.

Horatio shook his greying grizzled head. 'No, Mrs Bryant. That part is deeply troubling to me, I must admit. Usually, when Miss Nora was ready to retire to bed or after an occasion, she would take off her most valuable items and give them to me to lock up in her safe.'

'And she didn't do that after the party?' Matt asked.

'No, sir, I was tidying up after the staff she'd hired had all gone. Peggy had counted the money and that was bagged ready to be locked away. Miss Nora told me to lock up the money, but she didn't take off her jewellery.' Horatio frowned as he spoke. 'I told the lieutenant it was real odd.'

'Did you think she might be planning to go out?' Kitty asked.

Horatio sighed and shrugged. 'Miss Nora often stepped out

at night when it was late. Sometimes for a few minutes, sometimes longer. She would say not to wait up for her.'

'She didn't say anything the night of the party?' Kitty pressed.

'She told me and Peggy to go to bed as it was late. Looking back now, she seemed well, a bit distracted, I suppose. She kept twiddling with her wedding ring. She often did that when something was playing on her mind,' Horatio said. 'I admit I was exhausted, so I went right off to bed.'

'You didn't hear or see anyone come back to the apartment after the party had ended?' Matt asked.

'No, sir, the police asked me the same thing, but my room is on the other side of the apartment.' Horatio indicated towards the kitchenette area.

'Did Peggy say anything to you about Nora seeming distracted or keeping her jewellery on?' Kitty wondered if the girl had said anything. She knew from experience how servants would talk about their masters and mistresses.

Horatio scratched his head, furrows forming on his forehead.

'She did say something odd. I'd said as how Miss Nora must be tired. It was after we'd put the money in the safe and Miss Nora was gone to her room. She said that was probably what came of minding everyone's business.'

Kitty wondered whose business Peggy had been referring to and whether that was why she too had been killed? Had Nora discovered something about Peggy?

CHAPTER SEVENTEEN

Edgar emerged from Nora's bedroom at that point carrying a square, flat object wrapped in the flour sack under his arm.

'Ta ever so, old bean. It'll be strange for me having Lorena and Rudolph living here. Still, I suppose it's considerably larger than their place.' Edgar looked around a little sadly at the packing cases.

'The end of an era,' Horatio agreed.

'It's rather sad and somewhat surprising that Lorena is in such a hurry. Especially after poor Peggy's death here,' Matt remarked.

'Perhaps their lease is due for renewal,' Edgar suggested.

Horatio said nothing but Kitty thought the manservant's expression was very eloquent.

They said their farewells and went back downstairs to Edgar's apartment. Once they had divested themselves of their coats Kitty took a seat on the sofa. Edgar had placed his parcel down carefully on the small dining table.

'Well, Pa, are you going to satisfy our curiosity now and show us your mysterious bequest?' Kitty asked, her lips twitching in a smile.

'Yes, we are both agog at the secrecy,' Matt added as he took his place next to Kitty.

'I'm rather afraid you will be a tad disappointed,' Edgar said as he moved to the parcel. 'This picture was something that Nora and I both spotted about eighteen months ago at a charity auction. We both wanted it and got into something of a bidding war which drove the price much higher than I was prepared to pay. Nora, of course, eventually emerged victorious. She always used to joke that she would leave it to me one day in her will since I wanted it so much.' His expression sobered. 'Neither of us ever really thought that would be the case, or if it was, then it would be many years from now.'

'Now I am very curious to see this picture,' Kitty said. She hoped it wouldn't prove to be anything too risqué.

Edgar grinned and carefully removed the flour sack. He picked the picture up and turned to face them, holding it up so they could see it.

Kitty stared at it for a moment. 'Isn't that a picture of Exeter Cathedral?' she asked in bewilderment.

The picture was a watercolour showing the ancient stone building with the green in front and a young couple prome-nading in the foreground dressed in clothes from some twenty or so years earlier.

Edgar laughed. 'Yes. I wanted it as it reminded me of home. Norah wanted it because she and her husband are the couple in the picture. Look closely, you may recognise her. It was done as a sketch apparently when they were on honeymoon, years ago. She never saw the finished item and they lost the artist's infor-mation. When it turned up at the auction over here she was completely baffled.'

'It has certainly travelled quite a distance,' Kitty agreed. 'Who is the artist?'

'That's another tale. At the time he painted this he was quite unknown but he's since become quite in fashion apparently. At least that was what Nora told me. She was gloating about having acquired a bargain.' Edgar smiled. 'We used to tease each other all the time over it. If we had a slight tiff, she would say you're not getting the picture now. If I was cross with her, I would say she had better watch that picture or it might go missing.' His smile faded.

'You really were good friends, weren't you?' Kitty placed her hand on his arm and kissed his cheek. 'Poor Pa. I think she'd be happy though knowing you finally owned this.'

Edgar smiled back at her. 'I've no doubt she's perched on a cloud somewhere, glass of champagne in hand, hugging herself in delight at having pulled off one last jape.'

'It is quite a fine picture.' Matt had come to join Kitty and peered at the painting.

'Nora had it hanging in her bedroom where she could see it when she lay in bed. She told me it reminded her of happy times with her husband.' Edgar's smile had disappeared once more. 'I hope they catch whoever killed her soon.'

Kitty pressed his arm once more and wandered back to the sofa. Edgar carefully placed the picture back down on the flour sack. Matt had crossed to the apartment window and was looking out at the darkening sky and the whirling white flakes hitting the windowpane. Below, the street traffic seemed to have almost come to a halt with few motor cars still about. Instead, it was mainly the horse drawn carts and carriages that were still out in the snow.

Daylight was fading quickly now with the snowfall and Kitty shivered as her father turned on the silk-shaded lamps. It would soon be time to draw the curtains against the cold and the dark. It all made her question once more why Nora had gone downstairs, dressed in her evening dress and all her jewellery. It had been a freezing cold night and surely she could have seen whoever she was meeting in her apartment.

She had taken a moment to pull on her fur wrap and

Horatio thought she had been anxious about something. So, perhaps a meeting that she anticipated would be brief but where she had felt the need to impress. One she hadn't wanted anyone to know about. Maybe wearing her jewels might have given her confidence.

The question was, who could she have been meeting that would fit that bill? Mortimer? Titania? Rudolph? Or someone else entirely. Kitty sighed, she could even be on the wrong track. Perhaps Nora had been following someone and hadn't had time to change. She could have followed Peggy and either Peggy or whoever Peggy had been meeting had attacked her. It would help explain why Peggy was killed if that were the case.

She wondered how Lieutenant Tanfield's interviews with Titania and Mortimer Liggett had gone. Mortimer was certainly going to have a hangover later and she thought Titania would probably be suffering too.

Had they been telling the truth about what they had done on the night of the party? In a way she supposed they had given one another an alibi to some extent, although she could see they both still had opportunity to kill Nora. They could even have been working together. Mortimer might have changed his mind about divorcing Titania or he could have been covering for her if she was the murderer.

Kitty rubbed her temple, it was all very complicated and she didn't feel as if she was any further forward.

'You look deep in thought, darling?' Matt placed his arm around her shoulders as he sat next to her.

'I was thinking about Nora and wondering how Lieutenant Tanfield's interviews with Titania and Mortimer were going,' Kitty said.

Matt chuckled. 'I would imagine it would be very interesting. I'd like to have been a fly on the wall for those.'

Kitty smiled back at him. 'Me too.'

'I take it you haven't reached any new conclusions yet then about the case?' Matt said.

Kitty frowned. 'No. I think maybe it might be worth focusing a bit more on Peggy's murder. Where did that poison come from for instance?'

Edgar had seated himself back in his favourite chair and picked up his newspaper. 'What was that, Kitty, dear heart?'

'I was wondering where the poison that killed Peggy could have come from,' she said.

'Strychnine is in a good many things, isn't it? A bit like arsenic. I know Lorena had a problem in her building in the summer with various pests. Cockroaches, or was it rats? Hmm, they had exterminators in. Of course, this building too had an issue as we're so close to the park so it could have come from anywhere, I suppose,' Edgar said.

Kitty's shoulders slumped, it seemed that finding a source for the poison was not straightforward either.

'Where would poisons be kept in the building?' Matt asked. 'I assume the front desk would be the people organising the exterminators to come in. Would they leave anything here or would the pest control people have taken it away with them?'

Edgar peered at him over the top of his newspaper. 'I don't know. I suppose they would leave some in case the problems reoccurred. I think there is a cupboard just off the lobby which they use for all kinds of things. You know, stuff to clear the sidewalks and to polish the communal areas. That sort of thing.'

Matt gave Kitty a knowing smile. She knew her husband had sensed her immediate interest in the mysterious cupboard.

'You want to go downstairs to find this cupboard, don't you?' Matt asked her.

'Well, I've nothing much else to do right now.' Kitty made a ploy of pretending to examine her manicure.

'Darling, if it would make you happy to go and look at some mops and brooms, feel free.' Matt's smile grew wider.

'It would make me happy. At least it would settle some questions in my mind. I know the lieutenant said not to investigate any more but this is really just checking, isn't it?' Kitty jumped up, extricating herself from Matt's arm as she did so.

'If you say so, Kitty,' Matt agreed.

She could hear him chuckling as she made her way out of the apartment to the elevator. The lobby was busy when she arrived downstairs. The telephone at the desk was ringing and Enrique, the concierge, was arguing with a delivery driver who appeared to have the wrong address.

Kitty took advantage of the chaos to look around for the cupboard that her father had mentioned. She soon saw a discreet door next to the one marked *Staff: Private,* which she knew led to the kitchens and service area of the apartments. That had been the door Nora must have used the night she had been killed.

A quick glance revealed a keyhole in the cupboard door, and she wondered if it was kept locked. While Enrique's back was turned and he was busy with the driver, she took the opportunity to try the handle.

Much to her surprise the door clicked open, and she could see the cupboard was a generous size, lined with shelves from floor to ceiling at the back, with a stand for mops, brooms and buckets to the side.

The contents were arranged in an orderly fashion and sure enough on the shelf she could see all kinds of items for controlling pests. Flypaper, ant powder, weedkiller, rodent poison as well as cleaning products like caustic soda crystals and soap.

The telephone had stopped ringing but there was still the sound of raised voices from the desk, so Kitty picked up one of the packets of poison to examine the label.

'Have you discovered anything of any interest there, Mrs Bryant?' The cool, faintly amused tone of Lieutenant Tanfield's voice right behind her caught her by surprise. The box almost slipped through her fingers and onto the floor.

Kitty hastily stuffed the box back on the shelf and turned to face the detective. Her cheeks pink from being caught snooping. 'There seem to be lots of ways a resident of this building could lay their hands on poison if they so wished,' she said.

'Very true, and I'm surprised this cupboard was not locked.' The policeman glared at Enrique who had now returned to his desk to answer the telephone which had begun to ring once more. 'I do hope you weren't tampering with any possible evidence, Mrs Bryant, ma'am.' The detective returned his attention to Kitty.

'Certainly not, Lieutenant,' Kitty retorted indignantly, drawing herself up to her full five foot two inches.

'Hmm, then what were you doing in the supplies closet?' the policeman asked.

'I was curious. I kept thinking about poor Peggy and wondered where the poison could have come from.' Kitty folded her arms defensively and tilted her chin up as she answered.

'I see. So you weren't tampering with evidence or replacing something that you used to murder Peggy?' Lieutenant Tanfield asked.

'Certainly not, that's ridiculous,' Kitty snapped. She hadn't been sure at first if the policeman had been teasing her, but he certainly sounded serious enough. 'Why would I kill a woman I've only ever met once and know nothing about?'

'I don't know, ma'am, but you and your husband do keep popping up in this case despite me saying not to interfere. You found Nora's body and then Captain Bryant heard a noise and found Peggy's body. You tell me. You manage to get Mortimer and Titania Liggett drunk and come up with some cockamamie story and now I find you looking at a potential murder weapon.'

The lieutenant had taken out his notebook. Kitty was relieved it wasn't his handcuffs.

'Matt and I hadn't met any of these people before we arrived in New York. We came in response to an urgent telegram from Nora Dangerfield saying my father was seriously ill,' Kitty said.

'Step out of the storeroom, ma'am,' Lieutenant Tanfield said.

Kitty sighed and obeyed, exiting into the lobby with one last glance at the shelves.

The detective stepped forward and closed the store cupboard door with a firm click once she was out.

'Yes, your father, Mr Edgar Underhay, he seems to have made a very rapid recovery from his illness,' Lieutenant Tanfield mused, looking at her.

Kitty shrugged. 'One can do that when one receives the correct care.' Her tone was frosty. She knew her father had faked his illness to hide from debtors, but she wasn't going to admit that to the lieutenant.

'He and Mrs Dangerfield were very close friends. She knew him well enough to send for you and she left him a valuable picture in her will. A very personal gift.' The policeman tapped his pen against his notebook.

'They had been neighbours for some time and were good friends.' Kitty glared back at the detective. 'There is a story behind why she left him the picture. It has nothing to do with value.'

'Mr Underhay is known to us, ma'am. He has quite a record of petty and not quite so petty misdemeanours,' Lieutenant Tanfield said.

'I am well aware that my father is no angel, Lieutenant. However, there is a big step between petty crime and murder. He had no reason to wish to harm Nora or Peggy. He is devastated by Nora's death.' Kitty defended her father stoutly despite the sinking feeling in the pit of her stomach.

'Really? Mortimer Liggett says that your father had an argument with Nora a couple of weeks ago just before he became "ill".'

Kitty stared at the policeman. 'I don't know anything about any argument. Nora asked us to come to New York and she saw Papa at his apartment when we arrived. They were very cordial, and she invited us to her fundraising party. So, I think Mortimer may have been trying to deflect your attention away from him and his wife. They had much more reason to wish Nora dead than my father had.'

Kitty's voice had risen slightly during their conversation, and she saw Enrique glance in their direction as he finished on the telephone.

'I see.' Lieutenant Tanfield made some notes in his book.

Kitty bit her tongue, resisting the urge to ask the detective if he really did see, or if he just wanted to bait her in the hope of tripping her up somehow.

'If we are done here, Lieutenant, I should like to return to my family,' Kitty said as she prepared to walk away across the lobby.

'Before you leave, Mrs Bryant, a word of warning. I know you and your husband are private eyes in England. This isn't England and I don't care for meddling in my investigation. Now I thank you for your assistance so far, but as I said already, you need to stop. My department can handle this investigation perfectly well without your or your husband's assistance. I suggest you put Nora and Peggy's deaths out of your minds and focus on a nice, quiet, murder free Christmas,' Lieutenant Tanfield warned.

'And greetings of the season to you too,' Kitty said, before stalking over to the elevator.

CHAPTER EIGHTEEN

Kitty was kicking herself all the way back up to the apartment. She really should have better and wittier comebacks. It wasn't as if she had been doing anything wrong in checking out the contents of the cupboard. She was not in a good mood when she unlocked the front door of the apartment and went through to the sitting room.

Her father had given up on his paper and had his eyes closed while he sat beside the fire. Matt was at the dining table working on a jigsaw puzzle of a motor car.

'Is everything all right, Kitty, darling?' Matt asked as she entered.

She assumed the thunderous look on her face had probably tipped him off that all was not well.

'That wretched policeman!' The words exploded from her as she pulled up a chair next to Matt and told him what the lieutenant had said to her downstairs.

Her raised voice disturbed her father's nap and he opened his eyes and blinked owlishly at her. 'I did warn you what New York policemen were like, darling. They are not like your police in Devon,' Edgar said.

'Hmm, well it sounds as if we are all under suspicion, including you, Kitty,' Matt said in a sympathetic tone.

'How dare anyone suspect me. I've never even had a motoring offence.' Kitty was not amused. 'It makes me wonder if he is as efficient as we first thought. Surely, they should have checked those cupboards as soon as Peggy's cause of death was confirmed. And, it was still unlocked.' She huffed an indignant sigh as she finished speaking. 'Tampering with evidence, indeed. I doubt the killer would have left it there to be tampered with.'

'I agree. It does seem pretty slipshod if you ask me,' Matt said soothingly.

Kitty folded her arms. 'Well, I am not prepared to take this lying down. We need to find out who killed Nora and Peggy. It's blatantly obvious that Lieutenant Tanfield has no real leads.'

'Darling, neither do we,' Matt pointed out.

While this was irritating, Kitty had to concede her husband was right. Still, she was not going to be thwarted, there had to be some evidence or a clue that they had overlooked.

* * *

Matt could see by the look on Kitty's face that her meeting with Lieutenant Tanfield had left her feeling riled up and spoiling for a fight. Kitty was correct, however. This business of having two people murdered in their apartment block was definitely concerning. Even more so when the police appeared to have little to go on.

'Which murder do you want to look at first?' Matt asked.

He knew that Kitty wouldn't be able to settle until she had at least gone over everything they knew already. It didn't matter that the lieutenant had warned them off. He knew his wife had set her mind on solving the case.

Kitty frowned. 'I don't know. We know the two deaths are

connected, but we don't know if Peggy knew something about Nora's death or if she was involved in it in some way.'

Matt slowly turned a piece of his jigsaw puzzle between his fingers. 'Then perhaps we need to take a fresh approach to stop ourselves from going around in circles.'

'It's so aggravating. It's not like being at home where we would know everyone or there would be other people we could ask. Here, everything is against us; the weather, the city, the time of year,' Kitty finished with a huge, despondent sigh.

Matt pondered the problem for a moment before turning to his father-in-law. 'Perhaps you could help us, Edgar,' he suggested.

Kitty's father's eyes widened in alarm. 'Please don't get me involved in whatever it is that you're planning. I'm not up to crawling around on my hands and knees with a magnifying glass. Not with my back.'

'I don't think that's what Matt meant, Papa,' Kitty said.

'If you mean dish the dirt on my chums, I don't know if I can tell you more than you know already. Besides, a man has to have some principles and you heard what the lieutenant said.' Edgar attempted to hide behind his newspaper again, shaking out the pages as if he intended to immerse himself in the classified advertisements.

'Your dear old pals, Mortimer and Titania, were quick enough to suggest your name to the lieutenant,' Kitty pointed out.

Edgar lowered the paper and looked at his daughter. 'Hmm, you have a point there. Dear old Morty did rather attempt to chuck me under the bus.'

'Perhaps if we understand the people better then we might find something we've missed,' Kitty said.

'Perhaps start with Nora. What was she like? And what was her relationship with the others involved in this?' Matt said.

Edgar placed his paper on his lap. 'Nora was funny, sharp.

She could be extremely kind, but you had to do things Nora's way and she disliked being crossed. She was extremely wealthy and supported a number of charities. She always spoke fondly of her late husband and liked to reminisce. Is this the kind of thing you want to know?' he asked.

'Perfect,' Kitty assured him. 'How did Nora's personality affect those around her?'

Edgar's brow crinkled in thought. 'She adored Lorena, they were very close. Nora kept her on a tight leash though through her money. She paid for their apartment, all their expenses, that kind of thing. Lorena had a small independent income, but her father had left everything under Nora's control when he died. This would cause arguments between them.'

'And what do you think Lorena and Rudolph thought about Nora controlling their lives? You said she didn't really like Rudolph right from the start,' Kitty asked.

'No, Nora never really approved of Rudolph. I think she saw him for what he was, but he made Lorena happy. Nora would do anything to make Lorena happy. She was very generous to them. She would take them on holidays and cruises. She bought Rudolph a car which costs a small fortune to garage here in the city.' Edgar shook his head, presumably at the folly of this expense.

'You say Nora loved her late husband, how did she become involved with Mortimer? I mean, he's married to Titania, and I presume they were all friends,' Kitty asked.

'Nora knew them both from mixing in the same circles socially. Mortimer and Titania's marriage has been on the rocks for a long time. It's an open secret. Titania is the one with money and she doles out enough to keep Morty dangling. She often gets in arguments and causes scenes, especially if she's had a drink, and Morty smooths it all out for her.' Edgar paused, the lines deepening on his brow. 'Titania can be very difficult to live with I imagine. I know you saw Morty somewhat inebriated but that was out of character for him. Titania on the other hand drinks like a fish. Living here in the same block, I suppose it threw Morty and Nora together. They just hit it off,' Edgar said.

'It didn't bother Nora that he was married?' Matt asked.

'I think Nora was lonely and Morty was unhappy, so they provided company for one another. Nora said that Mortimer was going to divorce Titania and they were going to marry.' Edgar gave a slight shrug. 'I must admit I was sceptical. Morty has the spine of a jellyfish, but it seems Nora was right. He did ask Titania for a divorce.'

'I think we all know that Titania wasn't happy about that. How did Lorena and her husband take the news?' Matt asked.

'Lorena was not impressed. She had several arguments with Nora about it all. I think she found their affair embarrassing. Rudolph, I think backed Lorena. After all, Nora was the source of their income and if Morty started to interfere with that, well it could make life jolly uncomfortable for them I suppose,' Edgar said.

'Do they like Mortimer and Titania?' Kitty asked.

Matt thought this was a good question. He had only seen them all together for a short time at the party, but everyone had been behaving in a civil fashion until Titania had slapped Nora.

'Yes, I think so. I've never seen any arguments or disagreements. Lorena and Rudolph are always polite to Mortimer, at least on the surface. They are less tolerant towards Titania, but I think that's because of the drinking.'

Matt could see that Kitty was thinking about her father's assessment of the situation.

'You said before Nora was killed that she had been suggesting that Horatio Blackstock should retire, even though he's been in her service for years. Didn't you say Mortimer had first put the idea forward?' Kitty's nose crinkled as she tried to recall the conversation. A habit Matt always found endearing.

'That's true, and you said Lorena was eager to see Horatio

leave. Didn't she say he was nosey?' Matt asked, looking at Edgar and Kitty.

'I think Mortimer felt that Horatio acted as a spy for Nora. He was certainly always reporting back information about Lorena and Rudolph. In Morty's case I think Horatio was a tie to Nora's previous marriage.' Edgar sounded thoughtful.

'I wonder what Horatio told Nora about Lorena and Rudolph?' Kitty mused. 'Lorena sounded very scathing about him when she called to tell you about the bequest.'

'Lorena often sounds like that anyway. She isn't the warmest of people. I often wondered if she took after her father rather than Nora. I never met Nora's late husband. He had passed away several years before we became acquainted. Nora, on the other hand, was always warm and polite, even to Titania. Lorena can be very sharp,' Edgar said.

'What about Nora's relationship with Peggy? You said she had suspected her of being dishonest when things started to go missing around the apartment. Did she ever say why she thought Peggy might be involved?' Matt asked. He was curious to find out what exactly Edgar knew. He would have expected Nora to have dismissed a staff member if she believed they were stealing from her.

Edgar sighed. 'Nora had noticed things being moved around and then she noticed things disappearing. Small items, often from her silver collection. The thing is, she had a lot of items and would change them around when she had parties and events. It was hard to keep track and then, of course, the missing pieces would reappear again.'

Matt nodded. He had noticed the bijouterie cabinets of small silver trinkets when they had been at the party.

'Some of the cabinets were locked and Horatio had the keys. Those didn't seem to be affected so Nora suspected Peggy rather than Horatio. After all, he had been with her for years, why would he steal from her now? Especially as he wanted to convince her to permit him to continue working,' Edgar explained.

'Did Nora ever confront Peggy? Or let her know that she was thinking of dismissing her?' Kitty asked.

Edgar folded his paper and placed it on the side table, clearly finding the discussion more interesting than advertisements for Christmas toys and gifts. 'She didn't have any proof, and when things reappeared again, she thought perhaps she was making too much of it all. Peggy wasn't the smartest girl, but she was very pleasant and eager to please. There was no real reason for her to steal from Nora. I think she had dropped several hints about it. That's what I find so puzzling. Why was Peggy pawning Nora's silver? What did she need the money for?'

Matt could see Kitty thinking about Edgar's question. It was a good point and it felt as if they were starting to get somewhere.

'Perhaps she was helping her brother?' Matt suggested.

Kitty shook her head slowly, a lock of blonde hair falling onto her cheek. 'I met her brother and although he's obviously a working man he didn't seem in dire need of money. If anything, from the way he spoke, it was as if he considered himself fortunate compared to many people. He was open about Peggy writing to him weekly and I'm sure he would have said if she ever sent him any money.'

Matt snapped his fingers. 'The letters. Peggy went out to post letters the night she died. With it being so close to Christmas perhaps she thought they would get there quicker than if she left them for the concierge to deal with. I wonder if Lieutenant Tanfield ever found out if that was true and who they went to and what they said.'

'We know she wrote to a former neighbour and to her brother,' Kitty said. 'They would have contacted the police if there had been anything significant in those letters surely. We don't even know if she really had written any letters that day or if that was an excuse to get out of the apartment.'

'To meet someone you mean?' Matt asked. 'Perhaps the same person who she may have been lending money to?'

'Peggy was soft-hearted, she was the kind of girl who would do anything to please people. Gullible. If she had been rich, she would have made a good mark,' Edgar said thoughtfully.

'Pa!' Kitty said in a scandalised tone. 'Really.'

'Did she have a boyfriend at all? Anyone she ever mentioned?' Matt looked at Edgar. 'Anyone Nora ever told you about?'

Matt knew that Peggy was unlikely to have ever discussed her love life with his father-in-law, but he thought perhaps Nora might have found out something and she could well have raised the topic with Edgar.

'No one at all. Did Horatio know of anyone?' Edgar asked.

Kitty shook her head. 'No, her brother didn't know of anyone either.' She drummed her fingers on the tabletop, almost dislodging one of the completed corners of Matt's puzzle. 'She was in deep conversation with Rudolph on the night of the party. They were virtually concealed in that dark bit behind one of the big Christmas trees.'

'A liaison with Rudi?' Edgar suggested. 'Good heavens, that boy has been busy if that's the case.'

'Maybe,' Kitty said.

'We know Rudolph has a mistress. Peggy could have found out.' Matt looked at Kitty to see what she thought of the idea.

'Nora could have found out,' Edgar added.

'I presume though that this young woman Rudolph is seeing behind Lorena's back is not the first? That's right, isn't it? You said there had been a big argument back in the summer over a woman,' Kitty said.

'Good Lord, no, she's not the first. Nora knew of several, including the one in Hawaii. I know because she told me she had spoken to him about it. Apparently so long as Lorena never found out about the others then it didn't matter,' Edgar said.

'Was this Rudolph's view or Nora's?' Matt asked.

'Rudolph's. Nora only agreed to stay quiet because she knew how much Lorena loved Rudolph and they had been talking about having a baby. Nora desperately longed to become a grandmother.' Edgar looked at Kitty who was now rubbing her temples.

'Are you all right, darling? Shall I go and make us a pot of tea?' Matt suited his actions to his words at his wife's nod of agreement.

Matt headed into the kitchenette still mulling over everything Edgar had just told them. Any of the people they had discussed could have killed Nora and Peggy. Edgar had given them a lot more background, helping to fill in the gaps. Even so, he still couldn't see any new clear leads.

CHAPTER NINETEEN

Matt set the tea tray down on the coffee table near Edgar's chair. Kitty was pleased to see that he'd included a plate of biscuits. Perhaps something sweet to eat might help her to think more clearly. The chance meeting in the lobby with the lieutenant had been really distressing and her head was spinning now with all the new information her father had provided.

Edgar accepted his cup of tea from Matt and helped himself to a biscuit. 'So, what do you think has become of Nora's jewellery?' he asked, before leaning back in his seat. 'The apartment was searched, and it didn't come to light. Do you think whoever killed her took it or do you think that was a more opportunistic theft?'

'The police said they have alerted all of the reputable jewellers in the city, and presumably all the pawnshops. I don't know if even the less reputable places would want to touch it if the police have made it too hot to handle. There was a lot made of it in the newspaper,' Matt said as he passed Kitty the biscuit platter.

'Not even if it was broken up?' she asked as she helped herself to a couple more biscuits.

'The most valuable stones were quite sizeable. Whoever took the jewels might get away with selling some smaller stones I suppose.' Matt placed the almost empty plate back on the tray.

'Which is back to my question, did Nora's murderer take them? Or was it someone else?' Edgar asked.

'I suppose someone could have come across her body and stolen the jewellery later on, but I think it's unlikely.' Matt had obviously given the matter some thought. 'It would be too much of a coincidence and the weather was so bad that night. There were no clear footprints around her body, so I'd say they were taken by whoever killed her.'

'Do we think she may have been killed for the jewels? They were very valuable.' Kitty looked at Matt and then at her father.

'I suppose she could have gone to meet someone and been attacked after the person she had intended to meet had gone, or perhaps never appeared. It's possible she may have been lured into going outside so someone could rob her.' Edgar brushed biscuit crumbs from his tie.

'It has to be someone she knew though. Someone who knew she would be wearing expensive jewels that night and who she would have been anxious to talk to or trusted,' Kitty said. 'A stranger wouldn't have known any of that. From what Horatio has said she normally would have taken her jewellery off and locked it away so she must have felt safe.'

'That's very true, Nora was no fool. She would only have agreed to meet someone she knew well,' Edgar added.

'She must either have followed someone, Peggy perhaps? And didn't have time to remove her jewellery. Or she didn't want Peggy or Horatio to know anything about whoever she was meeting. Otherwise, she could have talked to whoever it was inside her apartment. This was something secret that she wanted kept quiet,' Kitty said.

'I wonder if something happened at the party?' Matt mused.

'Apart from Titania slapping her, you mean?' Edgar asked with a small chuckle.

'No, perhaps she saw or heard something, or someone approached her to meet with them afterwards,' Kitty said. 'That sounds possible. She was very relaxed and jovial wasn't she, when we arrived?'

'Yes, and even after the incident with Titania, she was upset and angry but she seemed perfectly fine otherwise,' Matt agreed.

'Oh, this is so frustrating. I wish we had the opportunity to talk to them all again. To see if someone lets something slip. It's so close to Christmas though now and it's just impossible. Tomorrow is Christmas Eve.' Kitty finished her tea and placed her cup back on the tray before snaffling the last biscuit.

Edgar suddenly sat up straight in his chair and reached for the telephone. 'Maybe not, my dear.'

Matt gave a slight shrug at this mysterious pronouncement and Kitty was forced to wait quietly while her father's call was connected.

'Felicia, darling, you know the little soirée you're holding this evening? May I bring a couple of guests? Thank you, yes, I'm much better now. Yes, my daughter and son-in-law are visiting from England.' Edgar winked at Kitty while he listened to whoever Felicia was on the other end of the call.

'Yes, darling, I know how much you adore London. I agree, it's so dreadfully sad about Nora.' Edgar listened to the response.

'I expect you did think of cancelling, but so many people would have been disappointed, and Nora would have wanted you to go ahead, I'm sure of it.' Edgar rolled his eyes and pulled a face at Kitty as he continued to listen.

She bit her lip and tried not to giggle at his antics.

'A simple memorial toast would be perfect, and you say Lorena and Rudolph are still coming. How jolly brave of them.

Yes, darling, much love, we'll see you later then. Toodles.' Edgar set the receiver back on its cradle and gave a small shudder of relief.

'Who was that?' Kitty asked, her lips twitching in amusement.

'Felicia Hogworthy, a ghastly creature I usually avoid like the plague if I can. She's having a pre-Christmas party this evening at the Madison Towers Hotel. She was one of Nora's chums, although Nora couldn't stand her either. I'm willing to bet my last dollar that either Mortimer or Titania will be there. Lorena and Rudolph are still going so you may get the opportunity to find something useful out.'

Kitty looked at Matt. 'Sounds like a plan for tonight then.'

'I'm surprised Lorena and Rudolph are attending so soon after Nora's death,' Matt said.

'No one wants to upset Felicia or your social diary will die a sudden and extreme death. No one likes her as she's dreadfully annoying, but she's as rich as Croesus and throws a good bash. Lorena and Rudolph will probably just put in a token appearance since Felicia intends to make some kind of speech in Nora's honour.' Edgar groaned at the thought. 'I had planned to plead my illness but now I shall have to show my face.'

Kitty laughed. 'Well, we appreciate your sacrifice, Pa. Just think that you are doing this for Nora and Peggy.'

It was something of a rush to get ready, but the hotel where Felicia was holding her party was only a short taxi ride from the apartment block. The Metropolitan Museum loomed in the night sky guarded by four imposing pairs of Corinthian columns as they passed by, its expanse so wide that it would be almost impossible to capture the entire building in a single photograph. The snow had finally stopped falling but it was now freezing hard. Kitty was relieved to see that the sidewalk in front of the hotel had been cleared of snow and ice and a uniformed doorman was ready to open the taxi doors.

The hotel foyer was full of expensively dressed men and women. The diamonds in the ladies' earrings and necklaces glittered under the light of the ornate crystal chandeliers as they handed in their coats at the cloakroom. The faint strains of jazz music drifted along the thickly carpeted corridor as they followed the crowd towards the function rooms Felicia had reserved for her party.

Once their names had been checked off at the door by a tail-coated hotel employee they were permitted to enter the party.

'I say this is frightfully swish,' Matt observed as they gazed around the room.

There were three smaller Christmas trees fully dressed in gold and crimson baubles and tinsel strands. Kitty estimated them to be at least eight feet tall. Then beside the area where the band were performing was a giant tree at least twelve or fourteen feet high laden with decorations.

Whoever Felicia was, she clearly was a very wealthy woman. Kitty wondered how her father knew her. He had been surprisingly reticent on that front. She was glad her dark-red satin gown was fashionable and that Alice had insisted she pack it. Edgar managed to secure a passing waiter and obtained three glasses of what they were assured was a special Christmas cocktail from his silver tray.

'Chin, chin,' Edgar said as he raised his glass before chinking it against theirs.

'Edgar, honey, you came. I was so pleased to hear you were better. Nora had told me how ill you'd been. This must be your daughter and son-in-law.' A woman, shorter than Kitty and as round as she was high, had appeared as if from nowhere to greet them. She was dressed in a fussy, formal gown and was laden with jewels.

Edgar dutifully performed the introductions.

'Oh my, and your first visit to New York and now all of this. How dreadful,' Felicia exclaimed.

The gold frilly satin of her dress and crimson sash reminded Kitty of a Christmas bauble, with her dark hair piled up on top of her head. The clips holding it in place were studded with rubies and diamonds. Kitty guessed her to be in her fifties.

'It was frightfully kind of you to invite us,' Kitty said politely.

'Oh, you just have the cutest accent, just like Edgar.' Felicia beamed at them and tapped Edgar's knuckles with a folded silk fan that matched her dress. 'I know how upset you must be, sweetie. You and Nora were such pals.'

'It has been awful. Are Lorena and Rudolph here? I should really go and thank Lorena for the small gift Nora left me,' Edgar said.

'They arrived a few minutes ago. I don't suppose they'll stay too long. I convinced Lorena her mother wouldn't have wanted her to lock herself away from her friends. It's times like this that you need to have support and something to take your mind off of things,' Felicia said.

Kitty smiled and remained quiet. She wasn't sure that she would wish to attend a party only a day or two after losing someone close to her in a violent and unexpected manner. Still, each to their own she supposed.

Felicia stopped a waiter and took a glass of the red-coloured speciality cocktail. 'Are you enjoying the drinks? I had these created especially for tonight. A festive treat, we've called them Felicia's Festive Fizzers. Isn't that fun?' She giggled before taking a sip. 'Now, I must fly, I've just seen Titania Liggett. Lorena told me all about that debacle at Nora's party, I must make sure she doesn't over do the drinks.' Felicia wrinkled her nose and vanished as swiftly as she had appeared.

'It seems Titania is here tonight as well, then. I wonder if Mortimer is attending?' Matt said.

'I doubt they have come together. I want a word with him though if he is here. Darned cheek trying to implicate me to Lieutenant Tanfield. After all I've done for him, too,' Edgar muttered. He took another sip of his cocktail. 'This drink is quite ghastly. It tastes like cough mixture.'

Kitty giggled as Edgar looked around for a spare tabletop and abandoned his glass.

'I think I see Lorena.' Matt indicated a gap in the crowd.

Kitty peered in that direction and spotted Lorena in a black-velvet dress with minimal jewellery talking to an elderly lady in bright-blue chiffon.

'We need to go over there,' Kitty said.

Her father nodded his agreement, and they threaded their way through. The music was louder now they were closer to the band and the air was filled with a pale-blue fuzz of cigarette smoke.

'Lorena, darling, I didn't expect you to be here this evening,' Edgar lied as he greeted her with a kiss on her cheek.

The elderly woman in the blue-chiffon frock had moved away.

'I must admit I didn't know what to do,' Lorena said. 'But you know Felicia and what she's like, so here I am.'

'She is terribly persuasive. You didn't come alone though I hope? Is Rudolph with you?' Edgar asked in a solicitous tone.

'Yes, he insisted on coming, although he is as distressed as I am over mother's death,' Lorena said.

'Thank you for letting me have that charming picture by the way. It means so much to me. Your dear mother knew how much I always coveted that little piece of home,' Edgar said.

'You're very welcome.' Lorena took a small sip from her cocktail and pulled a face at the taste.

'Horatio said you intend to move into your mother's apart-ment in the new year,' Edgar continued. 'I shall enjoy having you both as neighbours. It's so lovely when it's someone one knows.'

'Yes, he's supposed to be packing everything ready to clear for the decorators. Although, Rudolph is insisting we take a little vacation first to get over everything. We fly out tomorrow afternoon so we'll be there in time for Christmas Day.' Lorena glanced around as if looking for her husband.

Kitty was slightly surprised that the police were permitting them to leave the city. Still, they may have excluded Lorena and Rudolph from the inquiry.

'Jolly good idea. A change of scene will help take your mind off things. Let's hope the police nab whoever did this soon,' Edgar said.

Lorena responded with a wan smile. 'I'm starting to think she was mugged and that's why her jewellery is missing.'

'You would have thought that would have turned up by now,' Matt said.

'There's no sign of it yet. Lieutenant Tanfield says his department are on the case but who knows.' Lorena shrugged her bony shoulders.

'Dash it all, there's that cad, Mortimer.' Edgar spotted his friend in the crowd and hurried off in pursuit.

'Oh my, have your father and Mortimer had a quarrel?' Lorena looked surprised.

'A storm in a teacup,' Matt assured her. 'I'm sure they'll sort it out.'

'Mortimer is obviously very upset over your mother's death,' Kitty said. 'He was intending to divorce Titania to marry Nora, wasn't he?'

'Yes. Obviously, Rudolph and I were concerned when it became clear that Mom and Mortimer were having a liaison. No one likes to think of their parent making a fool of themselves with a married man.' Lorena pursed her dark-red painted lips. 'But then, when it became clear that Mom and Mortimer were serious about him leaving Titania to marry her, well, what can you do?'

'I suppose when people fall in love...' Kitty murmured before taking another sip of Felicia's Christmas cocktail.

Lorena snorted. 'Mortimer Liggett was in love all right. With my mother's bank account. He married Titania for her money and Mother was worth three times Titania's bank balance.'

'But presumably your mother was in love with him?' Kitty suggested.

'Mom only ever truly loved my father. No, she enjoyed having the power to get Mortimer away from Titania and he was very biddable. She was also very lonely, I think. Mom would say jump and Mortimer would say how high.' Lorena frowned. 'Speaking of angels or devils, Titania is headed over here. I really don't want to talk to her right now.'

Lorena made a sharp exit as Titania approached Matt and Kitty.

'I thought I saw Lorena over here. I wanted to tell her again how sorry I was about what happened the night of Nora's party,' Titania said as she looked around trying to see where Lorena had gone.

'How are you, Titania?' Matt asked. 'Did you and Mortimer manage to sort things out?'

Titania pouted and smoothed the dark-blue satin of her bias-cut evening gown. 'Oh, that man is being a nightmare. He's stopped talking about a divorce for now at least. Lieutenant Tanfield brought him home after you collected him from that bar.'

'Yes, he said he needed to speak to both of you about what you told us about the night of the party,' Kitty said.

'Speak to us! Interrogate us for what felt like hours. I had the most ghastly headache and he just kept right on talking.' Titania snagged a cocktail from a passing waiter.

'Oh dear,' Kitty tried to sound sympathetic.

'Then he kept on about Peggy's death. Did we know about her medication? Had Mortimer or I ever seen her take it? On and on, honestly, it was awful.' Titania took a gulp of her brightly coloured cocktail only to wrinkle her nose in disgust. 'Ugh, this tastes dreadful.'

'What did you and Mortimer tell him?' Kitty asked.

'That everyone knew how scatterbrained Peggy was about taking that darned tonic. Nora used to remind her as she would get giddy when she hadn't had it. We've both seen her take it many times. She wouldn't even usually measure it out. She'd just take off the cap and have a swig from the bottle while she was on the go.' Titania shook her head despairingly.

'Did Lieutenant Tanfield ask if either of you had argued with Peggy at all? I mean, he knew about you and Nora,' Matt asked.

Kitty thought that was a good question especially as Mortimer and Titania had been so quick to cast aspersions on her father.

'Why would I fall out with Peggy? She was Nora's assistant, and I don't quarrel with the help. I only ever saw her when we were at Nora's for a supper party or something. Mortimer must have seen her more than me, given all the sneaking around he was doing with Nora, but why would he argue with her?' Titania said.

'Did Mortimer argue much with Nora?' Kitty asked.

Titania glared at her. 'How the heck would I know? He'd never tell me if he did. Everything was just peachy so far as I knew.' Titania drained the rest of her drink, shuddering as she did so. 'Although, I guess they did have some kind of argument over him divorcing me. It was before the party. He came in one day in a foul temper, banging things around. I teased him a bit asking who had bitten him on the butt. He got angry and said I was the problem and to let him alone. I guessed then that she was pushing him to get rid of me so they could get married.'

'I'm so sorry. It must have been very difficult for you, especially with you and Nora being friends as well,' Kitty said.

'Friends?' Titania scoffed. 'I wouldn't say we were friends exactly. I mean we moved in the same social circles and living in the same block probably meant we saw more of one another than we would otherwise have done. But I wouldn't have called us friends.' She dumped her empty glass on the tray of a passing waiter.

'You told the lieutenant that my father had an argument with Nora a week or so before the party,' Kitty said.

'Well, yeah, it was a doozy. Something about some investment he had suggested to Nora or something. I know they didn't speak for almost a week, and they were real pally before. I guess they made up though. Morty used to get jealous of how friendly your father was with Nora,' Titania said.

'Is Mortimer a jealous man?' Kitty asked.

If he was, then perhaps he had been the one to meet Nora and they could have argued. He might have strangled her in a jealous rage. He could have taken her jewellery to make it look like a robbery or to provide himself with a financial cushion to enable him to still leave Titania.

'Oh yeah, he can get really petty and savage but he's all bluster. Morty is too lazy to do anything about anything. He used to get jealous of me when we first married. I was a catch, you know. Morty is my third husband. He hated when I spoke to any other man. Used to freeze me out for days.' Titania gave a regretful sigh.

'I think my father has gone to speak to Mortimer,' Kitty said. 'He wasn't too happy about what he told the lieutenant.'

Titania sighed. 'Like I said, we only answered the lieutenant's questions. Anyway I didn't come with Morty tonight. He lit out of our apartment without waiting for me, so I got a separate taxi. We argued again while I was getting ready. I wouldn't have come at all except Felicia can make life very difficult if you don't play ball. Plus, it's Christmas and I deserve a little fun.' She nudged Matt. 'Maybe I'll find myself a new beau for the new year, let Morty have his wretched divorce. See if he likes being broke all over again.'

Matt gave her a tight smile and edged slightly closer to Kitty.

'I suppose we should go and look for Papa,' Kitty said. 'It was nice to see you again, Titania. Have a good Christmas if we don't meet again before then.'

They moved away before the woman could initiate any further conversation.

'Her third husband! Gosh, New Yorkers lead a very different life to us,' Kitty said.

CHAPTER TWENTY

Matt looked around the room for any sign of Kitty's father. Matt had the advantage of being taller than Kitty so found it easier than she did to search for people in a crowd. It took him a moment before he spotted Edgar's silver hair and tall, distinguished figure.

'I think he's over there by the very big Christmas tree.' Matt took hold of Kitty's hand to avoid losing her in the crush near the dance floor and they threaded their way across the room.

Edgar was in conversation with two men. One, Matt immediately recognised as Mortimer Liggett, looking slightly crumpled, and as they drew nearer, he realised the other gentleman was Rudolph Briggs.

'Matt, my dear boy, there you are. I thought you and Kitty would be taking a turn on the old dance floor.' Edgar waved his hand in the general direction of the band. A three-piece ensemble with a male vocalist. 'Spiffing music.'

'Yes, it's wonderful,' Matt agreed. He noticed that Edgar no longer appeared to be annoyed with Mortimer so he assumed that they must have talked and sorted out their dispute.

Kitty let go of Matt's hand and edged around him, so he was

in between herself and Rudolph. It was clear to Matt that Lorena's husband made her feel uncomfortable.

'It's nice to see you and Lorena here tonight,' Kitty addressed Rudolph. 'It's probably good to get out for a few hours after everything that's happened.'

'Yes, that's what Felicia kept saying. We hadn't intended to be here, but she rang several times to ask us to come.' Rudolph had what looked like a glass of whisky in his hand and Matt wondered how he had managed to avoid the Christmas cocktails.

'I felt the same way. I hadn't planned to come tonight either but being cooped up in that wretched apartment with Titania sulking and pouting is enough to drive any man crazy,' Mortimer said. 'Even Felicia's parties are better than that.'

'I told Lorena to pack her bags so we can get away for a while. It's all been too much, Nora's death and then what happened to Peggy. We plan to get Nora's apartment redecorated ready for when we get home and then we'll move in. It's a bigger place than ours and has a much better view,' Rudolph said.

'Are you going somewhere nice?' Kitty asked.

'We're flying out to California tomorrow afternoon. Lorena has a distant cousin there, and she's invited us to stay. A change of scene and a few days sunshine will be a welcome relief,' Rudolph said.

Matt noticed Rudolph giving Kitty appreciative glances as he spoke. Matt placed a proprietary arm around Kitty's slender waist. The man was a menace it seemed whenever a pretty woman was around.

'Have the police excluded you both from the inquiry then, so that you're able to go away?' Kitty asked.

Rudolph looked surprised at her question, his brow crinkling into a frown. 'I wasn't aware that Lorena and I were ever suspects. Lieutenant Tanfield hasn't said anything to us.'

'Forgive us, perhaps things are different here than in England,' Matt said. 'In Devon, anyone close to the victims, unless actively excluded by the police, is asked to stay around until the culprit is caught. It's a precaution in case they have more questions or anyone they arrest tries to use you as their alibi.' He looked blandly at Rudolph, waiting for his reaction.

'He's quite right, dear chap, best get your vacation cleared with our police pals or they might think you and Lorena are the guilty parties fleeing the scene.' Edgar clapped his hand on Rudolph's shoulder in a friendly fashion.

'That's preposterous. Why on earth would anyone think Lorena or I would harm Nora? Nora was very generous to both of us. Lorena adored her mother,' Rudolph replied stiffly.

'Well, Nora and Lorena did butt heads from time to time,' Mortimer said. 'And I suppose it does depend on whether either of you have an alibi for where you were when Nora and Peggy were killed. After all there's more than one victim.'

'Lorena and I were together after the party. We went straight back home to our apartment. Lorena was upset after that business with Titania, and she had a migraine starting.' Rudolph glared at Mortimer.

'You're only two blocks down the street. One or both of you could have come back,' Mortimer persisted, before noticing Rudolph's angry expression. He raised his hands in a defensive gesture. 'Hey, I'm just saying what the police might be thinking. It's the same for all of us. Titania might even have to cancel her wretched new year cruise if this killer isn't caught by then.'

'And why would Lorena or I want to hurt Peggy?' Rudolph scoffed. 'Nora's assistant. It's rubbish, absolute nonsense.'

'It's not me you have to convince. It's Lieutenant Tanfield,' Mortimer said.

'He does have a bit of a point, my dear fellow. You know how the police can be, suspicious of everyone. I mean, did you or Lorena have any disagreements with Nora or Peggy recently?' Edgar asked.

'Who knows what goes on between a mom and daughter? Lorena and Nora would have little spats, but that's normal. As for Peggy, we knew Nora was worried that some of her things kept going missing or being moved. I spoke to her myself about it at the party since Nora was upset. Peggy was a sweet kid, I wanted to warn her that she needed to step up her game or Nora would fire her,' Rudolph said.

Matt guessed this must be when Kitty had seen Peggy and Rudolph together behind the Christmas tree.

'What did Peggy have to say about that? Did you ask her directly about the missing items?' Kitty asked.

'I just told her that Nora was concerned and asked her if she had noticed anything. I hadn't mentioned it to Lorena but at the time I thought maybe Nora herself might have been responsible. You know, memory problems starting or something with her moving stuff and forgetting she'd done it. Of course, now we know it was Peggy, but maybe Nora asked her to do it for some reason,' Rudolph suggested.

'Why would Nora do that?' Edgar asked.

'I dunno. I suppose she could have been trying to test out someone in some way.' He took a sip from his glass. 'Your guess is as good as mine.' Rudolph spotted someone he knew in the crowd and made his excuses.

'What on earth was that about?' Kitty asked, looking bewildered.

'Search me, dear girl,' Edgar said.

'And me.' Mortimer too looked equally confused by Rudolph's suggestion.

The music from the band finished and everyone applauded as the male singer called Felicia to the small stage.

'My dearest friends, we are gathered this evening for my annual pre-Christmas party and I do hope you will all have the loveliest of times,' Felicia announced as she took her place in front of the microphone. 'However, this year, we have lost a shining star from our midst, our dearest friend, Nora Danger-field, taken from us so cruelly. Before we go back to our celebra-tions, I'd like you to raise a glass to Nora's memory.' Felicia paused to hold up her own cocktail glass. 'To Nora, may justice be done and your memory live on.'

There was a ripple of assent from the partygoers as everyone dutifully raised their glasses.

The toast given, Felicia thanked everyone for coming, and urged them to enjoy themselves before relinquishing the micro-phone to the singer once more. The music and dancing resumed with the room soon returning to its previous buzz of activity and laughter. Mortimer wandered away and Edgar became engaged in conversation with a couple of ladies who had made a beeline for him.

'Shall we take a turn on the dance floor?' Matt asked, extending his hand to Kitty.

'We may as well enjoy ourselves a little,' Kitty agreed.

They abandoned their drinks on a nearby table and Matt took her in his arms. The dance floor was crowded and there was little room to do more than slowly circle the space. He always enjoyed dancing with Kitty and it was nice to do some-thing other than try to solve Nora and Peggy's murders.

'Felicia has a lot of friends,' Kitty murmured.

'The cream of New York society, according to your father,' Matt agreed with a grin.

They danced to a few more songs before Matt offered to brave the crowd at the bar to get them a drink that wasn't one of Felicia's Festive Fizzer cocktails. Kitty happily agreed, subsiding onto one of the few vacant gilt chairs just off the dance floor.

She was hot now from the exercise and the crowd and was looking forward to a refreshing drink. She fanned her face with her hand and looked around her, idly watching the crowd.

Evening-suited waiters were circulating now with silver platters of canapés and the room was noisy with music and the buzz of chatter and laughter. The huge crystal chandeliers sparkled overhead, and it seemed that everyone was enjoying the party.

Kitty twisted round to see if Matt had managed to get anywhere near the front of the polished mahogany and brass bar located near the entrance doors. She spotted Titania deep in conversation with a tall, distinguished-looking man who appeared to be plying her with champagne. There was no sign of Mortimer.

She couldn't see her father either, and guessed he was probably still entertaining the ladies who he'd been speaking to earlier. She spotted Matt near the head of the queue for drinks and relaxed back in her chair to look towards the dance floor.

She straightened up in her seat and leaned forward, uncertain at first if her eyes were deceiving her. Admittedly she had only met the woman once a few hours before and it had been a fleeting meeting at that. Kitty was sure, however, that the young woman who had been with Rudolph at the restaurant during lunch was here now.

He was standing close to her in a darker corner of the room as if not wishing to be seen or overheard. Her hands were in his and they looked very cosy. Kitty wondered if Lorena was still at the party, if she was, he was taking a big risk. She jumped up from her seat and sidled through the crowds, taking care that neither Rudolph nor his companion should notice her. She got as close as she dared, concealing herself behind one of the fluted-marble, Doric-style pillars that were dotted around the room.

'You promise you'll tell her when you get back?' Kitty heard the girl say. She was dressed in a pale-blue satin gown that looked cheaper than the ones the other women were wearing.

'Of course. I would have told her already but with her

mother being killed, well, it would have been too much,'
Rudolph said.

She had to strain to hear his responses since his voice was
lower than his companion's and he tended to mumble.

'Oh, Rudi, I'm so glad I managed to see you tonight. I don't
know how I'll bear it while you're away.' The girl looked up at
Rudolph with adoring eyes.

'Not much longer now, my darling. Anyway, you have your
Christmas present from me to open on Christmas morning and
we've been able to meet tonight.' Rudolph smiled at the girl.
'Don't forget to keep that other package safe. I don't want
Lorena trying to turn me over in the divorce.'

Kitty's eyes widened at this. Rudolph was obviously
promising marriage to the girl she had encountered at the
restaurant. He must love her a lot to give up his comfortable
lifestyle with Lorena. His girlfriend was obviously not wealthy,
and Lorena's own money seemed secure.

'I will. I'll do anything for us, you know that.' The girl
glanced around as if to see if they were being observed and
Kitty ducked back behind a fronded palm. Her pulse raced and
she hoped she hadn't been spotted lurking in the greenery.

She peered through the fronds to see the girl risking a kiss
from Rudolph before melting away into the crowd. Kitty
dodged back out of sight as Rudolph looked around, straightening his bow tie.

Her heart thumped as she waited a moment for Rudolph to
move away towards the bar, before she risked heading back to
where she had been seated before. The chair was obviously now
taken, and Matt was standing looking around the room with a
perplexed expression and a cocktail glass containing a drink of a
less lurid colour in each hand.

'I thought I'd lost you in the crowd. Where did you go?' he
asked, handing her one of the glasses.

'I spotted Rudolph meeting up with that girl we saw him

with at the restaurant at lunchtime,' Kitty said, before taking a grateful gulp of her favourite negroni cocktail.

Matt grinned at her. 'A spying mission then. He was taking a risk, wasn't he?'

'Absolutely.' Kitty smiled back and moved closer to him to tell him in a low voice what she had overheard.

'I must say I'm surprised,' Matt said after he'd listened to Kitty's story. 'Rudolph must have really fallen for this girl. She didn't seem as if she was on the same social level as Lorena and Rudolph from what you noticed, and he strikes me as a man who likes his comfort.'

'He could just be stringing her along, I suppose. He seems a real womaniser.' Kitty took another sip of her drink.

'I suppose so. I wonder what's in the package he's given her. He doesn't possess anything of his own, does he?' Matt said.

Kitty shrugged. 'Perhaps he's been saving up some money secretly or has taken something valuable that was Nora's or Lorena's so they would have something to live on after he leaves her.'

She could imagine that Lorena would not take the news of Rudolph abandoning her very well. She had already seen how she had reacted to Nora's death so she could see that Rudolph would swiftly find himself evicted and penniless. She had been quick enough to dismiss Horatio and Peggy.

Matt drained the rest of his drink. 'New York is very different to Devon. Everyone here seems to be having an affair or a divorce. It's so complicated. Mrs Craven would be mortified.'

'Grams would be too. It's certainly not what I expected,' Kitty agreed.

Lorena approached them. 'Have either of you seen Rudolph? I have the most terrible headache and I want to go home.'

Kitty thought the girl did look pale. 'I thought he was near the bar a minute ago.'

'I'll go and look for him for you,' Matt offered.

'Thank you.' Lorena gave him a grateful smile.

'That was a nice toast Felicia gave to your mother,' Kitty said.

'Yes, it was kind of her. There are a lot of my mother's friends and acquaintances here tonight. I must admit it's been quite wearing having to speak to everyone and hear them express their condolences when you know they just want some inside gossip on the investigation.' Lorena sounded quite savage, and she swayed on her heels.

Kitty looked about for a vacant seat and grabbed one from under an elderly lady's nose, earning herself a 'well really!' in the process.

'Here, have a seat. I'm sure Matt will track Rudolph down in a trice,' Kitty said soothingly.

Lorena rubbed her hand across her forehead. 'I'm sorry, Mrs Bryant, if I've been so out of sorts. You must think I'm awful. It's just that I'm finding it hard to believe that my mother is dead, murdered. It seems impossible.'

'I quite understand,' Kitty said. 'And then, of course, Peggy's murder as well. It's no wonder you're feeling the strain.'

Lorena gave her a tight smile. 'I must admit, when Rudolph suggested a vacation, I thought he was crazy, but I'm beginning to see the sense of it now. I can't wait to be on that airplane tomorrow.'

'Will you be away long?' Kitty asked. She couldn't help feeling guilty knowing what she had just seen and heard. Lorena was unlikely to have a happy homecoming if Rudolph did leave her for his girlfriend.

'Only until Christmas is over. Mother loved Christmas. She and Dad always made a big thing of it when he was alive, and Mom kept that up. Dad being an orphan he wanted to experience all the things he missed when he was younger,' Lorena explained.

'I can understand that. This time of year is often hard for many people, I think.' Kitty could see Matt returning with Rudolph. 'Oh, here they are.'

'Lorena, honey, let me get you home.' Rudolph took his wife's arm as she stood up from the chair. 'Thank you for looking after her.' He nodded at Matt and Kitty.

'Our pleasure. I hope you feel better soon, and enjoy your holiday,' Kitty said as the couple walked away.

'Are Lorena and Rudi going now?' Felicia had popped up like a plump Christmas fairy. Her beady gaze darting around.

'Yes, I think Lorena has a migraine and it's been hard for her, seeing everyone,' Kitty said.

'I must go and say my goodbyes to them. I expect I can catch them at the cloakroom.' Felicia hurried off in pursuit.

'What do you want to do now?' Matt asked. 'Fancy another spin on the dance floor?'

'Why not?' Kitty guessed it would be a while before her father would be ready to leave. There was always the chance too that they might learn something more about Mortimer and Titania before they went home.

She allowed Matt to lead her to the dance floor once more and they passed a very happy half an hour dancing. Edgar found them and took over from Matt to whirl Kitty about.

'I'm so glad you're here tonight to save me from the predatory single females of New York,' her father said as they danced past one of the women he had been speaking to earlier.

Kitty laughed, she always enjoyed dancing with her father as he was light on his feet. She told him about what she had witnessed between Rudolph and his girlfriend.

'Really? I must say I'm surprised he's taken such a risk. He's quite the dark horse, isn't he?' Edgar said as he manoeuvred them into a clear spot on the floor.

'You said he'd had other women that he's been involved with that Lorena hasn't known about?' Kitty asked.

'Oh yes, he is quite the Casanova. Nora was not happy with him about it. She didn't want Lorena to be hurt,' Edgar explained.

'Hmm.' Kitty wondered about that. It seemed to her that Rudolph could definitely be in the frame for murdering his mother-in-law. What if that package he had entrusted to his girlfriend contained Nora's stolen jewellery? And, if Peggy had found out what he'd done, then he could have killed her too.

CHAPTER TWENTY-ONE

Matt had secured some seats and a table when Edgar returned with Kitty. She sank down onto a chair and picked up the drink that he had waiting for her.

'Oh, this is lovely, thank you, darling. I am so thirsty.'

Matt and Edgar took their seats and the three of them settled back to catch their breath and to watch the other guests. Titania danced past in the arms of the gentleman Kitty had seen her with earlier.

'She seems to be enjoying the party,' Kitty remarked as Titania gave them a little wave with the tips of her fingers as she went by.

'Titania is never slow to enjoy herself,' Edgar remarked in a dry tone as they all gave her a little wave back.

'I wonder where Mortimer has gone?' Kitty asked.

'I saw him a moment ago when I fetched these drinks. He was propping up the bar,' Matt replied. 'It looked like he was settling in for quite a session.'

'Oh dear.' Edgar looked at him. 'Then may I suggest, dear boy, that we say goodnight to Felicia and make our way home *tout suite*. Otherwise, we could become enmeshed in a tricky situation. I have no desire to deal with an inebriated Mortimer again tonight.' He finished his drink in a couple of swallows and stood up to leave.

Matt could see what his father-in-law meant. He had no wish to deal with a warring married couple and a drunken Mortimer either. Kitty nodded her agreement and finished her own drink.

'I quite agree. I'm tired anyway now. All that dancing has absolutely worn me out,' she said.

They made their way to the door, only stopping to say goodnight and give their thanks to Felicia for inviting them. They retrieved their coats from the cloakroom and joined the queue of people waiting for the hotel concierge to obtain taxis for them.

Blasts of icy air filtered into the lobby every time the hotel doors opened, and someone left. Matt saw Kitty shiver and snuggle down deeper into her coat, pulling up the collar to protect her face against the cold.

'Not long now, darling, and we'll be home in the warm.' He placed his arm around her.

They were nearly at the head of the line when Kitty placed her hand on his arm.

'That's Rudolph's girlfriend.' She inclined her head towards a young woman in a worn wool coat with a knitted hat covering her fair hair.

The girl was standing at the side of the queue. She had her purse in her hand and seemed to be counting her money as if trying to see if she could afford a taxi. Matt guessed she had probably missed the last bus, and he wasn't aware of how the subway system ran.

'Excuse me, aren't you the girl I met at lunchtime today?' Kitty had spotted the girl's distress.

The woman looked at her and then Matt saw recognition dawn. 'Oh my gosh, yes, at the restaurant in the restroom.'

'We're just getting a cab now. We could easily drop you off somewhere on our way. It's such a beastly night,' Kitty offered.

Matt saw hope flare in the girl's face. 'Are you sure? We might not be going in the same direction.' She looked back at her purse with a troubled frown.

'I insist, we couldn't possibly let a lady travel alone on a night like this. Taxis are in short supply this evening and I expect the last bus has already gone,' Matt said firmly.

'Well, if you're absolutely certain. I would be really grateful,' the girl said.

The concierge beckoned to them to say they had a cab, and they got into the taxi. Edgar took the seat in the front while their new companion sat next to Kitty, with Matt on the other end of the rear seat.

'Where to, my dear?' Edgar asked her.

The girl gave the driver directions, and the cab pulled away into the darkened streets.

'I suppose I should introduce myself,' the girl said. 'I'm Sally Shaughnessy.' She then offered her hand and they shook it. 'I really am no end grateful for this. You have no idea.'

'I'm Kitty Bryant and this is my husband, Matt, and my father, Edgar,' Kitty said. 'I'm glad we were able to help you. It's dreadfully cold tonight.'

'It is. I was starting to panic a bit when I realised the time. The bus I was supposed to get didn't come and then it got so late I thought if I went back to the hotel I could try and grab a ride to get as close to home as I could. I really do appreciate this. Can I give you some money towards my fare?' The girl started to delve for her purse once more.

'We wouldn't hear of it. It's not much out of our way,' Matt fibbed.

He guessed Kitty had been keen to get the girl's address and wheedle some more information from her.

'Were you at Felicia's party?' Kitty asked in a friendly tone.

'I only stepped in for a moment. I had other business in the area.'

Matt saw colour creep into the girl's pale cheeks and he guessed she was trying to hide that she had been smuggled in by Rudolph.

'Hopefully you avoided drinking those ghastly cocktails,' Edgar joked with a mock shudder.

'Oh, I'm not drinking alcohol at the moment, I've kind of lost the taste for it recently.' The colour in the girl's cheeks deepened.

He saw Kitty give her a sharp glance. 'Well, you didn't miss anything, I assure you.'

The taxi had turned away from the bright lights of the broad main avenues to enter a poorer area where the lighting was not so good, and the storefronts had given way to shabby brick tenements with metal fire escapes. Tattered posters were pasted on the walls and Matt noticed an eviction notice pinned on a nearby door.

The cab pulled to a halt outside one such place. Edgar immediately jumped out to open the car door to assist the girl onto the sidewalk.

'Do be careful, my dear, it's jolly slippy,' he warned.

'I'll be all right, my place is just here. Thank you again. I sure do appreciate this,' Sally said, indicating a nearby entrance. She waved her leather-gloved hand in farewell as Edgar got back inside the cab and closed the door.

Matt gave the driver the address to Edgar's apartment, and they pulled away as Sally took out a key and let herself into her building.

'Well, we have her name and address now,' Matt observed as the taxi turned back towards the wealthier part of the city.

'Indeed.' Kitty seemed thoughtful.

. . .

It was almost midnight when the taxi dropped them back at the apartment. To Matt's surprise, Horatio was downstairs talking to the night concierge when they entered the lobby.

'Good evening,' Edgar said, greeting the manservant. 'Rather late for you tonight, isn't it, dear boy? No problems I hope?'

Horatio returned Edgar's greeting and said good evening to the rest of them.

'No, sir, no problems. It's just that I haven't been out of the apartment for a couple of days with all the packing and sorting for Miss Lorena. I wanted to make sure my parcels of gifts for my family at home made the morning post. Zavier here is going to drop them at the post office on his way home. I know they won't get there in time for Christmas Day but hopefully they won't be much after that,' Horatio said.

Matt could see a couple of small neatly wrapped packages tied up with string sitting in one of the cubby holes at the back of the desk.

'It's quicker than waiting for our mail carrier to come by, especially this time of year,' Zavier explained.

'I also realised I hadn't been down to collect Miss Nora's post.' Horatio picked up a bundle of mail from the countertop. 'I expect I shall have to telephone Miss Lorena after breakfast to come and collect it. It's probably Christmas cards but you never know, there might be something important in there.'

'We saw Lorena this evening. She and Rudolph are off on a vacation leaving tomorrow afternoon so probably best to get her to check it before she leaves in case there is anything that needs dealing with urgently,' Matt advised.

'Yes, I expect Lorena would like to get as many things in order as possible before she goes away. You know how she is,' Edgar agreed.

'Anyway, we had better get upstairs. It's been a busy night,' Matt said goodnight to the two men and Kitty stepped over to the elevator and pressed the button to call it down. They left Horatio to finish making his arrangements with Zavier and travelled up to Edgar's apartment.

Matt noticed Kitty was still quiet as she took off her coat, hat and gloves and warmed herself in front of the fire, before she offered to make them all a milky drink before bed.

'Not for me, darling. I'm turning in. I feel quite tuckered out. Felicia and her parties tend to have that effect on me.' Edgar kissed her cheek affectionately and said goodnight to Matt before retiring to his room.

'Matt?' Kitty asked, looking at him.

'Yes, please, if you're making a drink, that sounds lovely.' Matt settled himself in Edgar's chair while Kitty went to heat up the milk and add the cocoa powder.

He could tell she was busy turning something over in her mind and guessed that neither she nor he would sleep unless she talked about it. A warm drink would help them to settle and sleep more easily.

Kitty emerged from the kitchenette carrying two large mugs in her hands. She placed one in front of Matt and set the other one down on the other side of the table, before taking her place in the fireside chair opposite him.

'I feel quite exhausted now,' she said, unclipping her earrings from her ears and dropping them onto the table next to her cup. She rubbed her earlobes between her fingers to ease where the clips had dug in slightly.

'I'm not surprised after all the dancing.' Matt undid his bow tie and unfastened his shirt stud. He too was relieved to be back and relaxing.

'It's not just the physical exercise though, is it? I mean, at home I walk miles with Bertie every day. This is more mental tiredness, from trying to work out who killed Nora and Peggy,' Kitty said.

Matt inclined his head in agreement. He knew what she

meant. It was much harder being in a strange place, with time and the weather against them, to try to get answers. The police didn't want their help, and it was already Christmas Eve.

'Do you feel we learned anything new tonight?' he asked.

Kitty picked up her chunky pottery mug and cradled it in her hands. 'I think we learned that everyone there had a motive to kill Nora.'

'Even Mortimer?' Matt asked. He personally would have said Mortimer was low on his list of suspects.

'I think he could have killed Peggy, and he had the opportunity to kill Nora. We only have his word that she was going to marry him. She may have changed her mind and, of course, he'd already asked Titania for a divorce. He could have found himself with neither woman wanting him. Titania also said he has a jealous streak.' Kitty had obviously been thinking about this.

'He could have killed her in anger and then murdered Peggy if she had found out. We know he said she opened the door to him that night. We only have his word that she sent him away.' Matt tried the theory in his mind. Mortimer had been acting strangely since Nora's death, even trying to pin the blame on Edgar. It could just be grief but it could also be guilt.

'Titania could have murdered Nora to stop her from stealing Mortimer. She had already assaulted her on the night of the party. We know she's very jealous and possessive. Then Peggy could have realised and Titania could have killed her,' Kitty said.

'It's possible. Titania does have quite large, almost masculine, hands, and she looks like a strong woman. If she took Nora by surprise, she could have strangled her,' Matt agreed.

'Lorena could have murdered her mother to free herself from Nora's financial control of her and Rudolph.' Kitty paused and took a sip of her cocoa.

Matt could see she had started to relax now she was working through her theories.

'And we know Rudolph is having an affair with Sally and has told her he is going to ask Lorena for a divorce. I wonder if he knows how tightly wrapped up Lorena's money is?' Matt mused. 'He didn't accompany her to see the attorney to hear what was in the will.'

'That was odd, I thought. Still, they are all odd. Everyone is having affairs with everyone else. It's so confusing,' Kitty said. 'He did tell Sally too that there was something valuable in that parcel he has left with her.'

'That could be money, some of Nora's silver, or even her jewellery if he is our murderer,' Matt said.

He picked up his own cup and took a drink. It made him feel a little homesick. This was the part of the day he always enjoyed most. Sitting with Kitty, sipping cocoa or Ovaltine before bed, Bertie at Kitty's feet and Rascal curled up nearby while they talked about their cases.

'What did you think of Sally?' Matt asked.

'She doesn't have much money,' Kitty said. 'Where she lives is in quite a poor area. The Depression has hit hard there. I saw in Papa's newspaper about all the food queues. People are really suffering.'

'Yes, Rudolph must have fallen pretty hard for Sally if he is prepared to give up his life of comfort and ease to marry her,' Matt said. 'It's clear that financially, she and Lorena are in a different league.'

'Everything to do with these murders seems to be angled up in relationships, money and marriage,' Kitty said. She finished her cocoa and tried to keep back a yawn.

'Let's call it a night, time for bed, I think. It's our wedding anniversary now too since it's after midnight so we should plan to do something nice.' Matt smiled at her and finished his own drink. There would be time to think about everything in the morning.

CHAPTER TWENTY-TWO

Kitty woke surprisingly early the next morning despite their late bedtime. The room was still dark when she slipped quietly out of bed. She retrieved the small gift she had been hiding for Matt to celebrate their anniversary and took it with her. Matt was still slumbering peacefully as she made her way into the sitting room to turn on the fire.

The air was cool but not cold and she wondered if the apartment's heating had been adjusted at last. She drew back the thick curtains to look outside at the still dark streets of the city.

The horse-drawn delivery carts were already busy outside the shops and a few buses filled with workers went past mixed with cars and taxis. She made herself a pot of tea in the kitchenette and took a seat at the small dining table so she could continue to watch the street scene below.

She watched a man hurrying along the icy pavement and into their apartment block, followed shortly afterwards by another man leaving the building. She realised it must be the changeover of the concierge staff since Zavier had a load of packages under his arm as he walked away down the street.

Kitty sighed and poured herself some more tea from the pot.

Ever since last night she had felt as if the solution to who killed Nora and Peggy was right under her nose. She just wished she could think of what it was that was eluding her to make the whole thing make sense.

It was lighter now outside and the street was busier. At least it didn't look as if more snow was likely to fall. It was hard to believe it was so close to Christmas. The leather wallet she had bought for Matt inscribed with his initials and their wedding date lay on the table lovingly wrapped in tissue paper. She and Matt had married on Christmas Eve at the ancient church in Dartmouth two years earlier. They certainly hadn't foreseen that they would be celebrating their second anniversary in America up to their necks in murder.

She wondered how long Mortimer had been married to Titania since she had said he was her third husband. She had assumed they had been married for ages, but perhaps they hadn't. Was that why their marriage had run into trouble since it was Titania's third marriage? Perhaps it hadn't worked from the start and that was why Mortimer was intending to marry Nora instead?

Kitty sipped her rapidly cooling tea. Why had Peggy been taking Nora's silver and pawning it? She hadn't stolen anything, or had she? She tried to recall if Lieutenant Tanfield had said if anything was still missing.

During the conversation she had overheard before Peggy died, Lorena had accused Peggy of dishonesty and had said her mother had told her she was thinking of dismissing the girl. Had that just been grief, manifesting itself as anger? Or had Nora discovered something about what Peggy had been doing?

Nothing so far had been discovered to support a theory that Peggy needed money for drugs or drink or gambling. So, what had she needed the money for? Kitty poured the very last of the tea from the pot. It was quite strong now, so she added extra milk, thinking as she stirred the dark liquid in her china cup.

Peggy obviously needed small sums of money regularly in order to replace or retrieve the objects she'd pawned and then put back in Nora's apartment. Did she get the things back once she was paid? Or if she loaned the money to someone else, did she fetch them once that person had repaid her?

Everyone had seemed agreed that Peggy was not the brightest of girls but that she was kind-hearted and hardworking. Nora had trusted her with the money raised from the charity night, leaving Peggy and Horatio to secure it in the safe. Peggy could easily have stolen that money and disappeared with it after Nora was killed.

Peggy and her brother had both moved to New York from a small town. Exactly the kind of place that had been hit hardest and where people were the poorest during this difficult time. Kitty recalled the tenement where they had dropped Sally off just a few hours earlier. Peggy's brother probably lived in a very similar area. He had taken two buses to get across the city to collect her things after her death.

Peggy's brother was working and had seemed quite honest and forthright about his relationship with his sister. Despite living in the same city, they had kept in touch by letter. Peggy couldn't have been loaning her brother money as she didn't see him very often. She was certain too that he would have mentioned it as he knew nothing of her trips to the pawnshops with Nora's silver.

Could she have been supporting someone else with the money? Wiring small amounts back to her hometown? Kitty finished the last of the tea and shuddered at the strength of the brew. If that had been the case, then Peggy would have just sent it from whatever she could spare from her salary. She would have no need to pawn things, would she? Someone else had planted that idea in her head or had pressured her to do it.

Kitty sighed. Horatio had spent all his savings sending money for medicine and living expenses to his family. Perhaps

Peggy too had wanted to try and help some of the people who had helped her. She drummed her fingers restlessly on the tabletop.

Had Peggy been bright enough to think of taking Nora's things to the pawnshop herself after all? Everyone had stressed that Peggy seemed honest. Had she been persuaded by someone else that it wasn't theft? She had merely 'borrowed' the things and once they were returned, then no harm would have been done. Perhaps the same person who had benefited from the loans. Her thoughts raced around her head.

Kitty's father sauntered into the room dressed in his pyjamas and silk dressing gown.

'Morning, Kitty, it's nice and cosy in here. Anything left in the pot?' He eyed her empty teacup.

'I'll make some fresh tea. This one is empty,' Kitty said, rising from her chair and greeting him with a kiss on the cheek.

She busied herself in the kitchenette and returned a few minutes later with a newly laid tray. Edgar had seated himself in his favourite seat beside the fire.

'Thank you, my dear. I take it Matthew is not awake yet?' he asked.

'No, not yet,' Kitty said, seating herself opposite her father.

'Well, happy anniversary to you both for today anyway,' Edgar said as he stirred the tea in the pot. He passed a card to her.

'Thank you.' Kitty smiled affectionately at him as she opened it. She added it to the Christmas cards on the mantelpiece.

'Christmas Eve already.' Her father replaced the lid on the pot and arranged the metal tea strainer over the top of his cup. 'It seems to have arrived very quickly.'

'It does,' Kitty agreed. 'Papa, I was just thinking, about Peggy taking Nora's things to the pawnshop. Did she ever mention anyone she felt sorry for, or who she was helping in some way?'

Her father considered her question while pouring his tea. 'Hmm, Peggy was one of those girls who liked to be helpful. She was very soft-hearted. Nora told me once she found her sobbing over some tale of woe she had been reading in the paper about some children orphaned after a fire.' He set the teapot down and looked at her curiously. 'Why, what are you thinking?'

'Probably nothing useful,' Kitty admitted, 'but she must have had a reason for wanting sums of money for short periods of time.'

'True, and you think she may have been giving the money to someone with a sob story?' Edgar asked as he picked up the milk jug.

'Is that something she would do?' Kitty asked.

Edgar finished helping himself to milk and nodded. 'Oh yes, she would always put money in charity boxes or give children a few cents if she could. She had a kind heart.'

Kitty could see how someone could have manipulated Peggy into acting on their behalf. Persuading her that what she was doing wasn't stealing and that she was helping them to help someone else. It could have been that it wasn't Peggy who had a gambling, alcohol, or drug problem but the person controlling her.

If Peggy had wanted to stop what she was doing, they could have blackmailed her into continuing by threatening to tell Nora what she had done. Perhaps Peggy had said she would tell the police about who she had been loaning the money to, that could have been what signed her death warrant.

'You seem very thoughtful, my dear.' Edgar stirred the sugar in his tea.

'Oh, just turning ideas over in my mind about everything,' Kitty said. 'I suppose I should go and dress. I'm sure I've heard Matt stirring.'

Her husband entered the room as she spoke and came over to the fireplace. 'I thought I heard my name mentioned.' Matt was dressed, shaved and ready for the day. He kissed her cheek and handed her a small box tied with pink ribbon. Kitty gave him the present she had ready.

'Happy anniversary, darling,' Matt said as he unwrapped his gift.

'Oh, this is lovely.' Kitty admired her own present of the dainty little brooch. 'Thank you.'

'What are you two lovebirds planning to do to celebrate?' Edgar asked.

Kitty rose and tugged the belt on her dressing gown a little tighter. 'I don't know. We hadn't decided. I was just going to go and dress.' She felt quite frumpy seeing Matt dressed while she was still in her night attire. It was their anniversary so she felt she should make a special effort to dress up.

'Shall we go out for breakfast? Perhaps try the place in the park we were going to when we stumbled on Nora?' Matt suggested. 'We should do a few nice things today. We could watch the skaters in the park too.'

'That sounds lovely,' Kitty agreed. Perhaps a walk through the park in the fresh air might clarify her thoughts on the murders.

'You two go and have a splendid time. The tea house is quite lovely,' Edgar said, sipping his tea.

A little later, wrapped up against the cold, Kitty and Matt set off to walk through the park to the tea rooms. Kitty couldn't suppress a small shudder as they passed the spot where they had discovered Nora's body at the rear of the apartment block.

'Are you all right, old thing?' Matt asked affectionately as she squeezed his arm. 'You've been very quiet this morning.'

'I'm sorry. I can't help thinking about everything. I promise

I shall be better company when we reach the tea rooms,' Kitty said.

The fountain in front of the building, which probably looked delightful in warmer weather, was turned off and wrapped in sacking. Kitty presumed to protect it against the frost. The tea rooms had a weather-beaten sign announcing it as the Casino in the Park. The roof was high and tiled and styled almost in a Chinese fashion.

'Papa said it wasn't ever a casino, although that was what it used to be called,' Kitty said as they approached. 'He said it meant little house in Italian and was built for ladies originally.'

'It's an interesting place. The roof is very impressive.' Matt held the door open for her as they entered.

The restaurant was every bit as good as Edgar had said. It was decorated for Christmas and was already busy. They settled down near a window with a view of the park and ordered bacon and eggs. Matt toasted her with coffee, and they spent a pleasant hour before walking back along the wet paths where a slow thaw had begun to set in.

The snow which had covered the grass had started to recede in the areas where the weak sunlight had caused it to melt. Patches of green were now poking through, and water dripped from the black, bare branches of the trees. The park was huge, and they paused to watch the ice skaters on the lake for a while.

They reached the lobby of the apartment just as Mortimer was on his way out. He was wrapped up warmly in a dark-grey overcoat with a dark-red scarf and black homburg hat. He had a small stash of packages wrapped in brown paper under his arm.

'Good morning, did you enjoy the party last night?' Matt asked.

'As much as could be expected in the circumstances, obviously. Got home a bit late, no taxis.' Mortimer looked rather the worse for wear. Dark circles lay under his eyes and his skin was sallow.

'It must have been very difficult,' Kitty soothed. 'Are you off to the post office, too?'

Mortimer glanced down at the packages as if he had temporarily forgotten that he was carrying them. 'Yes, I missed the mail carrier so I thought I would drop them off. I doubt they will arrive on time but at least they will have gone. In all the upset over Nora and Peggy, normal chores seem to have escaped me.'

The lobby doors opened while they were talking to Mortimer and Lorena entered. She too was dressed for the cold in a sable coat and hat.

'Oh my, I seem to have run into everyone this morning,' she said as she wiped her shoes on the mat.

'We have just come back from breakfast in the park. It's our wedding anniversary today,' Kitty said.

'Congratulations to you both. Horatio telephoned early this morning to say there was a stack of mail here for Mother. I thought I should take care of it before we set off for the airport later,' Lorena explained.

'Are you going from Newark? I hope the runways are clear,' Mortimer said.

'Rudolph telephoned them and apparently all is well. I must admit it will be nice to feel some sun on my face. This cold is awful,' Lorena said.

'Did you say you were going to California?' Matt asked.

'Yes, I had better get a move on. It will take well over an hour to get to the airport and our flight leaves at two o'clock. I left Rudolph sorting out arrangements for when we get there. As it's Christmas Eve a lot of the car rental places and taxi companies are closing up early.' Lorena pressed the button to call the elevator.

Mortimer wished her a good holiday and left, while Matt and Kitty joined Lorena to ascend upwards.

'I hope you have chance to have a rest while you're away.

Perhaps the police will have caught your mother's killer by the time you return,' Matt said as the elevator started to slow for their floor.

'You would hope so, but I haven't heard much from that Lieutenant Tanfield so far,' Lorena said as Matt opened the doors once the cage had stopped.

They said goodbye to Lorena and returned to Edgar's apartment. He had dressed and collected his newspaper while they had been gone.

'Did you have a nice time at breakfast?' he asked, lowering his paper as they entered the room.

'It was lovely, thank you,' Kitty replied. 'We just ran into Mortimer and Lorena in the lobby.'

'I'm surprised Morty is still standing after the amount he was sinking at the bar last night,' Edgar observed drily.

'He didn't look too good, I must say. He was off to the post office with a pile of packages. It seems to be a theme lately. I expect it's all last-minute Christmas things.' Matt took a seat on the sofa.

'Lorena had come to collect Nora's post before heading off to the airport,' Kitty said, perching on the cushion next to Matt.

'It's all right for some,' Edgar grumbled. He folded his newspaper and set it aside on the table. 'A spot of winter sunshine sounds just the ticket.'

'It seemed to be thawing a little outside,' Kitty said. 'The air didn't feel quite as cold.'

'That's something, I suppose. Less chance of breaking one's ankles on the sidewalks,' Edgar said.

There was a short ring on the doorbell.

'I'll go.' Matt stood and went to answer the door. He returned a moment later accompanied by Lorena.

'I'm so sorry to intrude but I need to ask a favour.' Lorena looked at Edgar. Kitty thought she seemed annoyed.

'Of course, my dear girl, if it's in my power.' Edgar had risen from his seat when Lorena had entered the room.

'I have just been informed by Horatio that he is terminating his service today and will be leaving shortly. I suppose that now he has received that far too generous bequest from my mom's estate, all sense of loyalty is gone. Anyway. I have asked him to leave his keys with Enrique on the front desk and I wondered if you might have this key. Just in case of emergencies or problems while Rudi and I are away.' Lorena opened her black patent leather handbag and extracted a small bunch of keys, which she passed to Edgar.

'Of course, my dear, how very unexpected of him,' Edgar remarked as he accepted the key ring and slipped it into his jacket pocket.

'Could you check on the apartment after he has gone? There are boxes waiting for the movers, but I want to be assured that no damage has been done and nothing stolen. Although Rudi and I have removed everything we felt was of value already,' Lorena muttered.

'Certainly, did Horatio say where he was going?' Edgar asked.

'To his family, I think. I didn't ask for any details, but he definitely mentioned them. Something about his nieces. Thank you for doing this, Edgar, I do appreciate it. I expect I shall see you when we get back in the new year.' Lorena said her good-byes and Matt showed her out of the apartment.

'That's a turn up for the books.' Edgar subsided back onto his chair.

'Quite. Horatio didn't say anything last night when he was in the lobby. I thought he was all set to see his notice period out. I wonder what's changed his mind?' Kitty said.

'I don't suppose the idea of Christmas alone in an apartment full of packed moving boxes is very attractive,' Matt said as he retook his place beside Kitty.

'No, I don't suppose it is.' Kitty frowned.

CHAPTER TWENTY-THREE

Edgar announced that he had a long-standing lunch appointment with some friends and would be back late, leaving Kitty and Matt alone in the apartment.

Matt switched on the radio, hoping to catch a weather forecast and to listen to some Christmas music. Kitty listened with half an ear to the radio while her mind continued to puzzle over the murders.

'I wonder if Horatio has given Lorena a forwarding address,' Kitty said.

Matt looked up from the dining table where he was setting out another jigsaw puzzle. 'I don't know. Why would he, unless it's to arrange payment of anything he's owed? I must admit that murder investigations here are very different to those in Devon. Everyone here seems to be allowed to come and go as they please. It must be a nightmare to gather evidence.'

'I suppose it must be more difficult in a city to keep track of people. There are so many ways they can just disappear if they wish.' Kitty knew what he meant. In England, someone was sure to know where a person had gone and would be likely to see them on a bus or a train.

'That's true,' Matt agreed.

'I wonder why he posted the parcels of gifts if he is going home. There were only a couple of small packages. I saw Zavier take them to the post office this morning,' Kitty said. 'I mean, surely he'll be there before the parcels. They weren't very big and would have fit in a suitcase or even a coat pocket.'

Matt looked up from his puzzle. 'Yes, you're right. That is odd. I wonder how he is getting home to his family. He told me he had very little money left from his savings when Nora suggested he might retire. He said he had spent it on medical fees and medicine for his sister. Tickets are expensive and hard to come by last minute on Christmas Eve.'

'Then he was left ten thousand dollars in Nora's will because he was still in her service at the time of her death. He must have known about her will. Everyone says he was always snooping around.' Kitty had a bad feeling developing in the pit of her stomach.

'Peggy would have trusted Horatio more than anyone if he suggested she take Nora's things to the pawnshop. He could have helped cover up that they were missing until she could redeem the tickets,' Matt said. 'He had keys for some of the locked cabinets where the most valuable things were kept.'

'He may have needed money urgently for medicine or to pay for fees and given Peggy the money back when they were paid. It would be better for him if Peggy took the items to the pawnbrokers as the shop staff would be less likely to think they were stolen since she looked so respectable.' Kitty looked at her husband.

Matt nodded his head slowly. 'Then Peggy could have said she was going to tell someone about why she was pawning the silver. She wasn't the cleverest of girls, but she could have begun to put the pieces together.'

Kitty jumped up from her seat. 'We have to do something.

We have to confront him and tell that beastly Lieutenant Tanfield.'

'We may be too late. He could have already left. Did your father leave Lorena's key here?' Matt asked.

Kitty hurried into the hall to look inside the painted Chinese-style bowl where her father habitually left the keys. 'Yes, it's here.' She picked it up and waved it at Matt.

'Wait!' Matt cautioned her as she went to go for the front door. 'We need to make sure he's still there and let Lieutenant Tanfield know. If we're right, then Horatio Blackstock is a dangerous man. We can't just go blundering in there.'

'What do you suggest?' Kitty asked, her hand still on the door latch. She knew Matt was right to be cautious, but she wanted to catch Horatio and prevent him from getting away.

Matt moved to the telephone and called down to the front desk. Kitty waited at the entrance to the sitting room fidgeting with impatience.

'Enrique, do you know if Horatio is still here? Mrs Briggs told us he was leaving today, and we were hoping to say goodbye to him before he went.' Matt winked at Kitty.

'You haven't seen him leave yet. Thank you so much.' Matt replaced the receiver on the cradle.

'He's still in Nora's apartment, then.' Kitty's heart raced.

'I'll call Lieutenant Tanfield now. Open the front door and listen out for the elevator or any movement on the stairs,' Matt said as he picked the receiver up once more.

Kitty hurried back to the front door and opened it a crack so she could listen out for any movement from the penthouse floor. Matt was talking on the telephone, and she hoped he had managed to get hold of the lieutenant.

It was hard to hear what might be happening upstairs in Nora's apartment, so she crept out onto the landing to try and listen. She thought she could hear some muffled bumps and bangs from overhead as if boxes were being moved around.

Matt was still on the telephone, so she made her way quickly and quietly to the foot of the stairs that led from their landing to the penthouse floor. She knew from where she had overheard Lorena talking to Peggy just a few days earlier that she should be able to hear what was going on if she loitered in the stairwell.

She kept her back to the wall and slowly climbed up step by step. She thought she heard something but there was a wailing of sirens from outside the building. The noises up ahead seemed to have stopped now and she was about to turn around and head back down to her father's apartment when she heard a footstep on the stairs behind her.

'Mrs Bryant, whatever are you doing?' Horatio Blackstock blocked her retreat, preventing her from descending. He had a quizzical look on his face and a cold glint in his dark-brown eyes.

'Oh, my goodness, you startled me!' Kitty pressed her hand to her chest. 'Lorena said you had gone, and I heard strange noises so I thought there might be burglars in Nora's flat.' Her blood pounded in her veins, and she hoped he would believe her.

He must have gone down a floor in the elevator while she was on the stairs and probably saw the door was open to their apartment. She swallowed hard. If he had caught any of Matt's conversation, then he would know that her husband had been calling the police about him.

'Well, as you can see, it's just me. Why don't you come on up to the apartment? Take a look for yourself to put your mind at rest,' Horatio suggested as he moved a step nearer to her.

Kitty edged up a step to keep a space between them. His proximity was scaring her. 'Oh, it's fine. I should get back down to Matt. He'll wonder where I've gone.' Kitty tried to sound cool and collected.

'Oh, but I insist, Mrs Bryant. It would be terrible to leave and have someone thinking I'd stolen something that wasn't rightfully mine.' Horatio moved forward again, and Kitty realised they were almost at the landing.

She stepped up again and out onto the landing. A glance at the elevator showed her the cage was missing, probably where Horatio had used it to reach their floor. The sirens outside must have masked the sound of the elevator moving. The only way down from the penthouse floor was via the steps she had just climbed, and Horatio was now at the top of the stairs.

'I'm certain you are a very honest man, Mr Blackstock,' Kitty said.

'Are you, Mrs Bryant? Does your husband feel the same way? You two are both private eyes in England, aren't you?' Horatio continued to walk towards her, forcing her along the landing and the open door of Nora's apartment.

'England is very different to America,' Kitty said. She debated whether to scream for Matt. She knew this could push Horatio over the edge however and her intention at the moment was to keep him talking and keep him calm.

Matt would know where she had gone and would probably come upstairs to find her as soon as he was off the telephone.

'Are your bags all packed ready to leave?' Kitty asked. 'Lorena said she thought you were going to your family. That will be nice for Christmas, better than staying here by yourself.' She knew she was just making small talk but if she could keep him engaged, then it might buy enough time for Matt to reach her or for the police to arrive.

'Yes, ma'am, I'm all set to go. I got a bus route planned, ticket bought and my case packed. I travel light. Not many possessions,' Horatio said.

'I suppose that must be why you posted Nora's jewels on ahead in those packets that Zavier took to the post office for you this morning.' Kitty knew this was risky, but they were almost at the door to the apartment now and she didn't want to go inside.

'And why would I have Miss Nora's jewels, ma'am?' Horatio's voice was silky smooth.

'Because she owed you, didn't she? Years of not paying a very good wage, of not loaning you money to take proper care of your sister while she's been so ill. That jewellery was insurance in case she had taken you out of her will. Something to fall back on. It wasn't really stealing, was it? Not if it was in payment of a debt.' Kitty knew she was gambling that she had worked out Horatio's rationale for stealing Nora's jewels.

'I'm real glad you understand, Mrs Bryant. Peggy understood, leastways I thought she did.' Horatio had a calculating gleam in his eyes.

Kitty tried to appear relaxed as she listened for any indication that Matt might be coming up the stairwell.

'That was why Peggy helped you, wasn't it? Borrowing a few small pieces to raise some money if you were short of dollars to pay the medical bills before payday?' Kitty tried to keep the sympathetic note in her voice.

'Peggy had a good heart. She could see the problems I had. Miss Nora didn't miss looking at those things for a couple of weeks at a time. Peggy would get them back every payday,' Horatio said.

'You would rearrange things when you cleaned, persuade Nora that she was mistaken and they were in a different cabinet.' Kitty's keen ears thought she detected a faint sound behind Horatio on the stairwell. 'Peggy was a nice, respectable-looking girl, ideal to get the staff at the pawnbrokers to loan her money. It was too risky for you to go yourself. They might look at you and think you had stolen them.'

'I can see why you're good at your job, Mrs Bryant,' Horatio said.

'Then Nora decided to marry Mortimer, and he wanted you out, didn't he? No reminders of her previous husband and no one to spy on him and tell tales back to Nora.' Kitty noticed

Horatio's hands curl into fists at the side of his body. Large, strong hands with long fingers.

'Miss Nora always said that I was in her will. She promised my job was for life and that she would make sure I got my dues if anything were to happen to her. I'd seen her will when her lawyer came and brought a draft of it just after her husband died. I knew how much she had put down and that I had to be in her service to receive it. It wasn't a secret. It had been her way to keep me working for her rather than go someplace else for better money.' Horatio's hand tightened a little further.

'And Peggy was frightened she might get dismissed because Nora had started to suspect her of taking the silverware?' Kitty held her ground.

'She started to get scared. I thought Peggy was on the level. That she was a good, Christian girl. I always respected Miss Nora too when she was married, then she started seeing Mr Mortimer, breaking up a marriage.' Horatio shook his head. 'It wasn't right. I told her that. Mr Mortimer knew I didn't approve. Another reason to get rid of me. Then there was Miss Lorena's husband with all the morals of an alley cat. Miss Nora connived with him to keep it from Miss Lorena.' Little white speckles of spit formed at the corners of his mouth.

'She didn't want her daughter to be hurt, I suppose,' Kitty said.

'That's where she went that night. She crept downstairs to see Mr Briggs. She gave him money to get rid of the latest girl-friend. Told him the girl had to go and he was not to upset Miss Lorena. Miss Nora wanted a grandbaby. She thought I didn't know but I followed her downstairs and listened behind the door.' Horatio's nails were digging into the palms of his hands now and Kitty could see his knuckles had turned a pinkish white under his dark skin.

'You confronted her after Rudolph had left?' Kitty said.

'She accused me of spying on her. I only wanted to make

sure she was safe. She told me that was the last straw, she wanted me gone.' Horatio brought his hands forward, looking down at his fists as if seeing them for the first time. 'I don't know rightly what happened next. She went to go past me and I...'

His voice cracked and tailed off. Kitty suppressed a shudder at the description of Nora's death.

'And Peggy knew you had been out of the flat that night?' Kitty asked.

She saw a faint shadow move at the top of the stairwell and knew that Matt was close by.

'She knew that I wasn't telling the truth to the police when I said I had gone right to bed. I persuaded her that I had just taken some rubbish out. I knew I couldn't trust her though. She was one of Rudolph's conquests. I'd suspected it for a little while, but I saw them together the night of the party. He used to leave her little notes. I had to act fast as I couldn't be sure what she had told him already. I knew though that he would never say it was him that Nora was meeting. He had too much to lose, so for that part I felt safe.' Horatio dropped his hands back down, his voice taking on his usual calm conversational tone.

'But Peggy had to die,' Kitty said.

'She was as immoral as Miss Nora. There was no choice,' Horatio said, just matter-of-fact.

The elevator clanked into life, breaking the spell and startling them both. Before Kitty could move Horatio caught hold of her arms and pushed her inside Nora's apartment, slamming the door closed behind him.

Kitty caught a fleeting glimpse of Matt bolting onto the landing from the stairwell but too late to reach her. Horatio locked the door and slid a chain across to secure it further.

'Horatio, I really need to go and join my husband. Today is our wedding anniversary and it's Christmas Eve.' Kitty decided to try to appeal to the man, even though she thought her chances of success were probably slim to none.

'I'm afraid that's not possible right now, Mrs Bryant. I will need you to accompany me out of here so I can catch my bus.' Horatio appeared completely unmoved. His voice and demeanour as calm as if she had just stopped by the apartment for afternoon tea.

Matt was hammering now on the door to Nora's apartment and Kitty could hear him shouting her name over and over again.

'It's all right, I'm safe,' she called back to him, desperate to reassure him. She also wanted to try to keep the situation calm so she could attempt to plan her escape.

'Move away from the door, Mrs Bryant.' Horatio moved forward, blocking her from trying to release the chain or try the catch.

Matt stopped hammering on the door and Kitty guessed her husband would be trying to think of another way to help her. She felt in the pocket of her thick woollen cardigan and closed her fingers around the keys Lorena had left at her father's apartment.

She reluctantly obeyed Horatio's instructions and walked a few paces into Nora's spacious drawing room. Everything was now in boxes, the piano and furniture covered in dust sheets. Dusty marks on the expensively wallpapered walls indicated where pictures had been removed.

'Goodness, you have been busy,' Kitty remarked. A small brown suitcase stood near the piano stamped with Horatio's initials. There was nothing she could see at the moment that could be seized and used as a weapon.

'I wouldn't wish to give Miss Lorena a reason to not pay me my dues. I am sure if she could find a way of not giving me the money from Miss Nora's will, she would do so,' Horatio said.

A shiver ran down Kitty's spine. She was certain that Horatio's assessment of Lorena was correct.

CHAPTER TWENTY-FOUR

Matt's heart raced as the door of Nora's apartment remained firmly closed. At least Kitty had managed to call back to him that she was unharmed. He wished she had left Lorena's keys in the bowl downstairs instead of taking them with her. Then he could at least have tried unlocking the door.

When he had finished on the telephone, he had realised she was missing just after he had heard the clank of the elevator cage doors. He had crept up the stairwell following the sound of voices but had been unable to get onto the landing in time to prevent Kitty from being bundled inside Nora's apartment.

Horatio's confession had been chilling. Matt had lurked in the shadows hoping to find the right moment to jump out and rescue Kitty. Lieutenant Tanfield was on his way at least, and with extra manpower they should be able to break the door down if all else failed. Matt placed his ear to the door to listen. He could hear the muffled sounds of conversation, and he guessed that Kitty was probably trying to keep Horatio talking.

Matt looked around the landing trying to think of a way to get inside the apartment. He had heard Horatio sliding the bolt and chain across so picking the lock wouldn't work. The bolt would probably be too strong. Overhead he noticed a white painted wooden trapdoor in the ceiling, he assumed to provide access to a loft space. Perhaps, there might be another similar hatch door inside Nora's apartment.

He dragged over a large dark-green ceramic pot containing some kind of ornamental plant and placed it beneath the hatch. Praying it would take his weight he scrambled onto it, balancing precariously as he lifted the trapdoor and peered inside the roof space.

He gripped the edge of the hatch with one hand as he fished his cigarette lighter out from his jacket pocket with his other hand. He used the flickering faint glow from the lighter flame to peer into the gloomy attic.

It was a low space only perhaps three or four feet high. He could see there were some old boxes stored a few yards away and a rim of light that promised another trapdoor. The ceiling of the attic was flat like the roof of the building inches above it and he could see a quantity of cabling. He assumed that must have been installed when the building was converted to electricity.

Matt dropped his lighter back inside his pocket and using both hands levered himself up into the attic. He winced at the strain on the old shoulder injury sustained in the Great War. The ceramic pot toppled as he pushed himself upwards, spilling soil and bits of plant all over the landing carpet. He hoped the sound had been sufficiently muffled so as not to alert Horatio that something was happening outside the front door.

Once seated on the edge of the hatch, he retrieved his lighter once more to look towards where he thought he had seen the faint gleam of light indicating a second trapdoor. The palms of his hands were slippery with sweat as he assessed how to reach it. It was definitely an opening into Nora's apartment if he could get there.

He would need to ensure that he picked his way along the

supporting rafters or risk falling through the ceiling into the room below. The air in the attic was cold and he was forced to place his lighter back inside his pocket so he could use his hands to make his way inch by inch along a beam towards the other hatch.

The confined space and the darkness triggered his claustrophobia, another legacy from his time during the war when he had seen whole, deep trenches collapse in front of him. The sticky dark mud drowning men and even horses when the boards had given way, burying everything. It was one of the things that haunted his sleep, alongside the cries of wounded men and the sound of gunfire.

He listened out for Kitty and Horatio's voices as he inched his way across to the area where he had glimpsed the tiny rim of light. They were somewhere below him now and he heard Kitty say something about a bus.

Matt reached the trapdoor and patted his pockets until he located the small folding knife that he used for peeling fruit. He had found in the past that it was a useful tool when picking a lock or when prising open something that was stuck. He always tended to carry it with him, a habit he was grateful for now.

Matt applied it to the trapdoor, sliding it into the gap where the light was showing through and using it to lift the plywood door. Once he could grasp the edge of the door, he slid it quietly open just a small way so he could assess where he was within the apartment.

Looking down through the narrow gap he could see that he appeared to be above the bathroom. He recognised the green glass tiles and the black and white flooring surrounding the bath. Kitty and Horatio were still talking in the other room, their voices floating up to him where he could just pick out the odd word.

Now he knew where he was, he lifted the trapdoor clear so that he could lower himself down into the bathroom. He wanted to avoid dropping down onto the floor from a height since the sound would undoubtedly alert Horatio and he didn't want to put Kitty at further risk. The drop was also enough to turn his ankle if he landed awkwardly.

The bath was more or less directly below him, and he thought that if he was careful, he might be able to balance on the edge of the bathtub to break the drop to the floor. It was inevitable that he would make some noise, but he had to hope that he could be down before Horatio came to investigate.

* * *

Kitty heard a muffled thump from another part of the apartment.

Horatio immediately looked around and then reached out and took hold of Kitty's arm. 'Come with me.'

Kitty didn't have much choice as he marched her through the drawing room and in the direction of Peggy's former bedroom and the bathroom. His hold was tight on the top of her arm, and she could feel the bony strength of his fingers even through the thickness of her blouse and cardigan.

The door to Peggy's room was open and she saw it was empty. The bed stripped revealing the blue and white striped ticking of the mattress and the forlorn pillows devoid of their cases.

Horatio's hold on her intensified as he opened the bathroom door, shoving it with some force so it slammed back against the stopper in the baseboard. Kitty noticed a dirty mark on the side of the bath as if from a shoe and glanced upwards.

She stifled a gasp when she saw there was an open trapdoor above the bath. Had Matt made his way inside the apartment, and if he had, where was he? Kitty was given no time to think as Horatio released his hold on her to position his arm across her throat. He forced her against the front of his body. He held her so she was looking out like a human shield.

'Matt!' Kitty tried to call for her husband but pressure from Horatio's arm on her throat reduced her intended shout to little more than a squeak.

There was more noise outside the apartment now on the landing, with male voices and banging on the apartment door. Horatio pulled her backwards, retreating from the bathroom. Pressure from his arm against her neck made it difficult to breathe and Kitty wheezed as she tried to take in air.

She could smell the sweat from her captor's body, stale and odorous in her nostrils as she tried in vain to pull his arm away from her throat. Someone was battering something hard now against the door of the apartment and she guessed the police were trying to break in.

Kitty tried to drag her feet, forcing Horatio to pull her along, the heels on her shoes scuffling the carpet. She continued to try to break free while desperately wondering if Matt was in the apartment and if so where he might have gone.

There was a loud crash from the direction of the hall and Kitty thought that the door might have given way. Horatio turned as if to see if anyone had entered the flat. Kitty was feeling dizzy now, the pressure on her neck crushing her windpipe. She desperately struggled to try to free herself. Dots appeared in front of her eyes, and she felt herself beginning to lose consciousness when suddenly, without warning, Horatio released her.

Kitty staggered forward and fell onto her knees, wheezing and gasping for air. She looked around to see Matt wielding a frying pan from the kitchen and Horatio lunging at him with a roar like an enraged bull.

The sound of wood splintering came from the hall and two uniformed policemen burst into the room, their guns out of their holsters and ready in their hands. Lieutenant Tanfield ran in behind them.

Kitty was frozen to the spot as she watched Horatio grapple with Matt. Blood was gushing from a wound on the manservant's temple and his eyes bulged with anger as he tried to land a blow on Matt.

'Don't shoot!' Kitty's voice was croaky as she saw the police train their weapons on the men. She was terrified they would fire and hit the wrong man.

'Blackstock! Give yourself up!' Lieutenant Tanfield demanded.

Matt and Horatio were rolling around on the floor now, engaged in a deadly battle. Kitty watched in horror as Horatio had his hands around Matt's neck. The frying pan lay discarded nearby, and Kitty forced herself to crawl forwards on her hands and knees to try to reach it.

Finally, her hand closed around the handle, and she drew on her remaining strength to raise it above Horatio's head as he loomed above Matt, throttling him. As soon as she saw her chance she brought the pan down as hard as she could on Horatio's head.

The man fell forward onto Matt, relinquishing his grip. The police officers spied their chance and after holstering their guns placed handcuffs around Horatio's wrists. Matt rolled over to where Kitty was slumped against the side of the piano, the pan still in her hands.

'Darling, are you all right?' Matt took her hand in his as he gazed anxiously at her.

She managed a brief nod of assent before resting her head on his shoulder, unable to speak for a moment. Lieutenant Tanfield appeared to be barking orders at the policemen as they checked Horatio over.

Once satisfied his prisoner was secured and apparently starting to come round, the lieutenant came over to where Matt and Kitty were recovering themselves, seated on the carpet. He crouched down on the floor beside them.

'Do you need a doctor?' he asked, his sharp eyes assessing them.

'Kitty?' Matt asked.

She shook her head gingerly. 'I'll be all right,' she croaked.

Lieutenant Tanfield straightened up and issued more instructions to his officers as they half carried, half dragged Horatio from the apartment.

'Are you both able to walk?' the policeman asked.

Matt assisted Kitty to her feet, and she clung to his arm while she regained her balance. Matt had lost two buttons from his shirt and his lower lip was slightly swollen. Kitty knew her stockings were in shreds, and she had carpet burns on her knees. Her throat was sore, and she was certain that by tomorrow bruising would appear on her neck and her arm.

The lieutenant accompanied them in the elevator to Edgar's apartment. Once they were seated on the sofa, he went into the kitchenette to bring them both a glass of water. Kitty murmured her thanks and took several large gulps, the coolness of the drink soothing her sore throat.

'Right, now let me have it from the top,' Lieutenant Tanfield said, taking out his notebook.

Kitty, with assistance from Matt, managed to croak out the entire story of what Horatio had admitted and what had happened when she had been listening out on the landing. The policeman's bushy eyebrows rose towards his hairline as she recounted Horatio's admission to killing Nora and Peggy.

'And you say he has confessed to posting the jewellery he stole from Mrs Dangerfield to his family's home?' the lieutenant asked.

'Yes, he hid the necklace, earrings and bracelet in a parcel disguised as a Christmas present, then wrapped it addressed to himself at his sister's house. He said it was insurance in case

Lorena managed to get out of paying him the bequest from Nora's will,' Kitty explained.

'Well, he won't be seeing a dime of that money now,' the policeman remarked grimly. 'Thank you both. I had better get downtown to get Blackstock processed. I'll speak to the desk about securing Mrs Dangerfield's apartment.' The policeman put his notebook away in his pocket and headed off.

Once the door had closed behind him Kitty set down her empty glass.

'Are you certain you're all right, darling?' Matt asked. 'Can I get you another drink?'

'I would love a cup of tea.' Kitty looked at her husband. 'I'm so sorry, Matt, about what happened. I swear I was just listening on the stairs. I never heard the elevator. He took me completely by surprise.' She lifted her hand and rubbed a smear of dust from his cheek.

Her husband caught her hand in his. 'I know. I should have known better than to suggest that you spied on him. Trouble always seems to find you.'

'If you hadn't though, he would have been halfway across the state now. He would probably have escaped justice,' Kitty said.

Matt gently kissed her fingers. 'I'll go and make us some tea, and don't you dare move a muscle until I come back. I think we've had enough adventures for one day.'

'It's certainly a wedding anniversary to remember,' Kitty agreed with a small smile.

'You can say that again,' Matt said with a laugh as he rose from the sofa. 'Wait until your father hears about all of this.'

'Wait until Alice hears about it,' Kitty said. She didn't want to think about what her grandmother would have to say when she found out what had happened.

CHAPTER TWENTY-FIVE

The remainder of their stay in New York seemed to pass swiftly. A quiet Christmas followed by more interviews with Lieutenant Tanfield, then a riotous New Year's Eve party, hosted once more by the gregarious Felicia. A trip to the Metropolitan Museum and shopping in the sales.

Kitty waved Matt's white handkerchief from the ship's deck in farewell to her father until he was an indistinguishable speck on the dockside as the ship sailed out of New York. They slid past the impressive skyscrapers once more and the Statue of Liberty.

'I'm so glad our departure is happier and less worrying than our arrival.' Kitty snuggled up against her husband. The biting cold air sent colour into her cheeks as she watched the city slipping past them.

'Yes, it was a relief to discover your father wasn't at death's door, although I must confess, I think we could have done without the murders.' The corners of Matt's mouth curved up in a smile as he spoke.

Kitty shivered. 'I still can't believe everything that happened. I really do think my father should keep better company.' She wrinkled her nose in disapproval. 'I sometimes wish he would return to live in England, but then I remember how much chaos he always seems to bring with him.'

Matt chuckled. 'I know what you mean. Your father does seem to be a magnet for trouble.'

'Well, let's hope for a calm voyage back to England.' Kitty shivered again and turned to head below deck.

'Absolutely, the crossing can be rough this time of year,' Matt said as he followed her to go in search of hot coffee and a nice warm lounge.

Kitty and Matt were on deck again a few days later as the ship sailed into Plymouth. Kitty's heart lifted as soon as the familiar coastline of England came into view. The lighthouse on The Hoe just visible. They had telegrammed ahead to Robert Potter to ask if he or his father would drive to the city to collect them when they docked.

The outside air, although still chilly, was distinctly warmer than it had been in New York. The sky was grey and there was a hint of drizzle as they waited for the ship to slowly glide into place at the dockside.

'Do you see anyone?' Kitty asked as she peered out at the crowd of people waiting for the ship.

Below her she could see various workers readying to settle the ship at her berth, motor cars and small lorries, horse and carts as well as people waiting to meet passengers from the ship.

'I think we shall have to wait until we disembark, darling. The porters will take our luggage, and we can soon find if we are being met once we're on dry land,' Matt said.

Reluctantly, Kitty was forced to agree. She released her hold on the polished brass handrail and accompanied him down below ready to disembark. It took a little while to make their way off the ship, having ensured their trunks had been collected and to tip and bid farewell to the crew.

Kitty scanned the crowds on the dock once more as she descended the gangplank with Matt. She wondered who would have come to meet them, Robert or his father.

'Can you see someone?' Kitty stood on her tiptoes trying to see a familiar face.

There were drivers holding placards with various names who had clearly come to collect people. The porters were busy steering loaded luggage carts laden with trunks and carpet bags through the throngs of people.

Matt was much taller than Kitty so had the advantage of being able to see over some of the heads of the people around them.

Suddenly, Matt stiffened. 'I don't believe it! It can't be!'

The next thing she knew her husband had disappeared into the crowd, hurrying away as if his life depended upon it. Kitty remained where she was wondering what on earth was going on.

* * *

Matt scanned the crowd looking for the man he had seen a few seconds ago. He had to have been mistaken. There was no way it could have been the person he had thought he had seen. Yet he knew if he didn't catch up to the stranger and put his mind at ease it would trouble him for days.

At first, he thought he had lost him. The man looked so similar to others in the crowd. A black homburg hat, dark-grey overcoat and grey trousers. Then Matt spotted him walking quickly and purposefully away from the dock.

Matt hurried after him and, as if sensing someone was behind him, the man quickened his pace.

'Redvers!' Matt called the man's name.

The man turned his head to look behind him and Matt could clearly see his features. Their gazes locked and Matt's breath stilled in his throat. It couldn't be, and yet it was. Older now, but it was definitely him. The man turned and broke into a run, vanishing from view into a myriad of warehouses, storage crates and alleyways before Matt could gather his wits to follow.

He stood for a moment shocked by what he had seen, oblivious to the hustle and bustle around him as he stared at the spot where Captain Redvers Palmerston had been. Slowly he shook himself back to the present and looked around to try and find where he had left Kitty and their luggage.

'Matt!' Kitty was perched on tiptoe, waving to him.

He headed towards her, his mind still reeling.

'Robert and Alice are here to collect us. Are you all right? You just ran off without warning?' Kitty's expression was concerned as she took hold of his arm and peered up at his face. 'What happened? One minute you were there and then you were gone.'

'Yes, I'm all right. At least, I think so.' He gave her gloved hand a reassuring squeeze.

He hoped he was telling her the truth. Could he trust his own eyes or was his mind playing tricks on him?

Robert helped the porter load their luggage into the trunk of the car, securing the larger pieces with straps to ensure everything was secure. Kitty and Alice were chattering away ninety to the dozen about New York, Edgar and Christmas.

Matt found himself giving mechanical replies, unable to shake what he had just seen, or thought he had just seen from his mind. He noticed Kitty glancing at him a couple of times before they got into the car to drive back home to Churston.

Robert and Alice were duly shocked and fascinated by Kitty's tale of Nora and Peggy's murders and what had happened during their travels. Matt joined in only when he was appealed to by Kitty. He was shaken to his very core. Perhaps his experiences in the war were manifesting in a new way.

Once Robert and Alice had delivered them and their bags safely home and they had all been greeted by an ecstatic Bertie and an indifferent Rascal, Kitty turned to face him.

'I'm putting the kettle on and then I think you need to tell me what happened at the dock,' she said firmly once Alice and Robert had left.

Matt sank down on one of the black leather and chrome armchairs in the lounge. Bertie placed his nose on his knee and waited for Matt to rub his ears. If anyone could make sense of what he had just seen, then it would be Kitty. If not, then he was indeed losing his mind and he needed to see a doctor.

Kitty returned a few minutes later carrying a laden tea tray. She had removed her hat, and her blonde curls were still ruffled.

'Now,' she commanded, taking a seat and peering into the teapot to inspect the progress of the brew. 'What happened?'

Bertie switched his attention from Matt to the tea tray once his nose detected a plate of biscuits.

Kitty replaced the lid on the teapot and poured them both a drink, adding milk before passing a cup to Matt. She waited until he had taken his first sip.

'Well?' she asked again.

Matt stared at the tea in his cup. 'I saw someone. Someone I thought I recognised,' he said. He wasn't even sure how this was going to sound.

Kitty looked at him with narrowed eyes. 'Who was it?'

'This will sound crazy. Perhaps I am going crazy, Kitty. I followed him thinking I had made a mistake. That my mind was playing tricks on me. I knew though that unless I saw his face and knew it wasn't who I had thought it was I wouldn't be at ease,' Matt explained.

Kitty picked up her own drink. 'Go on,' she encouraged. 'Did you find him?'

Matt nodded. 'I followed him away from the crowds. He seemed to realise someone was behind him. I called his name, and he turned and looked at me.' Matt paused, his heart thumping now he had come to the difficult part of his story.

'So, it *was* the person you thought you knew?' Kitty asked. Her eyes were troubled, and he knew that she had sensed there was more to his story.

'I would be willing to swear on a stack of Bibles that he was Captain Redvers Palmerston. He was older, obviously, but I knew he recognised me as I had known it was him.' Matt's hand shook slightly, making his china cup clink against the saucer and some of the tea spill.

'What happened?' Kitty's tone was concerned.

'His eyes met mine. I recognised the nick at the bottom of his right ear. He lost part of the lobe when he was injured. I swear it was him, Kitty.' Matt paused again.

Kitty said nothing, waiting patiently for him to continue.

Matt licked his lips before carrying on. 'He took off as if the hounds of hell were pursuing him and I lost him in the alleyways by the dock.'

Kitty frowned. 'He was a brother officer?' she asked.

Matt inclined his head. 'We were comrades-in-arms. We were wounded at the same time and cared for at the same hospital where I met Edith.'

Matt drew a breath to carry on. It seemed so long ago now, recovering from his injuries and meeting his first wife who had been a nurse at the hospital.

'Redvers was more badly injured than me. He took longer to recover. Everyone thought he was getting better, but he didn't believe them. He called me over the one day and gave me a ring and a watch. He insisted that I keep it and pass it to his wife for his son if anything should happen to him. The ring had been in his family for years and the watch had been a gift from his own father.'

Kitty frowned. 'So what happened?'

'This is the part where you will think I have lost my mind.' Matt looked at her. 'He died a few days later. I went to his funeral and when I was well enough, I took the ring and the watch to his widow.'

Kitty stared at him in bewilderment. 'I don't understand. Then how could he have been at the dock today?'

Matt blew out a sigh. 'I don't know, Kitty. But it was him, it was definitely him.'

Kitty surveyed him with her cool blue-grey level gaze. 'You are quite certain?' she asked.

Matt swallowed. 'I know what I saw. He turned to his name. I saw a dead man, Kitty. A man I saw buried.'

She surveyed him levelly, as if making up her own mind.

'I don't believe you are losing your mind, Matt. I think that we have a new mystery to solve,' Kitty said. She squeezed Matt's hand and wondered what this coming year would bring them.

A LETTER FROM HELENA DIXON

Dear reader,

I want to say a huge thank you for choosing to read *Murder in New York*. If you enjoyed it and would like to keep up to date with all my latest releases, just sign up at the following link. Your email address will never be shared, and you can unsubscribe at any time. There is also a free story – *The Mysterious Guest*, starring Kitty's friend, Alice.

www.bookouture.com/helena-dixon

What could be more exciting than Christmas in Manhattan? The festive lights, the huge department stores, the glitz and the glamour. Yet, it wasn't that way for everyone at that period of history. Today, Macy's still has a Christmas parade and you can visit the museums, ice skate in the park and enjoy the sights! I do hope you loved *Murder in New York* and, if you did, I would be very grateful if you could write a review. I'd love to hear what you think, and it makes such a difference helping new readers to discover one of my books for the first time. You can get in touch on social media or through my website.

Thanks,

Helena

KEEP IN TOUCH WITH HELENA

www.nelldixon.com

 facebook.com/nelldixonauthor
x.com/NellDixon

ACKNOWLEDGEMENTS

My thanks to my fabulous support teams, the Tuesday zoomers, the Coffee Crew, South West Writers, and all of #TeamKitty at Bookouture. Special thanks to my outgoing editor, Maisie, for all of her knowledge of America, her unfailing support and her kindness. My thanks also to my brilliant agent, Kate Nash. Writing a book is a team effort and I couldn't do it without you.

PUBLISHING TEAM

Turning a manuscript into a book requires the efforts of many people. The publishing team at Bookouture would like to acknowledge everyone who contributed to this publication.

Audio
Alba Proko
Sinead O'Connor
Melissa Tran

Commercial
Lauren Morrissette
Hannah Richmond
Imogen Allport

Cover design
Debbie Clement

Data and analysis
Mark Alder
Mohamed Bussuri

Editorial
Maisie Lawrence
Cerys Hadwin-Owen
Sinead O'Connor

Made in United States
North Haven, CT
22 November 2024